Love Me Right

NAKIA ROBINSON

Right About It
Publications

Love Me Right is a work of fiction. Names, characters, places and incident are products of the author's imagination or are used fictitiously. Any resemblance to actual events, locales or persons living or dead, is entirely coincidental.

ISBN 978-0-9890982-2-9

Printed in the United States of America

Dedication

This book is dedicated to **Robert Lee Robinson** and **John H. Fraling**. You set the bar high. Your physical bodies may have been laid to rest, but I feel your spirits and I am so grateful to have you guiding me alone the way. Your love and words are always with me.

Acknowldgements

God, I thank you for bringing me this far. I pray that you continue to bless me with the ability to put words on paper in a way that people can connect and feel the story. I pray that you use me to inspire.

Mommy, again I thank you. Without your support I would not be where I am. I truly appreciate the sacrifices you made for me,

Nykidra and **Renny**. I love you and hope you recognize the jewel you are.

Antoine, thank you for pushing me and hustling these books, your support is not unnoticed. You made it possible. I'm ready for our next business ventures. We ARE A TEAM. **My children**, I love you.

Nyki, mogul in the making, God has so many great things planned for you. I am so proud of you. Many accomplishments thus far, but the best has yet to come. A leader, with you the possibilities are endless.

Renny, you have so much talent now build your business.

Lorenzo, your words make me do what I need to and prove what can be done.

My **grandmothers**, thank you for your love and support.

To **Mr. Lyndon**, without you I would still be lost, trying to get published. Your genuineness is a rarity in this publishing business. Your wisdom is priceless and I am sincerely grateful for you. I look forward to working with you for many years to come. SN: PF is looking for you, LOL

Jacci and Natalie I appreciate all the hard work and valuable tips. Thank you so much for the gems.

My Musa Egoo and wife Aylete, like I said before where I go you go. Thanks for always having my back and pushing me to do what I don't like to. MUSA, YOU ARE A BEAST AND THE BEST!

My fam, **Tyronna, Chaundre**, thank you for being my promoters Luv Ya.

Fam, **Dwayne "Big Shorty" Morris** and **Mechell**, thank you for your continued support. I know together we will make it happen. Mechell thanks for reading my manuscript and encouraging me. Big Shorty cant't wait to work on your script, can't wait for the world to see your talent.

Cretia, Y.E.S. Thank you for the continued support.

My **CF crew** thanks you for the support. Sorry for the wait, but I had to tell the story, RIGHT.

To **my readers** your support means so much. I pray that you feel the emotions of the characters and can visualize the script. Again thank you for supporting my dream. Please connect with me @ www.RightAboutIt-Publication.com, or Instagram Nykia8 or FB.

Yasmin's back and whew.......what a story....Enjoy *Love Me Right*.

Table of Contents

Intro......Epiphany

"I don't believe this! You lied to me all this time! I got over the affair. I accepted Yasmin like she was mine. I even signed the birth certificate and accepted his child! Do you know how hard that was for me?! Every time I looked at her, I saw him!" John Sinclair furiously spewed.

Those words answered many questions, reopened many wounds, cut deep, and confirmed how I always felt...I was never wanted.

I lie in bed staring in the mirror at my reflection, staring at my hazel-green eyes; hazel-green eyes I hated my entire life because they separated me and isolated me from my parent's love. I recall the many times my paternal grandmother would ridicule me saying I thought I was cute because of my eyes. She would constantly scold me, telling me I would never be good enough and would only serve as a temporary fascination. She'd insist that in the end, when the fascination died, I'd be like a used rag and tossed aside. I was taught my eyes would only cause me pain.

Now I know the reason for her hate. I was a constant reminder Michelle, my mother, cheated on her son. John Sinclair, the man I called daddy, was not my biological father. Yes, it was true I never felt the father-daughter bond, or love for that matter. However, deep inside, I sought for his affection and acceptance. Instead, all he and my mother's love was given to my younger sister, Ashley. At least he finally admitted he just tolerated me.

I don't know what hurts more, my parent's treatment towards me or Mr. Taylor's detachment. Mr. Lawrence Taylor, my best friend Landon's father. The man I've admired, the man who I always had a lot of respect and gratitude for is my biological father. All this time, he lied. Despite the many tears I cried due to forgotten birthdays or lack of affection, I didn't matter. He stood by ignoring how I felt, what I went through. He didn't care that I always felt alone. Instead, he disregarded me and my feelings like I was trash. I wasn't good enough. He showered the chosen one, Landon, with gifts and love, while I enviously watched and admired from afar wishing that John would love me just a tenth as much. How could he just constantly look me in my face and do nothing?

I can't stop the endless well of tears rolling down my face. I can't stop the pain that I feel in my heart. My head hurts as new questions arise and many walls are formed. My life has been a lie. How do I decipher the reality of what is? I can't escape the last twenty four hours nor can I escape the last twenty-four years. No matter how I look at this, it is an unbelievable mess. Where do I go from here? What do I do? There are so many questions with no answers.

I'm left here, broken. I finally had put all the hurt behind me. I finally embraced my future, me, and learned to love me. Now my past, my existence comes back, shattering what I fought so hard to build.

I just thank God every day for bringing Braxton into my life. Our journey began May 4, 2002, the day I graduated from college and declared my independence. Braxton came into my life when I didn't know how to love myself. Haunted by my paternal grandmother's words, I let my insecurities about my eyes hold me back. I was scared to trust and never had anyone to love me. Braxton changed all of that, he taught me about love. He helped me begin the process of loving myself.

From the first time we met, four years ago, he's called me beautiful, not my eyes. He didn't realize it then, but that meant so much. Hell, it still does. More importantly, he makes me feel beautiful. My favorite spot, in his arms, there, I always feel secure. I let go of my insecurities and embrace love.

Nonetheless, it wasn't all beautiful. We've had our share of problems, such as my miscarriage. This ultimately caused a year-and-a-half breakup. While the breakup was difficult for me, it was something I had to go through. It was during that time I learned to love Yasmin.

Time apart allowed us to mature, but it didn't waiver our love. When we did reunite, it was full speed ahead. Braxton surprised me with a trip to the Cayman Islands. My 5'11 inches, size twelve, golden honey complexion, statuesque body, stood with Braxton Simms. As the sun danced along the water, my marital union began.

Six months later, my heart still beats in sync with his. Even now, he's here holding me tight, helping me through the latest crisis. I pray he realizes how much I love and appreciate him. Like he's here for me, I'll always be there for him.

1

Flaws and All

"Hey Beautiful," Braxton kisses me on my forehead.

"Hey," I softly respond.

"Yasmin, I just want you to know when you're ready to talk I'm here.

I shook my head "no" as I squeeze tighter on his arm which is securely wrapped around me.

Do you want me to get you anything?"

"No, just hold me."

"I can do that," Braxton pulls me even closer. He gently strokes my face.

And that's when my tears began all over again.

"It just hurts. I thought I was finally over my childhood. You don't know how many times I cried myself to sleep, how many times I wished for some affection, asked myself why they hated me. I felt the hate they had for me. I watched as they doted over Ashley. How they made sure to show their love to her while all I received was criticism. You know I never had a birthday party, now I find out I was a mistake."

"Listen to me. You were not a mistake. You are right where you're supposed to be, here for me. I love you so much, beautiful. I wish I could take your pain away. I'm always going to be here for you. I thank God for you every day. I'm your family now. I'm not going to hurt you. You are my life and whatever you decide to do regarding your parents, I support you. Don't allow them to hurt you anymore. I won't allow for them to hurt you anymore. Truthfully, you don't need them. You have a family that loves you and wants you. My mother will disown me for you."

That got me to laugh a little.

"So you think it's funny?" He teased.

"Thank you, baby, I love you too. This is just one big crazy mess. Landon and I have been best friends for over 10 years. I've been to her house, and she's been to mine. Not one time did any of them tell us the truth. People always said we looked alike and asked if we were sisters. I still can't believe Landon is my sister."

"Yeah, I'm still shocked."

"I don't know what to do. I always loved Landon like a sister. I don't what will happen between us. I don't know what to do. Right now just thinking about this mess makes my head hurt. I know I'm mad as hell. Right now, I just want to do what they've done to me my whole life, forget they exist.

"Whatever you decide to do, I support you."

I stayed in bed for the rest of the day. Braxton stayed by my side the majority of the day comforting me trying to kiss my pain away. Lawrence called several times, but I refused his calls.

Later that night when Braxton went to the store, I decided to call Landon. I didn't know what to expect. Landon and I met for the first time our junior year of high school. That was over ten years ago. I had just moved into the area, so I didn't know anyone. I was use to staying to myself. One day, some fool assumed my quiet laid back personality was a weakness. Well I quickly embarrassed the fool, causing myself as well as others to get a laugh off how corny the fool was. After that incident Landon initiated a conversation and at first I was apprehensive. While we did have a class together, I never had any interest in creating a friendship. Truthfully, to me Landon was too loud and wild, and kept too much male attention. While she still is and does, we managed to ironically form a sisterly bond.

"Hey Land."

"Hey."

"This is crazy. I don't know what to say."

Landon always an outspoken diva got straight to the point. "Yas, I'm so fucking mad. I don't believe my father…Damn! our father lied!"

"Have you talked to him?" I asked.

"Yeah, he apologized and said he wanted the three of us to get together."

"I'm not ready for that."

"Have you talked to your mother?"

I sucked my teeth, "No, she hasn't called. You know she's worried about saving her relationship with John."

"I can't believe we're sisters."

"I know. I'm still in shock."

"Yasmin?"

"Yeah?"

"I want us to stay the same. It feels funny now, weird. I don't want this to make us feel uncomfortable around each other."

"Landon, you are my girl. This won't change that. It just confirms what we always felt. We're sisters."

"Yas, I just wished we found out sooner. I use to beg for a sister. Being an only child can be boring. I have to admit it will sound weird hearing you call him daddy instead of Mr. Taylor. We need a retail therapy day sponsored by daddy."

"Landon, I'm not ready for all that."

"Yeah, I guess."

I had to shake my head. Landon doesn't understand the severity of this and definitely can't relate to my pain. Landon and I talked for an hour trying to come to terms with reality.

As far as our father, my mother and John being a part of my life, I'm still undecided.

Later that night when I was laying in Braxton's arms, the phone rang. Braxton was already sleep so I answered it.

"Hello."

"Yasmin, why couldn't you leave well enough alone?!"

"What!" I said, shocked by the voice and audacity of the question.

"Why did you have that man in your house? You caused a whole lot of drama for what? Nothing!" my mother yelled.

"Why are you yelling at me?" I asked, upset.

"You know why! This is all your fault. I raised you. I could have had an abortion, but I didn't. I raised you and John treated you as his own. You had that man in your house and ruined everything. I should have aborted you when I had the chance. John left me and it's your fault. You are so ungrateful. Acting like you had the worst childhood. You had everything you needed. Now your selfish ass has sabotaged my marriage. This is your fault. Why, why, why?!" she yelled.

My mother has said and done things to me to hurt me deeply, such as the time I miscarried my son. I wanted my mother to hug me, tell me it would be okay. Instead, she told me it was for the best. According to her, I shouldn't have been having a child out of wedlock and should stop giving the milk away for free. No, I didn't cuss her out. I accepted what she said, blamed myself, and accepted her words. Never had I cussed her out, or disrespected her until now.

"You listen to me. Don't you dare try and blame this shit on me! You lied! You told John, Lawrence basically raped you. When in reality, your dumb ass was opening your legs for a smile. You're the one who was dumb enough to think he would leave his fiancé for you. You had the dumb look on your face when you found out you were just something to do. Don't blame me because your lies caught up with you. This is your fault, not mine.!" I said with venom.

"All my life, you made me feel unwelcomed. Every time you looked at me, I saw the hate. At least now, you're being honest. So you wish you would have aborted me? Well you didn't! Tell you what, how about I just be dead to you now?!"

14

By now, Braxton is up and irate. He snatches the phone and finishes my sentence, "Don't call my wife or house anymore. She has me now." Braxton slammed the phone down. He pulled me close. "I love you, beautiful."

"I love you," I cried.

He held me for the rest of the night. He did everything I needed. Kissing me and thanking God for me. And I thanked God for bringing Braxton into my life to love me.

2

I Love you More Than You'll Ever Know

"I'm going to miss you."

"I'm going to miss you too, beautiful. It's only for a couple of days. I'll see you in LA, next week for the BET awards."

"I'm not going to have anyone to keep me warm at night." I whined.

"You know I'm going to call you every night."

"I know, but I will be in our big bed alone for five days. The awards aren't until Tuesday." I whined again.

"You're spoiled."

"I know. You have me this way."

He laughed.

"I guess I'll just have to play with myself this weekend."

"You are so wrong, beautiful. Now you starting something. He pulled me close so I could feel the bulge in his pants.

I smiled, "Did I do that?"

He laughed, "Well beautiful, as much as I would love to be in you right now, I have a plane to catch. I do have to work, you're very expensive."

I hit him on the arm. "I am not, Mr. VP."

"Last I checked, we were living in a million dollar home that you picked out. You told me my little townhouse and your condo wasn't big enough. Let's not even mention the five carat emerald cut you have on your finger. That's love," he teased.

"You're the one who said you wanted a detached house. Your cocky self said, 'This way when you scream you won't disturb the neighbors.' Since you're complaining, I may have to upgrade you, Mr. Simms."

Braxton slaps my ass, "I claimed this."

"Wait till you see me on the red carpet. I bought this sexy dress that shows off all of my assets."

"Is that so?"

"I sure did and you won't be able to touch."

"Keep thinking that."

"I don't have to think anything. I know this because you'll be occupied with the other boring BET execs."

He laughed. "Now I'm a boring BET exec?"

"Yup, you sure are VP, another reason for me to upgrade. They're going to be a lot of options. I might have to find my singer or athlete since I'm hurting your pockets." I teased.

"I see you want to be a comedian today."

"We'll see. You know I wouldn't mind having someone sing to me at night. We both know you can't."

"You know I might just have to see if we can give you a little skit in the show. You got a lot of jokes."

"Just wait until you see my dress and I'll be putting the kitty kat on lock." I turn around and walk away.

Braxton grabs my arm, "Girl, you better come back here and give me some love. That's right! This kitty kat is on lock until Tuesday."

I hug Braxton tight like he was going away for five years rather than five days. "I'm going to miss you, baby."

Braxton kisses me on the lips before heading down the terminal to catch his flight.

✶

Later that day when I got home, I started cleaning up the mess Braxton left me. The Bethesda, house really was too big for just the two of us. I fell in love with it the first time I saw it. It was my dream house, decorated in rich neutral colors; a lot of browns, beige, and rust with some olive and coral colors. It was my tranquility, my therapy. A five-bedroom stone colonial with seven bathrooms, five fireplaces, sunroom, pool, 20 foot ceilings, sunken living room and master suite on three acres with a three-car garage. So big, so empty, I hope one day it'll be filled with kids. My heart pangs with that familiar pain. One day.

As I was finishing the phone rings. I assume its Braxton, but it's his mother.

"Hello?"

"Hey Yasmin. How are you, honey?"

"Hey Ma," I respond, unable to hide the disappointment in my voice.

"It seems you're not happy to hear from me."

"I'm sorry, Ma. I'm always happy to hear from you. I thought you were Braxton. I haven't heard from him since I dropped him off."

"I know. I'm just picking with you. You know my son, he always loses track of time. He'll call you right when you fall asleep."

"That sounds about right." I laughed.

"So other than missing your husband, how are you?"

"I'm fine."

"Well if you aren't doing anything Saturday, I need your help."

"Sure, what's up?"

"I need to get some things together for Jonathan's birthday party."

Jonathan is Braxton's oldest brother, Jeff's son.

"He's turning one already."

"I know. His first year went so fast."

I unconscientiously blocked Mrs. Simms. Jonathan turning one is bittersweet, A tear slid down my face as I thought about Bryan.

"Yasmin, are you there?"

"I'm sorry Ma. I'm here, my mind just drifted."

"There's nothing to be sorry for. I'm sorry if this is too much for you, I'll manage."

"No, it's not."

"Are you sure?"

I smile slightly. Since the first time I met Mrs. Simms, she's treated me like a daughter. Instantly, I formed a bond with her I never had with my own biological mother. Beautiful inside and out resembling Diahann Carroll, she could always tell if something was wrong.

"Yes, I still have my moments. It's been three years but I still think about Bryan every day. I just wonder what he would have been like. Who he would have looked like."

"I know, baby. He was your son, it's hard. Grieving is a process. Bryan was your baby, my first grandbaby, and he always will hold a special place in all of our hearts. It's okay to miss him."

"Thank you, Ma. You always know how to make me feel better. I know I can never replace Bryan, nor am I trying. I'm just wondering why I'm not pregnant yet. I was hoping I'd be pregnant by now." I say, rubbing my hand over my stomach, where the scar from my caesarian lies.

"Sweetheart, you've been married for less than a year, it'll happen."

"I'm just scared. I know my car accident ultimately caused my miscarriage. But the doctor also said I suffered a lot of trauma. I'm starting to think more damage was done then they thought."

"I'm sure you and Braxton will have more babies, just be patient. You will have another baby. I love my boys but I will at least get one girl. Yasmin, you're going to give me a girl."

I had to laugh, "If you say so. From your mouth to God's ears."

"Ok, we'll see."

"Thank you, Ma, and it'll be fun shopping with you Saturday."

"Alright, Yasmin, I'll see you Saturday."

✳

It was Friday I'd just gotten off work. I didn't want to go home because I would get lonely. So I drove around trying to figure out where to go.

My phone rang breaking me out of my trance. It was Lawrence. He has been calling daily apologizing, trying to build a relationship. Today, I don't feel like the apologies, so the call went unanswered.

Going to see my mother was not an option. Even though I told my mother not to call me, I am disappointed that she didn't attempt to apologize or make amends. I do feel bad because I haven't talked to Ashley. I never really could get close with Ashley, she was four years younger but I think maybe there was a little resentment.

I decided on Landon.

I headed to see Landon and my godson, well nephew now that the truth is out. I loved Eric like he was my own. He helped me cope with my miscarriage. He always put a smile on my face. Landon became pregnant a couple of months after I miscarried Bryan. It was difficult at first considering Braxton and I had gone from being engaged and living together to barely seeing each other to living in separate homes. But I put my issues aside and was happy for my best friend. It was hell, especially when Braxton and I broke up and Landon announced she was getting married. That was another big surprise. Landon was a diva and had made it clear on more than one occasion she was too young and pretty to settle for one guy. Landon always had men on standby and although she made more than enough money selling real estate, she made it known they weren't the only ones and the money must be right. The majority of the time, she dated athletes and not just any athlete. Like her, they had to be on top of their game, a star player. Landon loved her media attention. Surprisingly, Eric Ayers of the Washington Wizards got the diva pregnant and settled her down to a wife. I still can't believe it.

I rang the doorbell and waited for the diva. When she opened the door, I swear I saw steam. The diva, who was always dressed for the runway, had her dark-brown hair with blond tips styled in a spiked short do that looked like she just stepped out of the salon chair. She was wearing a jean Bebe green romper complimented by her nude peep-toe Christian Louboutin sling-back pumps. Her hazel- green eyes were piercing like she was on a hunt ready to kill her prey.

Now that it has been confirmed Landon and I were sisters, I couldn't deny our similarities. People always asked if we were sisters. We would laugh and dismiss it. Looking at Landon now I definitely saw our similarities. The golden honey complexion, the facial features such as our hazel-green eyes, high cheek bones or full lips, we were sisters. There were only a few differences. I'm 5'll, Landon is 5'7. She's a size 5, I'm a 10 - 12. She always wore short hair no longer than three inches. My hair was thick and hung six inches below my shoulders. Unlike me and Ashley, who didn't look related at all. However, don't assume Ashley is lacking in the beauty department. She's cute with mocha colored skin, short dark brown hair and stands at about 5'4.

"What's wrong, Diva?"

"Eric is about to get his privileges taken away?"

"Landon, what are you talking about."

"Yas, he needs to realize it's a privilege to be married to me. There are a lot of other men out there who would be more than happy to have me. He has the audacity to tell me the dress I'm wearing to the BET awards is too revealing and I'm not wearing it. Ha, I don't know how many times I have to tell him I don't take orders, I give them."

I just stood there and listened. I was not taking sides, but the last time I went to an awards ceremony with Landon her dress was risqué. The dress she had that night required my assistance and I have to give her props, she wore that dress. I could only imagine how risqué she would get. Especially since her size C breasts were still perky and her flat stomach showed no evidence of a baby.

"Yas, he has lost his dayum mind if he thinks I'm wearing another dress. I may have to explore my options when we go to LA."

I was not getting involved in this battle. "Where's my little cutie?"

"He's in the game room with big Eric."

I walked to the game room to get my baby with Landon behind me.

"So Yas, what are you wearing?"

"I picked out this bronze gown. I'm going Monday to add highlight to my hair. I'm debating if I want to cut it."

"Highlights and a cut, I'm impressed. How much are we cutting?"

"Calm down, I'm not cutting much, unlike you I like my hair, I want layers. I think if I add some blonde highlights, it'll bring out my eyes and compliment the dress."

"Do something different. Take some inches off."

"No, thanks. Me and my husband like my long hair."

Landon rolls her eyes, "Whatever! Please don't start talking about Braxton."

"Excuse me, don't start on my husband." They have this crazy love hate relationship. They tolerate each other only because they love me. When I first started dating Braxton, Landon was against it. She was jealous because I was spending so much time with him. She also thought he was too jealous and possessive, which he can be, but he's gotten better.

"I apologize, I know how you are about Braxton," she rolls her eyes again. "I admitted my mistake about Braxton, he loves you, makes you happy, so he cool with me. But I don't have to hear about it all the time."

"I see misery is trying to get some company but it's not happening. I'm going to play with my baby." I walked into the game room, "Hey, fellas!"

Little Eric's face lit up and he came running to me, "Mimi," his version of Yasmin.

Eric was so cute. He was only two, but I knew he would be a heartbreaker with his big grey eyes and caramel skin. He looked a lot like Landon. I didn't see Eric in him yet. Big Eric was tall, 6'5 with rich dark Hershey skin, wavy black hair and dark eyes that sparkled like diamonds. Very nice eye candy. Eric's best quality to me was his personality, always laid back. He had lots of sex appeal, with so many groupies, but he was always a sweetheart, never letting his stardom or looks go to his head.

"Hey Auntie baby." I scooped up little Eric and began tickling him.

"Hey, Yasmin." Big Eric said, giving me a hug.

"What's going on, Eric? Are you relaxing now that you're done with the playoffs?'

"I'm trying to, but your girl is driving me crazy. Did you see that dress she thinks she's wearing Tuesday?"

"Eric, Yas did not ask you about me. I've already told you I'm wearing the dress! You're the one who'll be looking stupid. If you think you're going to whine or complain in my ear all night, then you're mistaken. I will go to the awards by myself and party with whoever I choose."

"Landon, I'm getting sick and tired of your attitude. You're going to stop disrespecting me and talking to me like I'm a puppet. You're not wearing that dress."

"Eric, I'll talk to you any way I feel. As far as the dress, it'll be on my body."

"Landon, try me."

Before Landon could counter, I jumped in, "Listen, while you two go at it, little Eric and I are going to the mall. Matter of fact, I'll keep him tonight. He can keep me company."

"Thanks, Yas," said Eric. "Landon and I have some issues we need to handle."

"Eric there you go dragging Yasmin in this. This is between you and me. I told you, I don't care what you say, I'm wearing the dress!"

Little Eric was clutching on to me. I know he was ready to get away from his crazy parents. "Okay you two, stop it. Hello we have a baby right here. You know you shouldn't be fighting in front of him." I looked at both of them, "I'm going to get him some clothes and we will see you tomorrow."

I grabbed some clothes and toys for Eric and we jumped into my truck and headed to Chuck E. Cheese. We stayed there for about an hour, which was all I could take. Eric had a good time but I was more than ready to go, too many screaming kids for me. When we got back to my house I played with Eric for a while, then gave him a bath and put him in the bed with me. Five minutes later, he was sleep. I was glad because I was exhausted. But as soon as I fell asleep, the phone rang.

I pick up the phone quickly to avoid waking up Eric.

"Hello." I said in a whisper.

"Hey, Beautiful."

"Hey baby, how is everything? Are you enjoying LA?"

"I sure am. LA is giving me love since you neglected me."

"You are such a big baby. I gave you plenty of love but that's OK. I have someone to give me love tonight. He is so cute, handsome actually. His smile lights up the room and he already has me."

"You're still a comedian I see, trying to get me jealous."

"You should be jealous. He is the most handsome, sweetest fella and he loves to give me kisses. He's laying right beside me now. My only complaint is that he hogs up the bed like you."

"Oh, you're babysitting tonight for Landon. How is little Eric?"

I laughed, "Well little Eric is as cute as ever. I know you wish you were this cute. Big Eric and Landon were fighting over the dress she wants to wear to LA. They were driving me crazy, so I took Eric."

"Those two are a trip. Who was winning?" He joked

"I know, I wonder how they made a baby. You know who was winning. It seems Landon will be causing havoc."

"That's nothing new."

"I thought motherhood had slowed her down. From the looks of things, she might be picking up where she left off."

"They're that bad?"

"They're bad enough. They were yelling in front of Eric. I wasn't even there ten minutes before they went at it. I stayed out of it. You

25

know Landon has a mind of her own. Whatever I say will go in one ear and out the other."

"So Beautiful, what do you have planned for this weekend without me."

"Tomorrow I'm hanging out with Ma and Patrice. They're shopping for Jonathan's birthday party next week. I was going to take Eric home, but I might just keep him all weekend. He's good company. Eric and I probably will hang out, take pictures, get into trouble."

"Sounds like a plan, I'm going to let you get some sleep. I'll talk to you tomorrow"

"Alright, I love you."

"I love you, Beautiful."

3

Where Is The Love?

I was seated on the plane between Eric and Landon playing referee shaking my head as they both kept giving each other evil stares.

I told myself I refuse to let their drama ruin my trip.

"Landon, why are you so difficult?" Eric complained.

"I told you to get over it." She shot back.

"For real, I'm getting tired of your damn mouth."

"You know I don't care."

"Real talk, me and you need to have a long talk. This shit, your attitude, I'm fucking tired of this shit."

Landon yawned and I turned up the volume on my MP3 player.

*

The plane ride couldn't end fast enough. I was horny and ready to see my baby. Unfortunately, for me he wouldn't be able to meet us at the airport due to a last minute meeting. Instead, he arranged for someone to pick us up and take us to the hotel. It was still early, ten when we arrived. The show didn't start until eight, but Braxton wanted us there by six for the Pre-show. I found out via a note, along with flowers he left on the table, we would not be able to hook up until after the show. My hopes for a quickie had been dashed. I guess it was for the best. At least now my hair wouldn't get messed up. I looked in the mirror, admiring my long layers, so glad I added honey

27

blonde highlights. I laid my gown out and prepped my stuff for later. Landon and Eric were still barely talking. In fact, she advised me when we were going to our rooms that she would be getting dressed in mine. Five minutes later, she was standing at my door knocking with bellboy in tow carrying her things.

"Landon, why do you have to be such a diva?" I asked, turning around to face her.

"I'm not being difficult, I just don't feel like being bothered with Eric right now. Yas his days with me are numbered."

"Diva, you two are ridiculous. All of this over a dress?"

"It's more than the dress. He thinks because we're married I'm supposed to be a housewife that stays home and become a Betty Crocker. It's stupid of him to think that."

She was right about that. "Ok Diva, but tonight it's no girl slumber party. Get your own room or make up with Eric. Just letting you know after the awards, Braxton and I are out. You and Eric enjoy. I'll see you in the morning."

"Uh, you're kicking me out for a man?"

"Diva, please, no dramatics. It's not any man, it's my husband," I emphasized. "You're a big girl. Besides, from what it sounds like, you have your own after party planned."

"You know it. I will be partying tonight…alone."

"Land, do not start anything. You are married."

"I know what I am, but right now I'm not happy. I didn't say I was fucking anyone. I just will be enjoying LA."

"I'm not getting into this with you. Just don't call me until after twelve tomorrow."

"It's still early, what do you want to do?"

Let's just get some lunch and maybe do a little shopping. I want to be back no later than three, maybe two. From what I keep hearing about this dress, it may take you a while to get you in it."

"Ha, Ha it's not that bad, but that'll work. Are you ready?"

"Aren't you going to ask Eric if he wants to come?"

"No."

"You are terrible. I'll be back, I'll ask and you better be nice."

"I keep telling you I don't take orders."

"Land?"

"Yas?"

"I'll be back."

I went down the hall to Eric's suite and knocked on the door.

"Yeah, Yas, what's up?" Eric asked.

"Landon and I are going to get something to eat, do you want to come?"

"Obviously, Landon doesn't want me there because if she did she would have asked herself. I also see her stuff isn't in here either, so no thanks. Besides, I'm tired and I don't have the patience for the attitude. Truthfully, I'm getting tired of her attitude and her."

"Eric, you know Landon and I get ready together." I say in attempt to diffuse some of the growing tension.

"Yas, don't make excuses."

"I'm not and I'm not trying to get into your business but all this drama over a dress?"

"You know it's more than a dress. Landon is a spoiled brat that needs to grow up. She thinks the world revolves around her and she doesn't compromise. And that mouth! Where do I begin? I'm her husband not her servant."

"I understand Eric, but you know Land has always been blunt. She doesn't listen to me either. You married her. You knew how she was from the beginning."

"That's true but she needs to calm down. She dresses and acts like she doesn't have a husband or a child."

I agreed with him on that, but he knows how Landon is.

"Eric, you know Landon the more you tell her not to do something the more she will. Let her wear the dress. Like she said, you'll be with her. The less fuss you make the better. She'll move on."

"That's the problem, she's trying my patience. She's getting worse. All I want her to do is support me. You know like coming to some games and afterwards we can hang out. She came to one game. She did go to a after party, but did she come with me? No."

I took a deep breath. I was not prepared for all this.

"Eric, let's focus on tonight. I'll try to talk to her, but you know Diva doesn't listen to me. Let's try and have a good night."

"For you, alright."

"Are you sure you don't want to come with us for lunch?'

"Nah, I'm going to the bar. I need to mellow out before I can deal with Landon. Here, lunch on me," he peels off $500 and hands it to me.

"Good idea. Thanks brother-in-law."

"Yas, I don't know if Landon and I will be together in the future, but you've always been alright with me. I hope it can stay that way."

I gave him another hug, "Of course, but don't write Landon off just yet. You and I will always be cool. You are my handsome nephew's father."

Eric looked like his mind was a million miles away, "Yeah."

I went back to my room to see Landon in the mirror. "Are you ready, Diva?"

"As long as you're alone."

"You are terrible. Eric is not going, but he's treating us to lunch. He gave me $500."

"Cheap ass could have at least treated us to a massage. I need one with all the grief he's been causing."

"Diva, Eric is not bad. You should stop being so mean, acting like a brat. He spoils you and little Eric. He definitely not lacking in the looks department and from what you said many times before, he has plenty of bedroom skills."

"Whatever! Not good enough. Like I said, Landon needs freedom."

"Damn Diva, are you ever satisfied?"

4

You Da One

Landon and I had lunch and did a little shopping. By the time we made it back to our suite it was close to three. I kicked Landon out ten minutes later for my own sanity. I needed to take a long bubble bath and relax. Landon and Eric drama had me in a mood. I decided on Carol'sDaughter Ecstasyscent to get rejuvenated. It was in the bathroom, I found a note.

Hey Beautiful,

I'm sorry I couldn't be there with you

You just don't know how I wanted to welcome you to LA, my way

Tonight however be prepared, for now relax and enjoy your bath

I'll definitely be thinking of you as you say, I'm in my boring meetings

Anyway, I want you to know how special you are to me

Thank you for loving me and being you

Can't wait to kiss you tonight

I love you,

The best husband in the world,

Braxton

PS.

In the box to the right of the vanity

There's a little something special for you

I know it'll look good with your dress

You know I had to peek

31

That Braxton, I smiled. Opening the box revealed a beautiful gold diamond knot

eternity bracelet. He was right it would look good. My baby has taste. oh, how I love me some him.

I smile thinking of our first encounter. I've always had a lot of male attention, all fascinated by my eyes, but no one wanted to love me. It was always about my eyes until Braxton. He called me beautiful, something he still does to this day. He didn't realize how much that meant to me... hell it still does. My body tingles just thinking of how, even then, our bodies intertwined together, creating the perfect fit. When he wrapped his arms around me. I felt so secure. I knew it was where I needed to be.

Braxton gave me the gift of experiencing true love. I guess you can say we gave each other that gift. Unlike me, Braxton grew up in a loving home, attention and acceptances were never a problem. He was, well, still is, spoiled and decided he would be a player for life. He had no desire to settle at all until me. As he says, I flipped the script. However it wasn't always beautiful.

We've definitely been through a lot in our four years, including a miscarriage which ultimately caused a year and a half break-up. Although our break-up was very difficult for me, it was something I had to go through. It was during that time that I begin to love Yasmin. We both had some growing to do. We learned the importance of communication and what commitment means. When we finally did reunite, Braxton wasted no time going to the altar, surprising me in the Cayman Islands. Six months since our marital union, here I am.

Forty-five minutes later, I hear Landon knocking on my door.

"Time to get ready, Yas. Luckily, Eric wasn't in the room so I was able to take a bath. Now it's time for make-up."

Landon pulled out her dress and all I could do was shake my head. I'd say it was about a yard of material. The top of the dress looked and fit like a bathing suit and was a pretty gold color with a very low V-cut in the front that closed just above her navel. Her breasts were barely covered.. Around her hips was a Swarovski crystal belt. The bottom half extended only to her upper thigh. Although it was layered in material and did flair out you could still get a show. Basically, if she crossed her legs, you would get a peek. So yes, it was a bathing suit with a 3-4 inch skirt attached. Surprisingly, she was beautiful, not sluttish. Only Landon could pull it off..

"Landon that dress is a little risqué…" Landon cuts me off mid-sentence.

"Hush, Yas. At least it's not tight."

"Let me finish. You look good, fierce as always."

"Thanks, Yas. You know you would look just as good."

"I don't think so," I laughed. "If I had that on, Braxton would have a damn fit."

"Yas, please, forget a Braxton. You're too good. Braxton always has a fit with his jealous ass. He got your ass so far up in his you scared to move. I keep telling you show off that figure."

"Land, please, before Braxton was even a thought you wouldn't have caught me in that dress. That dress is only for you. As far as me being in Braxton's ass, it goes both ways. Unlike you, my man and I are happy, so don't hate."

"Yeah, whatever. Let's see what robe you wearing tonight."

"Diva, you need some don't you? Don't worry about what I'm wearing. I'll be getting just as much attention as you."

"Well, I'm not going to lie I wouldn't mind getting good dick, that'll definitely come later. With or without Eric is the question. For now, let me see this dress.

My dress was a bronze colored beaded dress embedded with gold accented crystal throughout. My 36 DD managed to stay intact held tight with crystal straps that criss-crossed in the back. Right below my breast, to just the top of my hips the dress were completely made of crystal. The bottom made of satin hugged my hips just right, then loosely flowed out to the floor, the split on the side that stopped upper thigh. Even with my matching gold accent crystal embedded four-inch stilettos my gown still scraped the ground.

"I must say, you look good, Yas. Braxton won't be able to keep his hands off you.

"Thanks, Diva. I know the media will love you."

"I aim to please."

I never was one for make-up. I did some mascara to lengthen my eyelashes and a soft colored pink lip gloss, my long wrap and golden highlights complimented my dress and eyes. Since my hair was so long, I chose long diamond earrings with a matching teardrop diamond necklace. The bracelet Braxton choose looked good with my dress and other jewelry. He has taste. The only other jewelry I wore was my wedding ring. I stood in the mirror admiring my reflection. Yes, Braxton wouldn't be able to keep his hands off of me.

At a quarter to six, Eric came knocking on the door. I was ready to go see my baby, but Landon was still putting the finishing touches on her look.

"Hey, Eric."

"Yasmin, you look beautiful," he turned to Landon, "Land, sweetheart you look beautiful too. I'm lucky I get to escort both of you beautiful sisters."

"Thank you, "Landon and I both said in unison.

The plan was to get to the show by 6:15 but with Landon finishing touches and traffic we made it there at 6:45. Landon and Eric were walking around doing photo shots. I stayed on the sidelines. I had my share of media attention when I dated Chauncey.

Like Eric, Chauncey was an NBA player. He was my rebound guy after my breakup with Braxton. Chauncey was an overall nice guy, very sweet. He sent me gifts along with lingerie weekly. The reason for the break-up, Chauncey, like me, had unresolved feelings for our exes. We dated for a little over a year, but my heart was always with Braxton.

I was on the sidelines watching Landon soak up the media attention when I heard a familiar voice.

"Hey Yassy, what's up?"

It was Geester, Chauncey's best friend. He was a rapper now turned actor.

"Hey Geester, I'm doing well. I know you're doing well. I see you're up for a couple of awards. Congrats on that and good luck."

"Thanks, Yassy. You're looking real good, girl. I know you're not here all alone." He said, giving me a hug.

Before I could respond, I heard another familiar voice coming towards me, singing D'Angelo.

"I want some of your Brown Sugar, ohh..."

I looked up to see Chauncey 6'7 frame looking as good as ever. His smooth butter skin and curly brown hair had me take a second. When I saw his pretty white teeth I reminisced a little about our relationship. I missed joking with him. He always greeted me with song hooks and made me laugh. Although Chauncey was cool, he was just there for sex, like I said earlier, a rebound.

"Hey Chaunce." I said, giving him a hug and light kiss on the cheek."

"Hold up, why he get a kiss? All I got was a hug." Geester whined.

"That's right, man, We got history."

I laughed.

"How you doing, Miss Lady? I see you look sexy as usual. Hmm and you always smell so good," Chauncey said, grabbing my hand. "You miss my sexiness don't you?"

"You are funny."

"Hold it, what's this on your finger?" He lifted my hand to examine my ring. "Nice, so you're a married woman now?"

"Yes, I am."

"Is he treating you right? Does he make you happy?"

"Yes and yes."

"He better, but I know he's not sexy like me."

"Still a sweetheart."

"Of course, where's your girl?"

"You know she's here causing Eric grief. Let's just say her dress is one of a kind. Something made for Diva."

He laughed. "Landon is still crazy, poor Eric."

"Poor me, I had to play referee and sit between them on the plane. I need a drink after listening to those two."

"They were that bad."

Before I could respond we had unwanted attention. This was another reason why Chauncey and I couldn't work.

"Chauncey, who is your date? Can we get a picture?" One of the photographers asked.

"For old time's sakes, miss Lady?"

"Sure."

I did a couple of shots with Chauncey and Geester. I wanted to ask Chauncey about his ex, Toya, but we were interrupted again by Javon.

Javon was Braxton's best friend, who I didn't particularly care for.

"Hey, Chauncey, Geester, Yasmin." Javon said suspiciously.

"Hey, Javon." they responded with equal skepticism.

"Yas, we going to catch up with you later. Holla if you need anything."

I gave Chauncey and Geester another hug along with kiss before they exited.

"You're bold aren't you?"

"What are you talking about?" I asked, annoyed.

"I'm just saying, hugging and kissing other men, an ex-boyfriend in front of your husband," he shifts his eyes and I follow.

I see Braxton talking to one of the other BET execs. He was maintaining his conversation without missing a beat, but from the stare I just received, I knew he was pissed. I focus my attention back to Javon. "That was nothing. It wasn't like that."

"Hey, I'm not the one you have to convince. For what it's worth, I believe you," he chuckled. "You know Braxton. How he is about you. How easily he gets jealous when you're with other men. But, you know what that's about, guilty conscience, skeletons in the closet."

"What are you trying to say Javon?"

He laughed, "Nothing, you're husband wants you."

I roll my eyes and walk over towards Braxton. His 6'4 athletic frame looked so sexy in his black tux. The way Braxton smooth caramel skin glistened under the sun had me ready to find a room for a quickie. Luckily, when I reached Braxton the other execs had left.

"Yasmin."

I took a deep breath to prepare myself. Braxton calling me Yasmin was not a good thing. He rarely, if ever called me by my name. I was always "beautiful." If he called me Yasmin it meant something bad or he was mad. I knew it was the latter. I took the opportunity to try and get a little affection, big mistake.

"Hey baby," I attempt to give Braxton a hug. He abruptly stops me. His piercing grey eyes shoot me a look that let me know he was pissed. The way his jaw begins to flex, I know not to press.

"Hey."

"I haven't seen you in five days, I can't get a hug?" I whined.

He stares me right in the eye, "Nope, not after you were hugging and kissing on other men. I don't want seconds, I mean thirds. Your lips kissed two other men and now you smell like them."

Is he serious? I bit my tongue. This is his job, I can't cuss him out now, but I most definitely will later. I thought we were passed his jealousy. "Fine, Braxton, I'll see you later." I turned to walk, but Braxton grabs my arm. Oh he was playing I thought. I turn around and smile, "Yes."

"The restroom is over there. You can freshen up. I'll be waiting right here for you."

My smile quickly turns into a frown. I turn around storming off to the restroom. Braxton had officially pissed me off. I wasn't in there a hot second when I heard Landon.

"Yas, you okay?"

"No."

I recapped Landon on the situation.

She laughed. "I don't believe I'm saying this, but you and Chauncey did look a little cozy. If I didn't know any better, I'd think you were together. I saw the way he held your hand the entire time you were talking, and the eye contact. Y'all looked so cute."

"Land, was it that bad?"

"Yas, the last time we were at a ceremony, Chauncey was your date and Braxton was the one with a dumb look on his face, full of regret. Tonight it was like déjà vu with you two. I was waiting for you to kiss."

"We weren't that bad."

"If you say so, but I actually felt bad for Braxton."

"Stop playing, I told him I was married." I grabbed a moist towel and dabbed around my neck. I refreshed my perfume and added some more gloss.

"You know I'm right. Well, I'm going back out to my sweetie."

I whipped my neck around and looked at Diva, "Who's your sweetie?"

"Eric, of course,"

"Alright, I'll see you in a few."

Five minutes later, I was standing by Braxton and he was still pissed. He still hadn't hugged or kissed me. He was barely holding my hand. I guess this will be a long night. We were doing the meet and greet with the BET people, but I wanted some alone time. I was tired of Braxton's attitude and needed him to get over it. Finally, right before the show was to begin I got a chance to pull Braxton to the side.

"I missed you, baby," I attempt to kiss Braxton on the lips, but he turns his head. Then he walks away without a word.

I stood there with a stupid look on my face for about five seconds.

"Come on before the show starts," he orders.

I wait for a few more seconds before following behind. When we made it to our seats, Landon and Eric were already there, holding hands, very cozy. Apparently, the tables had turned.

"Hey Eric, Landon," said Braxton.

Landon and Eric stood up so we could get by. From the look on Braxton's face I could tell he was shocked by Landon dress. He had a look on his face like, *"OK."* He looked at Eric who just raised his hands in defeat. I had to chuckle.

"So Braxton, any surprises during the show?" Eric quizzed.

"I'm not saying. You have to sit back and watch the show."

They continued to make small chitchat until the show started. While Eric and Landon joked and acted like a loving couple, Braxton continued to give me the cold shoulder.

The show was very live and entertaining. I was enjoying the show despite Braxton's mood. Things became even tenser when Geester performed. He had Chauncey on stage with him, and they needed two ladies out of the audience to help them out. I almost pissed on myself when Chauncey came walking down the aisle. I was panicking on the inside, but outwardly, I don't know how, but I kept a straight face. I looked forward, acting oblivious to what was going on around me. When he stopped at the row in front of me, I held my breath and prayed. They were answered because he picked some little J-Lo imitation who was acting like a crazed fan.

Landon nudged me then whispered to me, "That was close, too much for me."

I looked at her like, "You're telling me."

I glanced over at Braxton whom was still being nonchalant and ignoring me. When the show was over part of me was anxious to go back to the hotel but then again, I didn't know what to expect. This was definitely not how I planned to spend my trip. Braxton was right about one thing, I was spoiled. I haven't had a good night sleep since he left. I've tossed and turned since he left. From the looks of things now, it will be another sleepless night.

As we were exiting the show, Braxton pulls me close, grabbing me by my waist. "I have to talk to someone before we leave."

"Alright, I'll wait for you by the door. I'm going to tell Landon and Eric to go ahead and leave."

Braxton doesn't comment instead, he once again, leaves me alone. I find Landon and Eric who for the moment are still in love.

"Hey guys."

"You okay, Yassy," Landon gives me a hug."

"Where's Braxton?" Eric asked.

"He said he had to talk to someone, so go ahead. We'll catch up with you in the morning."

"You sure, Yassy?" Landon asked.

"Yes Diva, have fun for me."

Just as Landon and Eric were about to leave, Chauncey approaches us.

"Hey. Landon, Eric."

"Chauncey," Landon squeals as she gives him a hug.

"What's going on man?" Eric said, giving him a pound.

"Nothing much, just enjoying the off season."

"That was a good game you had against the Nets." Eric said matter-of-factly.

"Thanks, man."

"Chauncey, what have you been enjoying during the off season?" Landon asked.

He chuckles. "Nothing. The time off. I see your girl went and got married on me." He added, changing the subject.

"I know, surprised me too. She went away on vacation and comes back like, 'Diva I got married.' I was like what? I wasn't even there to partake in the festivities. All I saw was a picture."

"Landon, he didn't ask you all of that. That's enough." I warned.

Unfazed by my warning, Landon continues. "Didn't even have a chance to object if I wanted to, not that I would have, but still. I didn't get a chance to see my Yassy. She was at my wedding. I made sure of that. Silly me thought she would have done the same." Landon instigated.

I look at Landon and shake my head.

"You two are a trip, always entertaining."

"Ain't that the truth," Eric agreed.

"For the hundredth time Landon, it was a surprise. I didn't even know."

"It's all good though, as long as she happy." Chauncey smiled.

"I am."

"It didn't look that way earlier." Chauncey countered.

All eyes on me, before I could respond on cue, Braxton remembers me and comes over. I quickly made introductions.

"Chauncey, this is my husband, Braxton, Chauncey."

"Hey," Braxton responds without offering a handshake.

"Hey, man. Well, I'm going to the after party. Y'all have a good one. Congratulations, Braxton, you got a good one."

"Excuse me. Do you not see me standing here?" Landon interjected.

"Landon, you know you're in a class of your own. Hail to the queen."

"Thank you. I am one of a kind."

"Eric man," Chauncey pretended to be pulling out all his money, "Here man, you need it."

We all laughed at that, even Braxton.

"See you later. Eric and I are right behind you." Landon said as Chauncey walks off.

While Eric excused himself to the bathroom I took the opportunity to talk to Landon. Braxton had once again stepped away to talk to another business associate.

"Land, it was good seeing Chauncey, but I couldn't even look at him. He kept looking at me like, what could have been, what's up. Braxton obviously caught that too because now he's giving me the cold shoulder and a, 'What the hell is going on' look. I'm glad they're both gone. I need a minute to catch my breath."

Landon laughed, "I know. Eric and I both saw that. Braxton's probably having flashbacks of those old photos of you and Chauncey looking extra freaky on vacation. You two did make a cute couple. Didn't BET have you as one of their hottest couples? Yes, they did. Matter of fact, we both were listed, those were the days. I actually feel bad for Braxton." Landon instigated.

"Okay, Landon."

"Don't get mad at me. I'm just stating the truth. Another truth is Chauncey's whole swagger is on point."

"Chauncey's definitely looking real good."

"Yes, he is. He's always had sex appeal, but damn. He looks like he's been drinking milk. Are you sure his bedroom skills are lacking? I may have to teach him some moves, send him to Landon's boot camp."

"He's not that bad, he just needs to take his time. Stop sexing like he's still on the court trying to beat the time clock."

"Well, it's a good thing I'm married and he is your ex. Otherwise, that's one project I wouldn't mind getting involved with."

"Speaking of which, don't start any havoc. Landon, behave and be nice to Eric."

"Yassy, don't start. I am being nice."

"Yes, you are. I want you to continue to do that. I just want you to watch the flirting, hands and mouth."

She laughed, "This is LA."

"It is, just enjoy it with your husband."

"I will as long as he doesn't get too clingy or boring."

"Landon -"

Eric returns before I could continue my lecture.

"Land?"

"Yes, sweetie," Landon sang.

"Are you ready to go?"

"Yas, are you going to be alright by yourself?" She asked being sarcastic.

"Yes, Diva."

"We'll catch up with you in the A.M." Eric gives me a hug.

I stood around looking out of place, unattached for about fifteen minutes. Of course, I receive plenty of male attention. I alternated from diverting my attention to pretending to be engrossed in a text message, all the while making sure the wedding ring is in full view. I was doing whatever possible to avoid any attention. I still had yet to deal with Mr. Simms who had proven he was going to be quite difficult.

"Yasmin, I want you to meet my boss." Braxton said, before grabbing me and escorted me towards an older gentleman. At last, for the first time tonight Braxton held me like he loved me. "Mr. Johnson, This is my wife, Yasmin."

"Hello, Mr. Johnson, nice to meet you." I said.

"So nice to meet you, I've seen your picture, but you're much more beautiful in person."

"Thank you," I smile.

We made small talk for ten minutes while I pretended to be interested.

"Your husband is doing a great job at BET. You should be very proud." Mr. Johnson complimented.

"I am." I hug Braxton tighter.

"Well you two enjoy the rest of the night. Braxton I'll see you next week."

After meeting the boss, Braxton was cold again and I was too through. Before we left, we took a couple of photos. Braxton seemed to be in a better mood, but I wasn't. We stopped at an after party but it was all business. Braxton basically networked, so there was no dancing. Braxton still just managed to introduce me then he was back to ignoring me. I had a couple of drinks in hopes to mellow out my now attitude. Unfortunately, it didn't help. I made conversation with some, but Braxton still wasn't talking directly to me. On the way back to the hotel I sat on one end of the car and Braxton the other. I ignored him while he stared at me the entire ride. I did feel uncomfortable, but I remained calm crossing my legs, making sure to show plenty of thighs.

5

You Belong to Me

As soon as we enter our suite, the argument begins.

"Yasmin, why was Chauncey in your face? You were acting like you're married to him, disrespecting me, kissing, and hugging on him. Holding fucking hands!"

I just stood there and allowed him to vent.

"What the cat has your tongue now."

"No, are you done?"

"You want to be a smartass now?"

"Braxton, I'm tired, this has been a long day and I don't feel like arguing with you."

"And I did not want to look up and see Chauncey all in your face."

"Braxton, Chauncey was not in my face. We were talking"

"So what's going on, do you have unresolved feelings for Chauncey now?"

I look at Braxton like he was crazy, "Are you serious?"

"I asked didn't I?"

"Braxton, I thought we were over this jealousy thing you have. I married you didn't I."

"You didn't have to have him all up in your face. What kind of shit is that?"

"Braxton-"

"And him saying, I got a good one? What was that about? I know what I got."

"Well you need to start acting like it," I yelled, frustrated.

"So now I don't act like it. I don't do anything for you? I don't appreciate you?"

I let out an exasperated breath.

"Your words."

"I didn't say all that. I-"

He cut me off, "How the fuck you think I feel? You all up in his face like you're missing him."

"It was an award show, a gathering where people come together. They talk, socialize. It's what we do. Was I supposed to be rude like you were to me?"

He gave me that, stop being a smartass look.

I wasn't done, "Are we at a loss for words. Do we realize we were being irrational, frivolous and ridiculous?"

"Yasmin, I'm not in the damn mood for your smart ass mouth."

"I am not in the mood for your unnecessary foolishness. Listen, it's not that serious. It was innocent. Chauncey and I are friends, nothing else."

"It is serious." He unbuttons his shirt.

"We were talking. What? Really, again was I supposed to ignore him?"

"It looked like it was more than talking. Holding hands, looking like you were reminiscing about old times."

I was done with this argument "I'm sorry if you feel that way but what do you want me to do? It's over. I'm done with it. I did not come to LA to argue with you over Chauncey."

"I did not have you meet me in LA to see you hugging and kissing on Chauncey."

"Okay Braxton, you're right. Next time, I'll be more conscious."

"Next time?"

"Braxton you work at BET, Chauncey is in the entertainment business. Good chance we'll run into him again."

Braxton stood there for a moment just staring at me.

"What?"

"You don't think you were wrong?"

"Braxton grow up, stop acting like a baby. I said I was sorry."

Braxton stormed off into the bathroom and five minutes later I hear the shower running. I kick off my stilettos and made myself a drink. Braxton comes out ten minutes later wrapped in a towel. I was pissed at him, but horny as hell at the same time. We were supposed to be enjoying each other. And I still hadn't had a kiss. Damn, I married a jealous ass spoiled man, Pissed I am, but he looked sexy as hell with that towel. Caramel skin smooth, still damp from the shower, body toned, not as toned I admit as Chauncey's, but not bad at all. After looking at him I was ready to accept my defeat and beg for mercy. I ached to feel the strength from his back as he moved in and out of me.

By now Braxton is on the bed flicking through the channels. I walk over to Braxton. I attempt to kiss him but he refuses me.

"Braxton we haven't seen each other in almost a week. I apologized. Can I have a kiss now?"

He kept flicking the channel like I didn't just ask him a question.

"Braxton?"

Still he ignores me. You know what, forget him. I looked good tonight and I was going to party. I walked over to where I kicked off my stilettos and put them on. I checked my hair, reapplied my gloss and headed to the door. That got his attention.

"Where are you going?"

"Out!"

"Out where?" Braxton said, getting up and walking towards me.

"Out somewhere where my company will be appreciated."

"And where will your company be appreciated?"

"Anywhere, but here."

He got up in my face. "We're not done."

"Yes, we are," I put my hand on the doorknob and attempt to open the door.

Braxton put his hand on the door, preventing me from opening it. "You need to have a seat and calm your ass down."

"You need to get out of my way."

"Don't try me, Yasmin."

"Whatever."

Braxton picks me up, throws me over his shoulder, carries me over to the bed and throws me down.

Immediately, I attempt to get up, but Braxton isn't allowing it. "Calm down."

"Make me!" I challenge.

Braxton gets on top of me. His strong arms pin me to the bed. "You're a trip, giving me attitude after you were in the wrong."

I roll my eyes and sigh.

"There you go testing me. I'm working, look up and see Chauncey and you posing for the camera like you're together. Saying hello is one thing, but you took it to another level with the kissing and holding hands."

I look down to see his towel was lost during our struggle. Needless to say I was ready to feel my baby.

"Braxton, I'm sorry, really, I wasn't trying to disrespect you. You know I love you. Honestly, I never had feelings for Chauncey like that. You know he was my rebound guy after you. Baby, I don't want to fight." I say sweetly.

He looks at me, shakes his head and releases his grip on my arms. I take the opportunity to wrap my arms around his neck and pull him close. "You know you're stuck with me for life, till death do us part. I'm not going anywhere."

I could feel Sugar Daddy rising. He being in me was long overdue.

This time when I kiss him, he accepts. Braxton kisses me long and hard. I wrap my legs around his waist and continue to kiss him. Braxton abruptly stops and stands up grabbing me with him.

"Show me how much you love me. Take it all off." He orders.

I happily oblige.

I push Braxton on the bed, slid out of my dress, and kneel down on the floor in front of him. Gently I grab *Sugar Daddy*, my pet name for Braxton's thick 9 ½ long, smooth, caramel dick. It reminds me of the candy, once in your mouth guaranteed you can suck all day.

I seductively lick the tip before covering Sugar Daddy with my warm, moist mouth. At first I alternate from taking subtle nibbles to teasing him with my tongue. I take my time being extra nice and slow. Next I cover 1/4 of his dick with my mouth, sucking on my candy like it was stuck at the top of my mouth.

Braxton grabs my head. Gently, he pushes my head, indicating he wants me to take in more.

I don't. I place one hand on his thigh, the other on his balls, choosing to tenderly massage him instead, while being careful to add the right amount of pressure. Again, he presses on my head, this time pulling my hair. I add more pressure, sucking harder, massaging a little rougher. I stop and like my candy slip from my mouth. I lick up and down his shaft, than round and round letting the juices from my mouth coat him. I smile when I see a trickle of cream slid down. I take him in my mouth again, taking in only a quarter, but the most sensitive part. Allowing my mouth to savor him, I suck, suck and hold.

Braxton has both his hands on my head. I give him what he wants. I relax my throat and go further taking in more than half. Masterfully, I move my mouth up and down, pulling back yet again before he could reach his peak. I nibble at his tip, and then I lick, watching as more pre-cum trickles out and down his dick. Mouth open wide, I take in all of Sugar Daddy. Deep throat is what he got as I hold him in. Suck, suck, lick, suck, hold, and suck. Satisfied he enjoyed his treat, I let him have his release. But not before I pull away, allowing his cum to shoot all over the room.

I was more than ready to the feel him. I stand in preparation for my ride. I kiss him before bending down to straddle him.

Braxton takes his finger and begins moving it in and out of me. With his other hand he squeezes my ass, turning me on even more. I lift up, attempting to get him to slide in me, but he doesn't. He adds another finger to tease me more, moving faster and harder.

"I want some Sugar Daddy. Fuck me, Baby. Fuck me." I beg.

"Unh, unh."

"You know you want it. Give me the dick."

"Nope, you don't appreciate this dick," he antagonizes.

"Baby, I do. I need your dick." I whimper.

Braxton removes his fingers from me, takes that hand, grabs my ass and flips me. He's now on top, sucking on my neck, my breast, still teasing me, not allowing me to feel him. He uses his fingers again to tease me. I'm scratching his back, digging my nails in. I'm so wet and his fingers aren't reaching where I need them to. I push his hands away. Knowing Braxton would be turned on I use my fingers to please myself. Just like I knew, Braxton stops sucking my breast to watch me. I give him a show, playing with my nipples and moving my fingers, all the while giving him plenty of moans. I'm so wet, overflowing with desire that I share with him. I take my wet hand. Place it on his dick and massage him soothingly. It doesn't take long for Braxton to spread my legs into a split.

Braxton then rams his dick in me so far he takes my breath. I shudder from the pain. The pain soon replaced with pleasure. He's grinding so hard, taking control causing me to whimper, unable to talk. He bends down, kisses me hard, and then sucks on my bottom lip.

"Where's the smart mouth? You feel me fucking the shit out of this pussy."

I don't respond, just moan.

"Oh, we quiet now. How this dick feel? I'm hitting that spot. That's it. Damn, you wet. Ride this dick. Come on grind on it. That's my girl."

He lets up some. Lovingly he strokes my face. Intensely he kisses me as he hands continuously strokes my face. His dick strokes are now long, precise, and deep.

"You love me or this dick?" he asks

"Both." I moan.

"What did you say, Beautiful?"

All I can do is moan.

Long, deep strokes are stopped and he pulls out.

"Turn over." He demands.

I obey.

He grabs me by the legs, pulling me, to the edge. Grabbing my waist, he pulls me to him entering me vigorously. Taking one of his hands, he massages my clit. He was on a mission, he had a goal, and with each stroke his dick told me my pussy was his and only his. Telling me I could never get ecstasy like this from another. The mission, the goal is accomplished. I arch my back higher, giving him more of me, while I take in more him. His loving feeling so damn good I don't want him to stop. He grinds himself more into me, reaching that ultimate spot. He knows me, my body. He knows he's found his mark. His tease begins, light strokes, hard strokes, light strokes, finally a deep grind that sends me spiraling. I let out a scream as I feel my body reaching its sexual high.

I plop down from exhaustion. The clock read 3:08, but Braxton's energetic ass gets up, turns off the TV and lights. Braxton pulls out candles and incense, lighting them both. He comes back over to the bed climbing on top of me, dick hard, he moves my hair from my shoulders and begins kissing on me.

I turn my head to look at him, "What you do, drink a 5-hour energy drink?"

Smiling he says, "I missed you. Relax."

Braxton seductively places light, soft kisses down my back and butt. He takes the lit candle, pouring it over all the areas he kissed, aroused and ready for another round.

I turn over.

He pushes my knees to my chest and enters me slow. In and out he goes. I use my kegel muscles to squeeze him. He's in a deep rhythm, my pussy elated.

"Damn." He pants.

"Squish, squish, squish, squish," is the sound as he pumps in and out of me hard and my juices gush all over him.

The phone rings breaking my rhythm but not for long.

"Suck my nipples."

Pushing my legs apart, he does.

I begin moving my hips to match his speed. I wrap my arms around his shoulder while he nibbles on my breast.

Again the phone rings, this time nonstop. Braxton knocks the phone on the floor and is back to pleasing me in a matter of seconds.

He rolls on his back, pulling me on top of him.

I lay back slightly holding onto his ankles, creating the perfect V between my back and his legs. He sits up. My hips pump into him as he rubs my breast.

Simultaneously, the alarm in the room sounds, the sprinkler is activated and hotel security along with management comes bursting into the room.

"Ahhhh!" I scream.

"Is everyone okay?"

Braxton grabs a blanket to cover me. "What the hell?! This water is cold as shit!" Braxton yells.

I bury my head in his chest.

There is so much commotion going on and too many people. Just when I thought it couldn't get any worse, more people came. I hear Diva rushing in with Eric panicking.

"Yassy!" She stops abruptly, looks at us, and laughs. "I see y'all hot asses needed to be cooled off."

Of course there were some snickers among the room.

"Why are there so many people in my room?" Braxton asks annoyed.

"There was a complaint of loud noise, along with a small cloud of smoke. As you know it is against hotel policy to burn incense or candles. Several attempts to contact you were made, however it now appears the phone was knocked off the hook," said someone from the hotel management.

Braxton manages to sit up with me on top while keeping me covered. "We're fine, can we have some privacy so we can get dressed."

"Yeah sure, but when you get dressed we need to discuss what happened." Security made sort of adjustment and the sprinkler stopped.

Braxton nods.

Once the room was clear and the door is closed.

Braxton busts out laughing, "I guess it was too hot in here."

"Let me go! My hair is messed up and we're soaked. This is not funny, more like embarrassing."

"It was worth it."

I finally laugh, "You are such a freak."

"So are you. I told you before about that screaming. I can't take you anywhere," he teases.

Pouting, I give him a look and attempt to get up. I was so sore. This reminded me of our honeymoon in the Cayman Islands where I could barely walk for a week.

"You okay?" Braxton asked.

"No."

He comes over wraps me in his arms and kisses me on my cheek.

"I'm so embarrassed. I know I look a mess."

"No, you don't."

"Whatever. Let's get dressed. You know they're going to make you pay for this."

"I like how you said 'you pay,'" he laughed.

"You're the freak, you lit the candles, that's my story and I'm sticking to it."

"That's messed up, you going to leave me out there. You know you're an accessory."

I laughed. "You know I'm not leaving you baby, you stuck with me." I walked over and kissed him.

"You want more, come on quickie in the shower."

"No, let's get dressed."

Apparently, I left the suitcase open. I went to get my clothes only to discover they were wet. The sprinkler had soaked my clothes.

"No," I whimpered.

"What's wrong?"

"My clothes are wet. I don't have anything to put on. "

"We can get someone from the hotel to dry them."

"I don't think we should ask the hotel for any favors."

"Let's take a shower. Here, put on my shirt. Call Landon, tell her to go buy you something."

"Everything closed and Landon, pick me out an outfit?"

"Yeah, you right, I'll get you something."

"Ha, ha. That's alright. I'll stick with Landon."

Since the water was turned off in our room, I had to call Landon to let her know we needed to use her room. .

As soon as Landon opens the door the jokes begin.

"Hey, hot asses. Don't try anything crazy. I don't want a repeat of earlier. Matter of fact kids, separate showers. I can't take you two anywhere."

"Anyway Diva, when the store opens can you go pick me out something comfortable?"

"Of course."

"Nothing risqué, a size 10/12," I warn.

"In the meantime, can we get some privacy?" I ask, sweetly.

"Can we leave you two alone?" Eric joked.

"Ha, ha, go ahead and get your jokes. I know you wish you were creative like us."

"That's right, Beautiful, tell 'em. Don't be mad because y'all boring." Braxton comes behind and pulls me close."

"Ill… I don't want to see a porno. We'll be back in thirty minutes, freaks."

After they left, Braxton and I took a shower and he got his quickie. My hair was a big curly mess, so I pulled it into a ponytail. I was able to salvage a bra and underwear and I put on Braxton's t-shirt and a robe while Braxton went to talk to management. Landon came in shortly after Braxton left.

"Hey Diva, where's Eric?'

"Downstairs helping Braxton out."

"I'm so embarrassed. It seemed like the entire staff was in the room."

"Well at least you didn't end up in the ER like you did with Chauncey."

"Oh my god, don't remind me of that. This time the sex was definitely worth it."

"I can't believe Chauncey was that bad, him and his sexy self."

"He's without a question, sexy, but his skills are on the basketball court.'"

"Such a shame, my sweetie is multi-talented." Landon proclaims.

"Seriously, Chauncey is a sweetheart. He always treated me like a lady, very lovable, but you know. I didn't have a desire to try with him. I couldn't get Mr. Simms out of my system. Braxton has always been my love."

"Don't I know. Please don't start the Braxton record."

"Landon, I'm happy, despite the drama going on with my paternity. Braxton has been here, proving he's here for better or worse."

"Yeah, I know he loves you."

"He does. I know he stills feel guilty about the way he ended things after my miscarriage."

"You think so?" Landon commented seeming distant.

"I do. He's definitely proved he is committed, but…"

"But what?"

I took a deep breath.

"Where is this all coming from? You're back together, in love, married."

"Landon, with everything that has happened in the last month, I'm scared. Yes, I love Braxton. Yes, I know he loves me. But, all of this newfound truth has me so vulnerable. It's opened up a lot of insecurities. I have so many questions, doubts, fears. Now, I can't stop thinking something else is going to go wrong in my life. Sometimes I think I'm cursed. It's like it's not meant for me to be happy. I should always be in pain. That I should be on guard, always expecting the worst. All of this mess has me thinking about me and Braxton. I wonder if he will be able to handle another tragedy. Truthfully, I know I can't. When Braxton and I broke up, I never felt right. I had a constant ache that no matter what I did, or how much I tried, it would never go away. Then, I was dealing with losing Bryan. Three years later, I'm still struggling. It's so much. I'm waiting for the other shoe to drop. I'm scared."

Landon started crying.

"Land, what's wrong?"

"I'm sorry, Yas. Really, I'm so sorry. I never meant to hurt you. I'm sorry. I love you, you are my sister. I'm sorry I didn't mean to hurt you."

Now I was crying. "Land you didn't hurt me. I know you didn't know what to say to me after my miscarriage. You never lost anyone close to you. Truthfully, there's nothing you could've said. The only thing I wanted was my baby." I paused. "I was so hurt. I felt so alone. Everyone kept telling me, he's in a better place, or it'll get easier. It's ok to cry. No one understood how empty I felt. No one understood our bond. I would sing to Bryan, he would kick. He was growing inside of me, depending on me. Every morning I woke up and thanked

God. I couldn't wait until the day I held him. I couldn't wait to tell him how much I loved him and how happy I was he was in my life, but I never got a chance. There was nothing you could do. I'm not mad at you or anyone. I just have to grieve my own way. "

Landon grabbed me. "Yassy, I'm sorry, I should have been there more. I never meant to hurt you. I'm sorry for bashing Braxton the way I did. I'm sorry Yassy for being selfish. I'm sorry for not coming around you more. Yassy…"

"Land, I told you I understand. I had to grieve my own way. Bryan always will have a part of my life. I have to admit, when I found out you were pregnant with little Eric I was hurt. Not hurt because you were pregnant, but because I never got to see mine. I prayed that your baby was born healthy. When you gave Eric Bryan's name as a middle name that meant so much to me."

Landon started crying harder. "Yas, I'm sorry…"

Before she could finish the men walked in. Braxton immediately rushes to comfort me.

"Yasmin, what's wrong?" He asked with concern.

"Yeah, sweetheart what's going on?" Eric asked.

"We're fine." I insisted.

"Why are you crying, does this has anything to do with your parents?" Braxton asked.

"No, it's not that." I sniffed.

"Then what is it?"

"Yassy and I were talking about…Bryan."

"Yasmin, are you OK?" asked Braxton.

I could tell by his voice that he was a little shook by the mention of our son's name.

I stood up. "I'm okay now. Did you get everything straightened out?

"Yeah, we have another room," he responds, but it's obvious his mind is still on Bryan.

"Well it's after four in the morning. Since everything is shut down, I think we all need a couple of hours of sleep. Diva, don't forget my clothes."

"I won't."

I gave Land and Eric a hug before heading to our new suite. Once there, I took a few minutes to say a prayer for my baby boy.

Landon and Eric came knocking a few hours later. Landon handed me the clothes she picked out and I went to change. I pulled the clothes out the bag to see Landon picked me out a yellow colored BCBG tube dress. I was going to hurt her. The dress was cute, but not me. It stopped mid-thigh, clung, and I had too much breast for this dress.

"Yas, are you ready, I'm hungry." Land complained.

I walked out, "No, I need to buy another outfit."

"Yassy, you look cute, doesn't she fellas."

Eric and Braxton who looked to be preoccupied turned around.

Eric laughed. "Landon trying to clone you. That's definitely her style! You look nice, Yassy."

I looked at Braxton, "Baby?"

"It's up to you, beautiful."

"Land, I'll keep your dress on, but I need a jacket, can't have my breast popping out."

"Yeah, there is a lot up there."

"You think?" I said sarcastically.

"First we're getting something to eat. I'm hungry."

Damn Landon, you hungry again. You've been eating a lot lately," Eric said with a hint of inquiry.

"Shut up, Eric and come on!" blasted Landon.

Braxton grabs my hand and we follow Eric and Landon.

After we had lunch, we hung out in LA. It didn't take long for Land and Eric to get into an argument. Landon was upset after Eric wouldn't buy her a bracelet she wanted. But what pissed her off the most were the fans…female fans. Landon and I went to the boutique while Braxton and Eric went to the shoe store. Well, on our way to meet them, we noticed two females talking to our husbands. I admit, they were attractive. The girls looked like Kim Kardashian clones and were too comfortable. The one talking to Eric was touching, laughing, you know flirting.

"Eric has lost his mind letting that bitch in his face like that."

"Calm down Diva, as you told me it comes with the job."

"It does, but Eric doesn't have to be so friendly. I don't know why you're so calm, Braxton looks like he's enjoying the attention."

"Diva, when we go over there do not cause a scene."

"I am a scene, top priority and he needs to remember that. I gave up a lot marrying him," she said before storming off.

I, of course follow.

"Eric, sweetheart." Landon positions herself between Eric and his admirer.

Eric looks like he's caught.

"Landon."

Landon faces the chick that is talking to Eric, extends her left hand so the groupie could see her ring. "Hello, I'm the Mrs. And you are?"

"Nicollette," she says, with a phony laugh. Her friend tried to roll her eyes on the sly but Landon catches it.

"Are there something wrong with your eyes. I know it must be the way they were rolling. I suggest you get those fixed before they get you into something you can't get out of." Landon giggles.

Nicolette is bold, "Eric it was nice talking to you, again. Call me next week so we can set up a meeting." She extends her card but Landon snatches it.

"Image Consultant? Hmmm, interesting. Who is she, your helper?" She asked, referring to her friend.

Nicolette gave her a smile that said try me. "Kimberly is my partner."

"Really, I've never heard of either of you. You would benefit my husband how? With someone of Eric's status we need someone who is reputable, established, knows what they're doing. No one... how can I say this, naïve or injudicious."

"Landon." Eric warned.

"London, I am more than capable of handling the job. I'm a professional, my priorities are my clients. I make sure all are satisfied. I trust Eric will make the right decision."

"You've just confirmed one of my concerns. The name is Landon. Remembering a client as well as their wife's name should be your first priority. This shows the client you're sincere, give more of a personal touch. Basically, I'm not impressed, so here's your card back. You're services are not wanted or needed. You still have a lot of things you need to work on, but good luck."

That's my girl, I couldn't help but smile.

Eric had this look of disbelief on his face while Braxton stood speechless.

"Eric. Braxton." Nicolette said before turning away to leave.

Diva wasn't having it. "Nicolette, Kimberly, more needed advice for you, speak to all parties involved. Your people skills are terrible. And finally, if you're going to be image consultants at least keep up with the current fashion trend. Those outfits are hideous and last year."

"That's my Diva." I said, giving her a hug as Nicolette and Kimberly walked off.

"Yas, don't encourage her. Landon you took it too far. You didn't have to insult her." Eric scolded.

"Excuse you?! Don't have me insult you. You didn't have to allow that phony trick in your face. Furthermore, she insulted me. Are you stupid? Read between the lines, she wanted more than business. And you, standing there grinning with a goofy look on your face."

"Landon I was taking her card, not signing a contract. In my profession, I get approached by a lot of women. You know that. Flirting? That title belongs to you."

"Eric, this is not about me right now. Oh, and I caught the part, 'nice seeing you again.' The bitch wasn't even thorough or worth the time of this argument. Bottom line is she tried to get cute, but I exposed her for the ugly bitch she is. I'm just looking out for your best interest. You should be thanking me."

I intervened. "Ok you two, let's go. You two can finish this when we get to the hotel."

"There's nothing to finish."

"That's what you think," Eric said, before walking off.

Landon walked away like nothing was wrong and Braxton came over and put his arm around me. Yes, Braxton had a goofy smile on his face, but I wasn't mad about the incident. I decided to play with him.

"Don't try to be in my face now, you better find Kimberly. How easily I'm forgotten."

"Yasmin, don't even start. You know what I'm not even going to entertain this." Braxton said before walking off.

For the remainder of the day, Landon and I did our own thing and Braxton and Eric did theirs. When we did catch our nine o'clock it pretty much was the same thing. No one was talking.

L.A. had been nothing but drama. I was so glad to be going home.

6

Take Control

"See you later, beautiful," Braxton said on his way out of our bedroom door.

"Dag, no 'I love you.' No hug, just a 'see you later.'" I was sitting in our bathroom at my vanity preparing for a girl's night out with Landon. Unlike Braxton and me, Landon and Eric were still going at it.

"Sorry, beautiful, I'm running late," Braxton walks into our master his and her bathroom suite.

I look over to see Braxton dressed head to toe in Ralph Lauren. "You're always running late, that doesn't mean neglect me."

He smirks. "So I'm neglecting you now?"

"Yup."

"You're spoiled."

"I am, but you made me this way."

"Oh, lawd." he laughed.

"You did. So where are you going at tonight?"

"Just hanging out with Javon."

I roll my eyes.

"What was that for?"

"Nothing."

"I don't know why you don't like Javon."

"Did I say I didn't like Javon?"

"You don't have to your body language says it. What do you have against Javon?"

Not wanting to hurt his feelings on why his friend was an ass, I changed the subject. "Body language, huh?" I stood up in my matching blue Fredericks of Hollywood bra and panties giving him a seductive look and lick my lips. In my sexiest voice I ask, "What does my body language say now?"

Braxton comes over and kisses my neck. "It says you want some of Sugar Daddy."

He grabs my ass and then tries to remove my panties.

I stop him. "My body may say that, but right now my mind is saying I don't." I turn to face the mirror. "The mind has won. Now it's time for me to get ready for my night out. See ya."

"I need some love now," he grabs me from behind and started sucking on my neck."

"Remember, you were running late. You didn't have time to give me any love, as you said earlier. See you later."

He laughed. "So what are you and Landon doing tonight?"

"Haven't decided, but I know I'll be having fun."

"Um hmm, don't have too much fun, don't get into any trouble. I know how Landon mouth is and I know yours."

"Excuse you?"

"Excuse me nothing, I'm leaving for real this time, be good." He kisses me again before heading out the door.

Thirty minutes later, I was waiting for Landon.

It was the end of July and hot. I decided on a white skirt and silver glittery halter top with no back. Landon finally comes picking me up in her brand new Mercedes truck. When I get in, I know she's in a mood, but she looked good in her white Gucci spaghetti strap dress and Giuseppe Zanotti Pumps.

"What's going on, Diva?"

"Nothing much, I am so overdue for some fun."

"How's Eric?"

"Don't ask me anything about him."

"You two are still fighting?"

"Apparently, not enough, that what's the latest fight was about."

"Ok, what does that mean?"

"We weren't fighting enough because my ass got pregnant."

"Pregnant?" I ask, shocked and jealous. "Congrats."

"Yas, there's nothing to congratulate. The pregnancy was terminated the other day."

"What?"

"I told you one kid is enough, no more for me. Labor is a bitch."

I was instantly angry with her. Here I am trying to get pregnant and she's killing babies. How could she do that?

"Yas, what's wrong?"

"Landon, sometimes you can be so selfish. You should give Eric a little brother or sister."

"Yas, please, you and I both know Eric is more than enough. I love my baby to death. He's content being an only child if he wants someone to play with I can send him to your house. Matter of fact, why aren't you pregnant. I know your hot ass been fucking." She laughed.

I look at her. "That's the problem, it seems people that don't want kids seem to pop up pregnant and have them without a problem and abort them. Whereas, people like me, can't seem to get pregnant as you say, no matter how much there hot asses have been fucking."

"Yassy, I'm sorry, I didn't mean to upset you."

"Landon, it's your body, but prior to Eric you had no desire to have kids. I look at you now and I see how much you love him and he loves you, It's not like you can't afford it. You could have hired another nanny."

"It's too late now. Yas, I do feel bad. Honestly, I regret it."

"Land, why did you really do it?"

"I did it for all the reasons I said. The main reason is Eric and I have not been getting along at all. I didn't want to add another child to the equation, especially since I'm not sure if I want to be with Eric."

"How did Eric find out?"

"He decided to play detective. He saw me taking the pills they gave me afterwards. I had bad menstrual cramps and told him that's what they were for. He didn't believe me. When I went to sleep he took the bottle and did some research."

"Damn."

"Yeah, he is beyond pissed. I've never seen him so mad."

I didn't say anything but I was thinking, "*Hello, what did you expect to say I'm sorry and all is forgiven.*"

The line to get in the club was ridiculous, but since I was with the Diva, waiting was not an option. Once in the club, we saw why everyone was trying to get in. One of the Redskins was having his birthday party so there was a lot of media and other athletes. Landon wasted no time getting into the festivities. I followed along and did some dancing. It was hot so Landon and I made our way to the bar. I really didn't want any alcohol so I ordered a pineapple juice and Diva, Patron.

"Hey ladies"

I turn around and see Kevin's handsome 6'3 bronze frame.

"Hey Kev," Landon said giving him a hug and kiss. "Where you been?"

"Working." He looks at me with his dark ebony eyes.

"Daddy working you hard?"

"Mrs. Y.E."

"S" I finish. Kevin adopted the idea of spelling out the initials of my name, Yasmin Elaine

Sinclair, at the time. Strange, but that's Kevin. Kevin works at our "father's" law firm. Things were still awkward between us. At one time, we were real close. Kevin always

was interested in pursuing a romantic relationship with me, but I didn't have those feelings.

Anyway, we had a big fight and things haven't been the same.

"How you doing?"

"I'm doing well and you."

"That's good. I miss my friend. It's been over a year, you're married now. Why can't we get along."

"We are."

"Let's dance."

"Yassy, be nice." Landon warned.

"Come on, Kev, Landon. Let's see if he can handle both of us."

We danced with Kevin for a while. I admit it was fun, I did miss Kevin too.

"Ladies, it's been fun."

"Kevin, you're leaving us?"

"Yes, I need someone to wrap up with tonight."

"Do your thing," Landon approves.

Landon and I head back to the bar for a drink.

"What's the matter Yassy, no cranberry and grey goose tonight."

"Nah, I'm cool. I'm having a good time."

"Yassy, look to the right, that's Reggie Bush. He's a sexy chocolate thing. He's a little too young for me, but for him I'll make an exception. I need a little fling, time for me to get into network mode."

"Diva, slow your roll, you're married. I know you and Eric are having problems but don't add to it."

"Yassy, that's why I love you, big sis. Even before we knew we were, you were always looking out for my best interest. You care and don't want to see me in any trouble," she gave me a hug.

"I love you too, Diva. I'm glad you know then, that I lecture you out of love and not just because I want to ruin your fun."

"I do and I appreciate it all, but you know I never listen, holla," Diva strolls over to Reggie and begins her seduction.

I shake my head and laugh.

While Landon was getting closer to Reggie I decided to do a little dancing. There definitely were a lot of sexy fellas. The one guy I was dancing with looked familiar. I didn't know whether he was an athlete or not, Landon kept up with that, it didn't matter either way. He was tall, 6'7' butter skin, cornrows, deep dimples and pretty white teeth.

We danced to Ludacris's "Money Maker, Busta's Touch It remix and TI's Why U Wanna." He kept trying to pull me close and I tried to keep a distance. On Jay Z's, "*Show Me What u Got*", I grinded a little too hard. His dick got hard and he was trying to grab my breast. I walk away to the bar and of course, he follows.

"What's up, sexy?"

"Hello."

"I like those sexy cat eyes. You hypnotize people don't you?"

"No." I laugh.

"What's your name?"

"Yasmin and yours?"

"I like that. You know my name."

"No, I don't."

"Give me your number and I'll tell you." He winks.

"No."

"What are you trying to play hard to get. I don't have time for games."

"No games, just not interested."

He starts laughing.

"Yeah right, you want my number then?"

"No."

"Alright sexy, my name is Cory."

"Thanks for the dances, Cory. Have a good night." I got the bartender's attention and ordered another pineapple juice.

"Something about you, sexy I like. You really don't know who I am."

"No I don't, but it doesn't matter, I'm married." I held up my ring.

"You don't dance like you're married."

"How does a married person dance?" I ask scrunching my face.

"Not on another man's dick. You couldn't be my wife."

I chuckle. "You were the one pulling my ass on your dick. Notice when you got too comfortable the dancing was over. And I'm not your wife, nor do I have a desire to be. So, we're good, no worries."

"I like you, so let's cut the games. I'm a star, sexy, and I'm not trying to get caught up in the relationship thing. You're married, good for you. But like I was saying I like the way your ass felt on my dick. Now I want to feel how my dick will feel up in you. I won't tell."

Before responding, I lick my lips. "I don't like games either. I like your directness." I paused, he smiles and I was feeling devious. "I am one of a kind. I'm not going to lie. My pussy does stay wet and tight. You know from the way I move my ass that I can handle my business. However, cute as you are, I'm married, and my Sugar Daddy is the only one allowed to get this treat."

"Sexy, I like your sassiness."

"Thank you, my husband loves it."

"Never a dull moment with you. So really, what's it going to take to get with you?"

"Cory, I'm serious. My husband has this on lock. His dick fits it like a glove."

He pulls out a card, "Here you go, sexy. Give me a call when you ready to have some fun."

"No thanks, Cory. It was nice meeting you."

Cory looks at me and shakes his head before walking away.

"Go, Yassy, messing with ballers now?" Landon takes a seat next to me.

"What are you talking about?"

"Cory Johnson, MVP of the 2006 NBA season."

"Oh, he kept saying, 'You know my name.'"

"You're clueless when it comes to sports."

"So, I don't want an athlete, I'm with who I want."

"Yeah, yeah."

"What happened with Reggie?"

"I told him buying property in the DC area would be a good investment."

"Oh, so you're putting your real estate license back to use?"

"Yes, I am. You know I'm good at what I do. I sold you your house."

"Yes, you are Diva."

"I'm going back out there to mingle. You coming?"

"You go ahead. I'm going to chill for a minute."

I was sitting at the bar when I noticed Braxton. He was dancing with this bitch, Lisa Stevens. Lisa was Braxton's co-worker, who technically, was married, but from what I see, is constantly unable to stay out of my husband's face. I can't stand the bitch. It's been that way since I first met her at BET and nothing has changed. I played it cool and observed. I could tell she wanted him to dance more intimately. She kept trying to back it up. I know his dick better not be hard because the bitch is tacky. She was wearing an ugly yellow pants suit. It was tight and made her look like Spongebob, really she had no curves, flat ass and b cup chest. She did have a decent weave tonight that was shoulder length. Her make-up, as usual, was all wrong; red lipstick, pink blush, foundation two shades too light on her brown complexion? Come on.

The bitch grabbed Braxton arm. Oh, she's getting a little too comfortable. I decided to stay incognito and observe. I watched as

Lisa buys drinks. Generous are we? Braxton drinking Hennessey straight, what's up with that. I know she's not trying to get him drunk. Still I sit calm while she orders some drink with a cherry. With her drink, she does the swirl the cherry on the tongue act. I continue to watch Braxton, he doesn't look impressed. That's right my baby knows she's not worth the time. Oh hell no, the bitch is whispering in his ear. I quickly get the bartender's attention.

"Hey, you see the guy over there talking to Spongebob's sister?"

He laughed, "Yeah."

"I want you to take him some Crown Royal. Tell him it's from Beautiful."

"He looks occupied, sweetheart."

I chuckled and stood up. "Do you really think I can't get his attention?"

"You ain't even nice, but you're so right."

The bartender takes the drink to Braxton. Placing the drink right in front of him he steps out the way to nod in my direction. I smile.

Braxton smiles and I give Lisa the 'try me' smile. Braxton quickly excuses himself and leaves her looking stupid. I stroll to the dance floor and start to dance.

It doesn't take long for me to feel Braxton come wrap his arms around me and we begin to rock together.

"What you doing, Beautiful, following me?" He joked.

"I need too. I don't appreciate you being so friendly with Lisa."

He laughed.

"I'm not laughing. She's overstepping the boundaries. I've been nice because we both have to work with the trick, but my patience is running thin."

"You're jealous now? We were just having fun."

"She nothing to be jealous of, she looks like SpongeBob. It's about respect and I'm going to have to tell the bitch off."

"Be nice, beautiful."

"I told you I've been too nice, but enough about 'desperate.' Show me how happy you are to see me."

"How do you figure?"

"I can see in your eyes," I looked up at him. "Feel it in your touch, but the main reason I know." I paused, "Sugar Daddy gives you away every time."

He pulls me close, kissing me on the check. The DJ started playing Justin Timberlake's "My Love", and I turned around and started grinding. Braxton grabbed my hips and we moved in sync like we always do. Braxton began to nibble on my neck and my eyes literally rolled in the back of head. He knows that's my spot.

"You like that, beautiful?"

"Baby, yes I do. I have something planned for you tonight."

"Really, what do you have planned for me?"

"I'm thinking about making an investment on some equipment."

"You and your investments."

"You should be glad your wife is a financial advisor, especially with the way you spend and I know you will like this investment."

"Can't wait to see it."

"Can't wait to show you."

We danced to Busta and Kelis' "I Love My Chick,' and the DJ played Amerie's, "Take Control of Me". I felt the music and began a little provocative dance for Braxton. I grinded up and down his body then bent over and shook my ass. I had a couple stares, one of which I caught with my peripheral vision was Cory, but I didn't care. I smiled and kept doing my thing without missing a beat. Braxton grabbed me by the waist and in a swift move had his hand up my shirt.

"Umph Umph umph, I should be mad at you coming out the house without a bra. Funny thing is when I left you had one on."

"I couldn't wear one because of the shirt."

"Unh huh, you're lucky I didn't see you dancing with anybody."

"Like you were with Lisa?" I counter.

"I wasn't dancing with her like that." The DJ was playing Lloyd's, I Want You.

"Ha, ha, what I can't dance now?"

"I didn't say that, but you stir stuff up, teasing, flirting."

"I do not."

Braxton had his hands on my hips again and he slid his hand on the side where the slit was. Next thing I felt was his two fingers moving towards my clit.

"Baby, stop. Are you forgetting where we are?"

"It's a lot of people in here just close your eyes and go with the flow."

I leaned back and allowed Braxton to play with my clit. He was arousing me, had me moaning and ready to cum. I was startled when he stopped. I opened my eyes to see Javon; a pain in the ass. Braxton guided me to the bar. I excused myself and went to the bathroom. It was hot. I wet some paper towels to put on my face. On my way out, I saw Landon.

"Diva, I see you're unwinding."

"You too, I saw you with Braxton. You need to get a room, but you were killing them girl."

"Braxton was the last person I expected to run into but what time are you trying to leave. I'm partied out and it's too hot in here."

"Your hot ass is always hot. What'd you expect with all that 'come fuck me' dancing you were doing? Get a ride with Braxton."

"Ha, ha, why do I have to get a ride, we came together."

"I'm not quite ready to go."

"Landon, don't get into anything."

"Yas, I'm long overdue. I rarely go out now, just making up for lost times."

"I know Diva, but be careful."

"I will. Go see if you can get a ride with Braxton and let me know. Besides, Kevin is still here."

73

I went to the bar to see Braxton talking to Javon and Cory. Cory sees me approach and puts a devious smile on his face.

"Hello again, Yasmin."

"Hello."

Braxton gives me a look that said, '*how the hell do you know him?*'"

"This one right here," Cory points at me. "I'll give her props she's sexy and she knows it. She got a sassy ass mouth too, a big tease."

"Is that so?" Javon instigated.

Braxton looks at me and I could tell he is getting pissed. He was quiet, waiting for Cory to finish his story.

"Yeah she is. She gets you first with her eyes. Then with the body, she's got some moves."

"I was dancing. I did not tease you at all. What did I tell you?"

He started laughing. "After she enticed me and shit, she holla's I'm married."

"No teasing, you did that to yourself. I was straight to the point."

"You're a handful. I bet you drive hubby crazy."

"I do, but he loves me. Don't you, baby?" I walk over and give Braxton a kiss on the lips.

Cory starts laughing. "Braxton, I thought you were crazy when I find out you got married. Now I know why you are, she's definitely unique, no disrespect intended."

Landon came over, "Hello, fellas."

"Hey," everyone greeted her.

"Yas, I changed my mind, I'm going to leave. I can drop you off."

"Ok, give me a sec."

I lean into Braxton and whisper in his ear, "Don't keep me waiting too long. Let me show you how much I love you tonight. My tongue needs a taste of Sugar Daddy." I licked the back of his ear.

"Always starting something, I'm right behind you. We took separate cars," he grabs my ass.

"Cool, wait thirty minutes before you leave. I have to get prepared."

He nodded, and then winked.

"Come on, Yas."

I turn around and said goodbye to everyone.

*

An hour later, everything was in place, from the smoke machine, to the pole I purchased for my strip tease. Glittered and oiled all over wearing a silver zippered halter top, that stopped right above my navel with sexy pleated skirt. I wore silver sheer stockings, and a garter that had the word "sexy" written on it. I completed my outfit with silver 6" stilettoes and thigh high boots. Massage oil waited in the bedroom. I placed notes from the front door to the guest room.

When I hear Braxton pull up, I turn off all the lights leaving on only a strobe light creating stars around the room. The smoke machine and music are turned on when he climbs the stairs. The radio plays Nelly Futardo's "Say it Right". Braxton enters the room unsure of what's going on. I step through the smoke, he can't help but smile. I kiss him, then I guide him to the bed.

Kissing him again, I unbutton his shirt.

Braxton tries to pull down my panties, he is stopped. I back away. I shake my head and finger to indicate, no. I walk to him again. This time I straddle him backwards, giving him a lap dance he'll never forget. I take both of his hands, gliding them all over my body. Sugar Daddy is aching to come out. I gyrating my body onto the floor ending up in a split.

"Damn, my baby got skills. I'm in love with a stripper." He declares.

I ssh him.

I bend forward, giving him a clear view of my assets. I begin a seductive dance with the floor.

Braxton so impatient has stripped. He tries to join me on the floor. I stop him by standing up, playing with zipper on my top.

The next song, Akon and Snoop's "I Want to Fuck You", begins. I shove Braxton back on the bed.

I unzip my top, revealing silver pasties. I watch as Braxton licks his lips. I smile. Then I jump on the pole, wrapping my legs around, swirling, grinding to the floor. I stand up, remove my skirt, revealing my naked body. Next I get on the pole, slide down halfway, letting my legs down so I can sensually glide up and down the pole. Jumping on the pole again, I bend backwards. Spreading my leg wide into anther split, I rotate my hips, demonstrating my belly dancing skills.

Braxton's amazed, fascinated, enjoying the way the light bounces off my glittered body. He pulls out his wallet. He starts throwing all his cash, credit cards, anything of value.

It isn't until the third song plays I allow him delight. Jill Scott's "Imagination" now plays. I lift myself from the ground. I walk over to him, placing my leg over his shoulders.

Braxton turns around, grabs my ass, pulling my sweetness to him. He hungrily tastes me with him.

I'm taken aback by his aggressiveness, nonetheless enjoying every second. My knees buckle, he grabs me and lays me on the bed. Braxton is on his knees. He pulls me towards him, starting off real slow, licking me like a lollipop. He starts sucking my clit, I can't speak just moan. Nothing compares to what I'm feeling now. He starts fucking me with his tongue. The way he is curling his tongue in me has me begging for mercy, pleading with him to give me the dick and fuck me hard. He stops, but then he begins to nibble on my clit. Got-fucking-damn! My knees clap his head. I can't take it. He pulls away and proceeds to take long slow agonizing licks up and down my clit to my ass. I grab at him, the sheets, my nipples, I am about to explode. He stops. He smirks, taking in enjoyment of me squirming and being frustrated I didn't climax. I'm throbbing, yearning for him to be inside me. He obviously forgot this is my show, and his tongue wasn't done with my pussy. I take two fingers, moving them in and out of my pussy. My hands are soaked from the waterfall of pleasure falling from me. I take the two fingers I used to pleasure myself and place them in Braxton's mouth. He sucks on them like I knew he would. I remove my fingers from his mouth and repeat. It doesn't take long for Braxton to push my hands away. He picks up exactly where he left off, slow agonizing licks. Soon he has fingers in me, playing me like a piano causing me to sing. Licks become more aggressive, again, I'm gasping, grabbing on him, pleading for him to fuck me. When he starts sucking on my clit, I can't control it anymore and let my orgasm flood his tongue.

He climbs on top, entering me. Nice and slow is the theme. The way he slides in and out of me with so much expertise is a crime. Damn, he feels so good. Floetry's "Imagination" plays. I can't help but smile.

There are so many things that we can do.
Use your imagination.
You can taste, you can touch, you can make moves.
Use your imagination.
Use your imagination.

Yes, there's no need for me to fantasize, I am in ecstasy. He's moving so slow, he's teasing me again. We kiss obsessively. Powerful strokes follow. I hold on as he pumps his dick in me. He hits every spot. He always knows exactly what to do and my body responds. Clenching onto him, I spread my legs wide waiting for him to explode in me. When he does, I follow.

It's not long until we both drift off to sleep.

7

I Wanna Be Loved

"Hello, Lawrence." I step into the foyer of his French Country Style home.

"Thanks for coming, Yasmin"

I ignore his gratitude. Instead I look around, feeling out of place. Even though it wasn't my first time here, now I feel like a trespasser. I notice now the many pictures of Landon on display. I'd be lying if I said there wasn't any animosity. Looking around it is evident she is loved…a Daddy's girl, wanted, prized. Like my mother's home, I am the imposter, the reject. Yup, just like my mother's, for every twenty pictures of Ashley, there was only one of me.

Lawrence approaches me for a hug. I refuse. This wasn't a happy to see you meeting.

Since this whole fiasco has come to light, I admit he's been consistent. Despite my anger and uncouth remarks, he still calls at least three times a week. For the most part the conversations are short, no longer than ten minutes. I tell myself I don't need him, but deep down I know I want acceptance from one of my parents. Which is why when he asked to meet with me, I agreed, but I never would admit it to him.

Lawrence led me to the study and we both took a seat.

"How are you doing?"

I gave him a look that said cut the bullshit.

"How's Braxton?"

"Fine."

"That's good. Yasmin, I'm glad you have Braxton in your life. I know he truly loves you. You two are good together, you look good too," he chuckles, uneasily.

Annoyed by his analysis, I asked, "How do you know? You barely know Braxton or me. True, your blood may run through my veins, but you don't know me. I've been coming to this house for ten years as your chosen daughter's "best friend." You and I never formed a relationship, or bond for that matter. Throughout the last ten years, I was only Landon's best friend, so other than a 'hello,' maybe a 'how you doing,' you don't know much about me."

"I wasn't there physically, you're right. You and Landon met, automatically you formed a bond. I didn't want to disrupt that. I provided financially. At the time, I thought you were happy with John and your mother", he defends.

"You were selfish. You did what was best for you. While you were happy living your lovely life, I was miserable. I guess I should be happy that Michelle thought there was a possibility I was John's. She finally admitted if she knew I was yours she would have aborted me." The tears were falling. I was mad at myself for allowing myself to cry.

Lawrence walks over to me and hugs me.

"Don't touch me. Don't try to comfort me now. Where were you when I was growing up? Here with your family, ignoring my existence. You weren't there when John's mother was taunting me. Saying I thought I was cute. Telling me my green evil monstrous eyes would only cause me heartache. Or when she'd say I'd never be good for anything other than a fling. How no one has or will ever love me. You proved her right, gave me away without a second thought. You let John, who she said hated me, raise me. I believed her every word for a long time. Go ahead. Tell me what my mother has already confirmed. Tell me what you really want to do. Tell me let's just go back to the way things were. I'll just be Landon's best friend."

"Yasmin, I never knew. I'm so sorry you had to go through that. I want to be a part of your life."

"Whatever. I'm not done. Let me fill you in on other highlights of my life. Now about mother, there's so much she's done over the years. The thing that hurts the most is my miscarriage. Do you think she was there for me when I lost my son? Do you think she gave me words of encouragement? No, she didn't. All I wanted was a mother's love and acceptance. Instead, she gave me a pep talk. She said, 'Yasmin, things happen for the best.' And she lectured me on how I wasn't married and should stop giving the milk away for free. Then she told me to get over it."

"I'm sorry. Your mother should have been there for you."

"And what about you? Evidently I didn't matter to you either. Do you know how alone I felt? Do you know how all I wanted was for my mother and father to once hug me, love me, and tell me it would be alright?"

He's speechless.

I continue, "It only took me 27 years, but I finally love Yasmin. I love me and I'm not going to allow you or anyone to make me feel anything less. I'm happy. I love me. I have a husband that loves me and you know what, his family, especially his mother, accepts me," I chided. "She gave me more love in one day than both you and Michelle combined ever did my entire life. You know that is so sad and pathetic. Biologically, you are my parents, but that's where it stopped. I am who I am despite both of you. I don't need you. Without the love from any of you, I survived."

I looked at Lawrence who was sitting there speechless with tears in his eyes. Was this supposed to move me?

"Why so quiet? Lawyers always have something to say?" I finally ask

"I'm so sorry, Yasmin. You're right. There's no excuse for what I did," he pauses, "I took the cowardly way out and I take full responsibility. I should have handled this better, taken responsibility."

I sat there mute.

"I know this is hard to believe Yasmin, but I do love you. Again, you're right, I did a horrible job of showing it. I deserve for you to hate me. I didn't do right by you. I should have been there for you. I honestly thought I was doing the best thing by keeping quiet. I looked at your accomplishments and assumed your mother and John were there for you."

"Her name is Michelle. I'm dead to her now. Haven't you been listening? She blames me for ruining her marriage. She wishes I was never born. It is her request that I don't call her. Apparently, the only thing I've caused her was grief."

"WHAT?! The audacity of that woman. I swear."

"Don't get upset or show concern now. As you stated before, you knew how evil she could be. I know you're thinking how did I hook up with her let alone get her pregnant."

"Yasmin, I don't regret you. I wish I would have fought for custody and raised you and Landon like sisters. I truly was happy the way you and Landon bonded. I feel so bad, guilty for keeping you apart. I'm glad the two of you have remained so close despite everything that's going on. I messed up. I missed out on having you in my life. You're so right, despite all the heartache you've survived. I'm so proud of you. You are beautiful, strong smart, mature, young lady and I was stupid for not including you in my life. Please allow me to be a part of your life now. Allow me to be the father you deserve, show you the love you deserve, be there for you. Please give me another chance."

I could see Lawrence crying and pleading with me in his eyes.

I stood up prepared to leave. I felt better after getting things off my chest but it would be a long time before I could trust Lawrence. I'm not sure I wanted him to be a part of my life. I was going to take it one day at a time.

"I appreciate you being honest, admitting your mistakes. But I need time. I can't promise you anything."

"I understand you have every right to be apprehensive. I appreciate and will value any time you give me."

"I have to go. I have to meet Braxton at one."

He smiled, "I'm grateful you found Braxton. I know Braxton will do anything to protect you. I see the way he looks at you and I see how much he loves you. You deserve to be happy."

This time I smile. "I love him."

"I know you do. Yasmin, thank you for coming, I regret I can't change the past. However I swear to you in the future I will be a father to you.

I didn't respond I just left out the door, wiping my tears.

*

On my way to Mrs. Simms annual cookout I get a call from Landon asking me to keep little Eric for the night. I really wasn't up for it, but Landon sounded upset. Before I could ring the bell, Landon had little Eric and his bag ready.

"Thanks Yassy, I appreciate it. I'll pick him up tomorrow.

"Land, what's going on? Talk to me."

"Yassy, I'm fine. His car seat is in my car. See you Mommy man."

Landon gives Eric a kiss. Then she closes the door.

I was a taken aback but I wasn't in the mood to try to figure out Landon's theatrics.

When we arrived at Mrs. Simms, I checked my face for any signs that I'd been crying. I was still a little emotional and felt a migraine coming on. The last thing I need is for Braxton or Mrs. Simms to fuss over me. Unfortunately, my eyes were puffy. With sunglasses on, Eric and I headed in back for the cookout.

"Hello everyone," I say. Eric lets go of my hand running to be with the rest of the kids.

Braxton comes over to hug me. Then he kisses me. "How is my Beautiful doing?"

"Fine now." I return his hug.

"Aww, look at the newlyweds. Yasmin turned Braxton from a Playboy to a little punk. " Vincent, one of Braxton's three brothers, teases.

"Vincent, leave Braxton alone." Mrs. Simms scolded.

"Braxton always the mama's boy."

"I'll show you a mama's boy."

Vincent and Braxton always had some competition going on.

83

"Sure you want Yasmin to see you get your ass beat?"

"Watch your mouth," Mrs. Simms cautions.

"Vincent, that's your problem. Always running that mouth, all talk no action. That's why you can't keep a girlfriend." I retaliate.

"Listen to Yasmin speaking up for her husband. Actually, I can keep one I just haven't found one worth keeping."

"No, no one wants to keep you."

"Ha,ha, I see you and hubby got jokes. My new one is on her way. So watch it."

"How long you plan on keeping this one?"

"That's yet to be determined." He rubs on his chin like he is in serious thought.

Vincent's last few girlfriends have been just that, tricks who he used for a video or somecommercial he was doing. I do give him credit, despite Vincent being a hoe, he, like his brothers, is smart. He worked in the entertainment industry as a videographer doing a lot of work for A-list clients, Chauncey and Geester included.

"Come on let me beat you in some basketball," Braxton taunts.

"Are you coming to cheer your man on?" Vince asks.

"Nope, he can handle you. My baby has skills."

They run off to the court.

Eric came up to me for me to tie his shoe.

"Eric is getting to be so big and handsome. He's definitely all boy, a roadrunner. All my

boys were handfuls, but Braxton, woo!" She shakes her head.

"Yes, he is a handful, but that's my baby." I laugh.

"Yasmin, you don't look too good."

"I'm fine."

"You need to eat something. You've lost weight and have a tired look. You need to take it easy." Mommy lectured.

"Stress, I promise to take it easy. Matter of fact, can you watch him. I think I should lie down."

"Yasmin eat a little something for me."

"I really don't have an appetite. I'll eat when I wake up." I gave her a kiss. I found one of the empty bedrooms for a nap.

I don't know how long I was asleep or what I dreamt. I was awakened by Braxton stroking my face and him softly placing light kisses on my cheek.

"Sleeping beauty, are you feeling better."

"A little," I yawn.

Braxton pulls me in his arms, cradling me. "I'm here if you want to talk about Lawrence."

"I actually feel better about Lawrence. He admitted he was wrong and wants to build a relationship. I just don't know what I want."

I let out a frustrated moan.

"What's the matter, my beautiful, Yasmin?"

"I hurt for such a long time, it's still hard to believe I'm finally happy. I'm scared something will happen to us."

"We straight, I'm committed to only you. I love you. If I have to keep telling you every day, I will. I'm not going anywhere."

I smile.

He pulls me closer.

I sit up in his lap. "I've just been emotional lately. I want a baby and I'm frustrated that I'm not pregnant yet. We can never replace Bryan but I want to have another baby. Ever since we lost him I feel like part of me is missing. I like the whole pregnancy thing, the belly, baby moving and kicking, the bonding."

"Relax, it'll happen."

"I know all this drama going on with my paternity and the stress I know isn't helping I'm trying to relax and block out this entire issue."

"I'm here for you, beautiful."

"You married a mess."

"No, I married beautiful, Yasmin. Beautiful inside and out, I'm very fortunate to have you. I love you."

"You love me?"

"You know I do. You're a part of me. Yasmin, I love everything about you. You're the only one I want. I want to make you happy. I don't want to see you hurt. I want to take away the pain. Tell me what you want me to do."

"Can I have a kiss?"

"You know you don't have to ask for that. I can give you more than that," he kisses me and begins to caress my butt.

"You always trying to be all up in Yasmin," I giggle.

"That's right, let me get some."

"You'd think you never got any. Sometimes three times a day, chill."

"You just don't know how good you feel. Come on."

"I do know how good I feel." I tease.

"Who's cocky now? You should be giving me some then."

"Um no, this is your parents' house and there are too many people here. Somebody will walk in."

"I can lock the door and we're married."

I kiss Braxton hard giving him my approval. He got on top of me I could feel Sugar Daddy hardening.

I broke away from our kiss. "Mr. Simms, lock the door."

"Give me another kiss."

"No, if I do you won't get up."

He laughs. Ignoring my request he starts sucking on my neck, then my lips arousing me.

Just as he was about to pull up my shirt his brother Vincent busts in with company in tow.

"Damn Vincent, you ever heard of knocking?!"

"Damn Braxton, you ever hear of going to your own house?!" He countered.

"Why you in here anyway, what you want?"

"Punk, you should have locked the door."

"Yeah, well, what you want?"

"Yasmin, Ma looking for you and I wanted to introduce y'all to Ty. Ty this is my brother Braxton and his wife, Yasmin. "

I looked her over and this one didn't look to be hoe-ish as the others. Her mult-colored maxi dress was cute, complimenting her bronze skin. Her long brown hair was straight and pulled to the side. Face round held innocence, but her eyes said something different.

Uncle Charles soon follows. "Hello," he looks over Vincent girlfriend for the moment.

"Hello." I respond.

Uncle Charles was Braxton's outspoken uncle. Always saying what he wants, not caring what it is. He reminds me of John Witherspoon but he dressed in the current fashion. He had his share of women to, having several different girlfriends since Braxton and I have been together. I give him his props; he was very handsome for an older man. He stood 6 feet, with mocha colored skin, salt and pepper, more pepper. He kept his hair cut low, matching goatee, definitely in shape with a lot of swagger for an older man. Uncle Charles started calling me Sweet Thing the first time we met. He, like the majority of the family was shocked to see Braxton serious about someone. Braxton, at the time, was upset because Kevin stopped by my place. He thought Kevin wanted me. Anyway Uncle Charles sensed how Braxton really liked me and knew he had an attitude about something. He started calling me Sweet Thing to irritate his once playboy nephew who was now in love.

"What you two knuckleheads up to? Y'all fighting over the room. We got other bedrooms. I'm charging $100 an hour, but it'll be $200 if you don't want me to tell your mother."

I laugh. "How's my Uncle Charles doing?"

"Vincent got another groupie." Uncle Charles whispers.

I laugh again.

Ty just stares at us.

"What you starting Uncle Charles?" Vincent inquires.

Uncle Charles laughs, "I'm talking to my sweet thing."

"Unh Hunh, Uncle Charles. I came to see if Braxton was ready to takes this ass kicking," joked Vincent.

"Only one has an ass kicking coming is you." Braxton boasts.

"I got money on my baby. You looking kind of round around here," I pat his rounding belly.

"I guess I'm going to have to embarrass you too," said Vincent.

"I'm not scared of you. You can't run. My baby got this."

"Yasmin, I'm going to get you back. Watch your back." he says laughing.

While Braxton ran off to the court, I changed into my brown and gold V-neck one piece bathing suit. I wrapped a sarong around me before joining the festivities.

I smile when I see Horace talking to an attractive female. Horace the second oldest was

the quietest out of the bunch. He, like his dad, Mr. Jeff was a doctor. Mr. Jeff an anesthesiologist while Horace is a cardiologist. She put me in the mind of Rachel True, Mona from Half and Half.

I was just about to go say hi when someone grabs me from behind. In a matter of seconds,

I'm dangling upside down. I reach for anything I can hold onto.

"You not laughing now are you?" Vincent declares.

"Vincent, put me down!" I scream my heart ready to jump out of my chest.

"Are you scared?" He antagonizes, bouncing me up and down. Causing me to feel like I'm about to fall on my head."

"Yes, now put me down."

He laughs.

"Man, if you don't put my wife down."

"With pleasure" he chuckles. He lifts me up high, throwing me in the pool.

I go down deep, my body quickly adjusting to the cold climate. I resurface with hair everywhere, out of breath.

"Are you Ok? I told you I was going to get you back" He laughs.

"I'm going to kick your ass."

"Ooh, Miss Goody, cussing at me."

Braxton is laughing.

"You punk, you were supposed to be defending me. Instead you let this chump get me."

"I told you he is a punk."

"I'm a punk now" Braxton asks, pretending to be hurt.

"You sure are. I guess I'm going to have to do what you couldn't."

"Is that so?" Vincent challenges.

Vincent jumps in the pool. Braxton follows.

Despite them dunking me a few times, I give both of them a hard time. I out swim them both, also throwing in as many free shots as I can. Kicking, slapping both of them in the head. Not long after, the other guests start joining in with the exception of Vincent latest concubine.

After my pool workout, I finally make it over to Horace and his date, Monica. Horace left us alone to go play basketball with his brothers. We went through the pleasantries; she's 29, works in HR for the state government. She has a three-year old son and has never married. I got a good vibe from her. Now when Ty came over…

"Hello, ladies."

We both return her greeting.

"This is a cute little place."

My in-law's place was gorgeous three-story Victorian home with circular driveway, pond and cobblestone over 6,000 square feet. Her comment instantly told me she was snobbish, which basically put me on alert.

"So you like space?" I inquire.

"Yes, I do. But this is decent."

"I think it's lovely."

"You really have settled." She turns up her nose.

"Excuse me?"

"I'm sure you've been in more exquisite homes, considering you dated Chauncey. Speaking of which, you should have took Chauncey to the altar and got that six-figure alimony check. His sexy self is making moves. Well I hope you were smart enough to get something."

"Ty, are you slow and think we're friends or know me well enough to analyze myrelationship with Chauncey. I don't need Chauncey or any other man for money. I make my own legitimately, unlike you, who chooses to lie on your back and hoe for a profession."

"Like your husband isn't. He's been around. I've heard and seen plenty. So that honest sanctified act is bullshit. I know how your girl, Landon operates and I know Vincent and Braxton well. We all travel the same circuit. Don't get upset because you settled. You have a decent compensation prize. A five-figure alimony is okay, your ring can be pawned for a good price and I know the dick is excellent."

"So you fucked my husband?" This shit right here. Oh I was about to go in.

"No, my friend Melania has, along with a few others I know. But if he anything like his brother," she smiles. "Men like them never change. You marry them for benefits, not love. Like I said, I guess you got dickmatized and said "yes" too soon without exploring all of your options. I mean your ring isn't bad. I'm pretty sure that set him back, but hey, that's his fault, make it your gain."

I look over at Monica and she looks like she's enjoying the entertainment. Is this chick really sitting here telling me about my husband? Seriously! Talking to me like we're discussing the weather or something.

"First off, you don't know me or my husband. You've only seen me. Obviously, you've been studying me, trying to get notes. You know who my husband and I dated, seems like you're trying to get to my level. So why would I take advice from you? What do you have? Let me give you some advice. You are a hoe. You and I never were or will ever be on the same level. Chicks like you shelf life is short. Like milk it gets sour and old and then you have to throw it away because it stinks. You continue to be the best hoe you can be while you can before you expire. One more thing, talking about I settled. No, you are settling. Your compensation prize is a trip to the clinic. "

Braxton, Vincent and Horace catch the end of conversation and all look at me like I'm crazy.

I smirk, sitting back in the chair and start a conversation with Monica.

Ty got up and left.

Landon called as we were leaving the cookout, deciding she wanted her baby. I was glad.

My migraine was back. I didn't know if I could handle Mr. Eric. I was too tired so I had Braxton drop off Eric.

Braxton comes home in a bad mood.

"Hey, you."

"Hey."

I could tell something was troubling him.

"Baby, everything okay?"

"Yeah."

I walked over and kiss him. It is returned half-heartedly.

"Braxton, are you sure. I can tell you're upset."

"Yasmin, I'm fine, just leave me alone, please."

He called me Yasmin, something was definitely wrong. I swear sometimes Braxton is like Dr. Jekyll and Mr. Hyde. He has more mood swings than I do. I wanted some loving tonight. From his mood, that won't be happening tonight. So I give him attitude back.

"Braxton, I don't know what you're problem is, but you and your attitude can sleep in the guest room."

"You sleep in the guest room."

"We'll see who sleeps in the guest room. I'm sleeping in my bed with or without you."

Caught off guard, too tired to argue, I ignore his comment. I go upstairs to avoid his latest mood swing. Making sure I slam the door behind me. After I enter the bathroom, I turn on the water for my shower. I remove my underwear. Rubbing the scar on my belly I see my period had started. Another month, another disappointment I still was not pregnant.

8

Whenever You're Around

I woke up to see Braxton sitting on the couch in the sitting room of our master bedroom suite staring into space.

"Are you okay?" I ask groggily.

"Yeah."

I looked at the clock to see it is 12:35 in the morning.

"Baby, come to bed."

"Nah, I'm aw'ight."

"Braxton, you know I can't sleep without you." I whine.

He didn't respond or move.

"Baaaby,"

"Yasmin, please, just go to sleep."

By now, I'm out of the bed walking over toward the couch. Braxton is irritated, huffing and puffing. I attempt to give him a hug, a kiss. He stops me.

"Why are you being such an ass?"

"I told you leave me alone, I don't feel like being bothered."

"Braxton-" He interrupts me.

"Yasmin, please not now. Let me think."

"What is your problem? For the past few weeks you've been acting like you don't want to be bothered with me."

He sighs, stands up and grabs some clothes.

"What are you doing?"

"What does it look like?"

"It's twelve in the morning. Where are you going? We both have to work in the morning."

"If you would have left me alone I wouldn't be going anywhere."

"Stop being an ass and talk to me."

He ignores me, continuing to dress.

"Braxton, where are you going?"

"For a ride."

"It's after twelve, there's nowhere for you to go. Braxton, I know when something is bothering you. I don't know what your problem is, but I'm getting tired of your mood swings. What's so hard about talking to me?"

Braxton looks at me. For a moment it looks as if he will. Then he turns, leaving out the door.

Braxton, for a while now has been very distant and difficult, on edge. Even though we've been intimate, I can feel him holding back. Something is off. Every time I try to talk he pushes me away. Honestly, I'm scared. It reminds me of the time I miscarried and he broke things off. My gut tells me something isn't right. His attitude has me thinking Ty's comments and assumptions may be dead on.

The next morning when the alarm awakes me, I notice Braxton asleep beside me, arm securely wrapped around my waist. Part of me was happy he was there. Another part pissed that he left in the first place. Normally I woke Braxton up with a kiss, but this morning I hit the snooze button for him. I got up, picked out my outfit then took my shower. Since it was Wednesday Hump day I decided to be spicy with Carol's Daughter Almond Cookie to get me over the hump. After my shower, I walk out nude. In my bedroom, I see Braxton is up. He stares at me while I dress. I make sure to take my time, deciding also I wasn't speaking to him until he apologized. Because of the unusual cool September weather I slid on a pair of tweed slacks that made my booty look extra round along with a cream fitted button down shirt. I pull my hair into a bun, leaving hair out front. I slip on my brown pumps, before looking in the mirror one last time. I continue to ignore him. Not turning around to acknowledge his presence, I leave out of the door.

Once I got to work I had a hard time concentrating. I call Landon but there is no answer. Braxton definitely was not an option. Since I had nothing else to do, I decided to call Lawrence. I know I was desperate, irritable. He's still been calling me at least three times a week trying to build our relationship. He answers, asking me out for lunch. I agree to meet him at his office.

As soon as I step off the elevator to head to Lawrence's office I run into Kevin.

"Hey Mrs.Y.E.S."

"Hey Kev." I give him a hug.

"You're hugging me again. I'm surprised."

"Kevin, don't start."

"Bad mood, well at least you look good."

Although he was right, I still gave him attitude. "Excuse you, Kevin. I always look good."

He laughs.

"Am I funny now?"

"No, but I can see being around Diva and hubby has changed you. Both of their moodiness has rubbed off on you."

"I'm still the same ole Yasmin, You're the one who doesn't know what to say out of your mouth. Isn't that the reason we stopped talking."

"I thought we were over that. As you told me it was just sex, not that serious."

"Let's go to your office, Kevin."

Once when were in his office I had a few choice words for Kevin. He chose the wrong day.

"Kevin, why are you bringing that up? That was a long time ago. It's over, a bad mistake."

"Calm down. I was just playing."

95

"Believe me I am calm. The subject of you and me is nothing to be playing about. I thought we agreed to forget it happened."

"When did we agree to do that?"

"Kevin when I saw you at Zanzibar you were cool. None of this came up. Why are you being an ass, bringing this up now?"

"I apologize, Yas, really I am just playing."

"Don't joke about that. We agreed to forget. It never happened, okay?"

"Alright, I'm just surprised your jealous husband still talks to me after finding out." He laughed.

I didn't say anything. I stood there ready to slap Kevin.

He stopped laughing. "Braxton doesn't know. That explains why he speaks. So you decided to keep a secret from hubby. That's messed up," he shakes his head.

I roll my eyes.

Kevin continues, "There should be an honesty clause in the wedding vowels. You each should be allowed one secret. I guess that's why my salary increases with all the divorces I handle."

"Ha, ha Kevin, anyway can we forget about what happened and not bring it up.

"Yas, you and Braxton are married now. He's obviously the person you want, not me. You should be honest. Technically y'all weren't even together then. It doesn't count. He'll get over it."

I look at him like he was crazy. "You know damn well how jealous Braxton is. Like I said, it never happened. Besides it was over a year ago. No need to open that door."

He laughed. "Yeah, you're right your husband has some issues. But um, Landon knows and you know she can run off at the mouth unconsciously."

"Stop talking about my husband. As for Landon she has no reason to bring that up."

"I apologize."

"Kevin, the reason I stopped dealing with you is because you acted as if you were cross-examining me. I am not on trial with you. I'm supposed to be your friend. A friend is what I need. In the future, I expect you to be more tactful."

"You're right."

"Anyway, I came here to see Lawrence. Goodbye."

"Yas, I'm sorry. I really do miss our friendship. I know you're married to Braxton, but it'll be nice if we could hang out sometime. You and Landon are my girls. Can I get a hug?"

I gave you one.

"Yasmin."

Although annoyed, I obliged.

Sleeping with Kevin is one secret I pray Braxton never finds out about. Technically, like he said, Braxton and I weren't together. In the process of reconciling, but Braxton will not see it that way.

I left Kevin's office and went to meet Lawrence. I managed to block out my issues with Kevin as well as Braxton. It felt weird going to lunch with Lawrence. I didn't know what to expect. I never spent any time with John since he held a lot of animosity towards me. Although Lawrence was late, it did feel good to have a father.

For the remainder of the day, I somehow managed to get a lot of work done. I missed Landon and my little cutie, Eric. On my way home, I decided to stop by.

When I arrive at Landon she looks so depressed. Depression was something I never imagined Landon going through. Landon is always live, if anything she'd be causing depression, not being it.

"What's going on, Diva?"

"Hey Yas, what made you stop by?"

"I missed you and of course my cutie, Eric."

"You look nice today."

"Thank you, Diva. What are you and my baby up to?"

"Nothing much, Eric actually has little Eric."

"Aww, Eric hanging out with his daddy. I'm surprised you're not out shopping."

"Yeah, what's going on with you?" Landon said quickly.

"Let's see, I need a drink. Braxton's being an ass, so is Kevin. My period came for the month so that means no baby and I still have cramps along with a migraine."

"A lot is going on."

"Yeah, what's going on with you?" I look at her to see her body tense, "What's wrong Land?"

"I'm fine. I thought you and Kev made up?"

"Kev, doesn't know what to say out of his mouth. But Land what's going on. Are you and Eric getting along? Land, I love you and I'm here if you want to talk."

A tear rolls down her face and she hugs me.

"Land what's going on?"

"Yas, I don't want to talk about me and Eric."

"Land, you're upset. Talk to me."

"Yas, please drop it."

"Land, you're crying. Please tell me what's wrong."

"Yas, I appreciate your concern, but please I don't want to talk about it. Yas, I am really tired. I'm going to lay down. Can I talk to you later?"

"Now putting me out sounds like Diva."

She laughed.

I got up and head to the door. "Land, call me if you need me."

"Thanks, Yas. Thank you for always having my back. I love you."

"I love you, too."

When we open the door Eric is walking up the driveway with my baby.

"Hey, big boy," I said, reaching for him.

"Mimi." He runs toward me.

I pick him up and smother him with kisses.

"Hi Eric, How's it going?"

"Yeah Yas, you're leaving right. I need to talk to Landon."

I was shocked to say the least, Eric has always been friendly towards me. I knew I had to leave to let these people handle their business but, I was concerned for my sister.

"I'm leaving now. Do you want me to take Little Eric?"

"Nah, he's cool." Eric took his son and walks into the house.

I walk up to Landon because something was up.

"Land, I can stay. Eric is upset obviously. I don't want him to take his anger out on you."

"Yas, I'm fine. Eric isn't going to do anything crazy."

"Land, are you sure?"

"Yas, go home and enjoy your husband."

"Call me if you need me. It doesn't matter the time."

The last 24 hours have been crazy and I was ready to go home and relax. Seeing Eric so upset alarmed me, I prayed him and Landon would work things out.

I get home about nine, Braxton is already sleeping. Even though I said I wasn't speaking until he apologized, I broke that rule. Like I said, it's been crazy, I needed some comfort. After my shower I slid into bed, wrapping my arms around him, kissing him before drifting off to sleep.

The next morning however, when I awoke he was gone.

9

Love You 4 Life

I finish my work up around one. I decided to surprise Braxton at work for a possible treat. Prepared I was in my beige colored mid-thigh skirt with pink wrap around shirt. As I was going into BET, I ran into Chauncey.

"Hey, Ms. Lady," He gives me a hug.

"Hey, Chauncey, what brings you to BET?" I return his hug. Making sure then to step back, allowing distance between us.

"I'm here on business and you."

"Came to visit hubby."

"I see you are definitely wearing that skirt. Easy access, huh? I'm jealous."

"Whatever, Chauncey, how's Toya?"

"She's cool, we're taking a break."

"Chauncey!"

"I know, but you know me. I still have a little of the playboy in me. And it didn't help that I had another kid."

"So the baby was yours?" I asked referring to the baby he conceived during our relationship. Chauncey is now up to three kids, three baby mamas, equaling too much drama.

"Yeah."

I shake my head, letting out a laugh.

"What?"

"Yeah, then you need to be here talking business to keep that money rolling in. I guess I should say congratulations."

"I apologize for that."

"Apologize for what?"

"You know, the baby."

"Chauncey, it's okay. Actually, it's not okay to cheat. I do accept your apology, things happen for a reason. Besides that was a long time ago. I'm married now and you're....doing you."

He laughs. "I miss joking with you."

"Oh, I was just a joke?" I say, pretending to be hurt.

"See, you're mad cool. I miss you, Yassy. Why you have to go and get married on me?"

"Um, didn't you just say you were still living the playboy lifestyle? I was done with that. I was ready to take it to a new level."

"Damn, I miss you, always straight to the point, no games."

"Only way for me to be."

"So, you sure you're happy?" He flirts.

"You said it earlier. I'm wearing a skirt, easy access," I smile.

"I'm jealous," he laughed.

"You should be." I tease in return.

"Um, Um, Umph, reminisce on the love we had," He sings.

I can't help but to burst out laughing, "Nice seeing you again, Chauncey. I'm going to find my husband."

"No need, looks like he's coming out of a meeting. I would stay to say hi, but I don't think your husband would appreciate me having a hard on."

I was in no way in the least interested in Chauncey however his comment by instinct caused my eyes to widen. Take a peek down south.

He laughs. "I caught you looking. I see you like what you see. You know you're facial expressions gives you away all the time."

Damn, double damn. Damn for Chauncey catching me, but got damn for Braxton seeing me with Chauncey. To make matters worse, I couldn't hold back my laughter.

"Have a good day, Chauncey." I finally manage to say.

"You're too, sexy." He nods to Braxton. Turning around, he heads the other way.

I was standing in the corner where Chauncey left me trying to decide what to do. Since Braxton was still engaged in conversation I decide to wait in his office.

I took a seat on the couch located in his office and wait, and wait, and wait. I wait so long I end up falling asleep. It's not until Kim Braxton's secretary came in at 3 to drop off papers that I wake up. I found out that Braxton took a lunch. Of course I am furious. I was going to wait for him but I decide this conversation had to be done at home, no room for interruptions. I left a note telling Braxton to meet me at home at five.

On my way out of Braxton's office I see him with the bitch, Lisa Stevens.

"Braxton, your tie is a little crocked. Let me fix it for you."

"Hello Lisa," I say, coldly.

"Yasmin. Isn't it nice to see you," she said sarcastically.

"Well, I'm on my way out."

"Aww, so soon." Lisa says in a phony concerned voice.

"Yeah, I have to get some things together."

I am not in the mood to be phony. I walk up to Braxton slid my arm through the back of his jacket. I pinch the hell out of him, he jumps. I make sure to snuggle real close. I wanted Lisa to have the illusion he was aroused by my touch. I stood on my tippy-toes then whisper in Braxton ear, "See you at five, don't be late," I emphasize.

Then I pinch him again. "Bye, Lisa."

Braxton arrived home at 5:44, he was being a smartass.

"I said be here at five."

He looks at me without saying a word.

"I told you not to be late," I say very calmly.

"Yeah, well, what's so important?"

"What the hell is your problem?" I ask now annoyed.

"I don't feel like arguing with you. If I knew you were going to act all crazy. I could have stayed out."

"Crazy, you ain't seen crazy yet."

"Yasmin, I'm not for it. I didn't come home to hear you yap your gums."

"Well, I'm not for this. I'm tired of you treating me like I'm some chick you met on the street and don't want to be bothered. I'm your wife. You're treating me like I disrespected you, like I'm the enemy.

"Well I know you didn't show me any respect today when you were flirting with Chauncey. That's the second time you've done that shit at my workplace."

I cut him off, "Saying Hi is not disrespectful. You've been acting like an ass for the last couple of weeks. I've tried talking to you but you push me away. What is your problem?"

"Anyway, today you were acting like a trick on the street. No, I take that back. Actually more of a groupie, the way you were all in Chauncey's face laughing and giggling."

That did it. I swung at him. Trying to hit Braxton in his mouth, I miss. He was quick, catching my arm. Then on reflex he grabs the other one.

"Now you want to be Laila Ali, what the hell is your problem?"

"You! Now get the hell off me!"

He still has my arms. I try to knee him in the groin. He let's go, grabbing his balls to protect them. Damn he was fast.

"Have you fucking lost your damn mind?"

"Fuck you, Braxton. Watch this trick slash groupie walk out the door."

He didn't say anything until he saw me grab my keys.

He walks up behind me, placing both arms around me. "I apologize. I was wrong,. I shouldn't have said that."

I remove myself from his embrace. Turning around, I face him. "That's the problem. You've been saying and doing a lot of things you shouldn't. You act like you don't want to be bothered. I've given you your space. Now you're calling me a fucking trick."

"I didn't call you a trick. I said you were acting like one."

"Whatever, it's the same thing," I say walking away.

"I also said you were acting crazy, doesn't mean you are." He smirks.

"I don't know where all of this jealousy or insecurities are coming from. Braxton there's no reason for you not to trust me. I told you before we were married I had no feelings for Chauncey. Hell, I thought about you the entire time I was with Chauncey. In all actuality, I wouldn't have even been with him if you didn't break up with me. Speaking of which, you're acting the same way you did when you decided a committed relationship was too much for you. I asked you before we got back together if you could handle a relationship. You told me you were in it till death. You surprised me with our wedding. Now it's like déjà vu. Braxton, are you having those same thoughts. Let me know now because I will bring death to you."

Braxton walks up to me. Putting me in a bear hug, he kisses my cheek.

"I'm sorry, beautiful. I love you. No matter how I get. Believe me I am committed to you only till death. I have no regrets. You are my life."

"Then why are you pushing me away?" I ask, frustrated.

"Beautiful, you married an ass. I'm sorry just a lot of pressure on me."

"Braxton, you can talk to me. But you need to know I'm not taking this bullshit."

"I know, beautiful. You know my temper I don't handle pressure well."

"I understand that Braxton, but you can't take your frustrations out on me. "

"You're right. I apologize."

"What's bothering you?"

He loosened his grip around me and took a seat on the couch. "You know me. I can be difficult and cocky at times. I made a bad business decision."

I scrunched up my face, "Oh, how bad?" I asked, taking a seat next to him."

"It was bad, but I managed to fix it."

"You want to talk about it?"

"Nah, not really just pressure comes with the job I know. Messed up at work and now I'm messing up with you."

"Baby, you can talk to me. Remember our vows, we promised each other to communicate. We also promised to be honest. This is it, me and you, I'm not going anywhere."

"You promise?"

"I promise. Baby, stop shutting me out. Whatever's bothering you, just like you got my back, I got yours. "

He grabbed me in his arms and nestled me. "Yasmin, I apologize for being an ass, really. I meant everything I said to you when we were married. I'm sorry I haven't been keeping my promise to make you happy. I do love you." He kissed me. "You just don't know how much I love you, beautiful. I know I am difficult and do stupid things, but never doubt I love you. Promise me you're with me. I can't deal with you leaving me."

"Braxton, I'm not going anywhere! I'm committed to your bi-polar ass. I'm with you for better or worse. You're stuck with me."

"You're stuck with me."

He then hugs me tighter. Repeatedly placing light kisses on my face. For the remainder of the night he made love to me without penetrating me at all.

10

Too Late to Apologize

I was so ready to collapse. I couldn't wait to get home into my bed. The only thing I want to do is sleep. I've been so exhausted lately, having migraines, no energy and still no real appetite. Now I'm starting to get these minor anxiety attacks. I know it's due to stress.

Lawrence has been keeping his word and has been consistent with trying to build a relationship with me. My mother on the other hand, hasn't tried to contact me neither has Ashley; that really hurt. Landon was still distant. No surprise she and Eric are over. Since Landon's breakup with Big Eric she's been clinging to little Eric, so I rarely see him. I can understand, so I let her know I'm here when she's ready. While Braxton has been very, very supportive, my gut is telling me something still isn't right and let's not even think about the baby situation.

As I pulled into my driveway, I notice Landon's car was there. She's brought Eric to see me. He always puts a smile on my face. It's been too long and I need some sunshine. I rushed out of the car anxious to see my baby.

As soon as I open the door, I hear a lot of yelling. Braxton and Landon are arguing about something. Female institution tells me to stay quiet and listen. Slowly, I walk toward the kitchen.

"Landon, why the hell are you doing this now?" Braxton yelled.

"Because I have too! You see how keeping secrets hurt us?" Landon cried.

"You waited all this fucking time!" Braxton's still yelling.

"I know I know I was wrong. I didn't want to think it was possible!" Landon yells back.

"So now you ready to just come here to clear your conscience?"

Braxton wasn't yelling but I hear the aggravation in his voice.

"Yes, I can't do it anymore. I'm tired of lying."

"It's always about you. It's always when you're ready whenever it suits you."

"I told you I know I was wrong. I didn't want to hurt Yassy because she was already hurt. I didn't want to lose our friendship. She's always been there for me."

"Ain't this some shit. You didn't want to lose your friendship, but it was okay for me to lose her?"

"Look, you're married now so it worked out."

"You just don't get it."

"I do get it, but she has to know the truth."

"You're right! But how the hell you just going to show up at my house and dictate today is the day you want to tell the truth?" He was yelling again.

"Look, I told you I'm tired of lying and I'm not leaving until she knows the truth."

"When I found out you were pregnant, I asked you, Landon is there a possibility the baby is mine? You said, no. My gut told me you were lying but I ignored it. When I saw him at the mall I came to you and asked you to tell me. You still said no. I lost years with my son. Now you're going to break up my marriage because you finally get a fucking conscience."

My heart stopped. The air that filled my lungs had been knocked out. All I could do was stand there with my mouth open while my body went into shock. My head was spinning, still in disbelief. I felt dizzy, confused. I tried to refocus, but I couldn't.

"I have to tell her. I can't lie anymore." Braxton's and Landon's ongoing argument broke my trance.

Wait, rewind, Eric is Braxton's son. No, no, no please, God, no please, no God, please no. No, this is not true. Eric's father is Eric Ayers. Landon and Braxton don't even like each other. They only deal with each other because of me. How or when could they have been together? They both couldn't have looked me in the face for the last two years and lied. Besides, little Eric, he looks like…

For the second time, the wind was being knocked out of me. My mind is telling me to breathe, but my body is disobeying. No, no, no, this is not happening. I fell back against the wall, causing a loud thump that startled all of us.

"No. How, why, what," I babble.

"Yasmin?" Braxton says calmly.

"Why!" I yell as the truth at last hit me, reality beginning to set in.

They both look at me and I feel hot tears running down my face.

"Eric's your son?" I asked, feeling my body tremble.

Still they just look at me. Both stand there in shame, never looking me directly in the eye or face.

Air is sucked in, in an attempt to calm my now pummeling heart. Air however does nothing, brings in no relief, only more pain.

Silence remains the dialogue between us.

"I know both of you hear me fucking talking to you. Now answer me!" I yell, frustrated.

"Yas, I'm so sorry it was a mistake," Landon cries.

With my body still trembling, I ball my fist. I ask, "What was a mistake?"

"Braxton and me."

"Yasmin, I didn't want you to find out like this?" Braxton said, apologetically.

"Really? Were you going to take me out, tell me at dinner? Or were you going to fuck me and tell me then? Sorry, you didn't get to play out any of those scenarios. Did you want to wait till tomorrow? Either way, it's all fucked up."

"Yas," Landon cried.

"Eric's your son, Braxton?" I said dismissing Landon's pleas.

"Yeah."

The tears flow as I unconscientiously shake my head no. "Have you been together all this time?"

"NO! It was a long time ago," Braxton spoke up.

"When?!" I yelled.

I know I could have done the math myself but my mind, nor my brain was functioning properly. Honestly, I couldn't accept the answer.

They just stood there not saying anything.

"When?!" I yell again. I had to hear them admit that they hurt me when I was at my lowest, when I wanted to die.

Landon spoke up. "When you miscarried you were going through some things."

Braxton interrupts, "You pushed me away. One night I ran into Landon."

"Is that supposed to justify it, make it alright?"

"No, Yasmin, I'm so sorry." Braxton apologizes.

"How many other times were you together?"

"Yasmin, it was only one time," Braxton confesses.

"So, I miscarry. I'm devastated, depressed, mourning. My best friend, no, I'm sorry my sister and my fiancée at the time hookup and make a baby. You make a baby after I lose mine. Talk about loyalty."

I'm trembling from hurt.

"It was a mistake," Landon cries.

The tears are falling. It's getting so hard for me to breathe. "I went through hell when I lost my baby. Bry…" I paused.

Another revelation. The little calm I had subsided while my anger raged. I pick up the closest thing, a vase, threw it at Landon. Unfortunately, I miss. I lunge forward to literally try to kill her. At that moment all I had for her was hate. I hit her in the face with my fist. She fell back against the counter, holding the right side of her face. I went to wrap my hands around her neck, but Braxton restrains me.

"You fucking BITCH! I was there when you had Eric and you gave me some shit about honoring my son. Your son has my son's name. He was almost born the same day my son died. What is this a joke? All this time you knew there was a possibility Braxton was the father?" I lectured Landon. "Smiling in my face giving me that speech about how my baby could live on. This is so fucked up, but what should I expect, you've never been anything but a selfish bitch anyway. Always what you want doesn't matter who gets hurt." I broke away from Braxton restraint and lash out at him.

"You're protecting her now. You can't let your baby mama get hurt. So you love Landon now. Why the hell did you come back into my life? What the hell did I do to either one of you? Why did you do this to me? Why?" I cried.

I started throwing punches at him, but my punches had no effect. He was able to restrain me, putting me in a bear hug.

"Yasmin, I love you. I'm so sorry. I'm sorry I hurt you."

"Bullshit, you don't do shit like this to somebody you love. Fuck love, you don't do this shit period."

Still he restrains me. "GET THE FUCK OFF OF ME!" I scream as I unsuccessfully try to squirm out of his grip.

"No, calm down."

"Don't tell me to calm the fuck down. You have a fucking son with my sister. There's no calming down. Take your damn hands off of me," I rage, full fury set in.

Reluctantly, he releases his hold of me.

Instantly, I feel light headed. My body feels like fire, my legs are unstable. Angry with my body for being so defenseless, I take hold of the counter to prevent myself from falling.

Landon tries to come over and touch me. "Yas…"

"Don't fucking touch me you fucking, bitch. You knew how difficult my miscarriage was. You knew! Knew how I felt about Braxton yet you constantly told me not to limit myself and your ass has a baby by him. You were there when we broke up. You saw how I was so depressed, most days I didn't get out of bed. I cried on your shoulder and you would throw insults. You were my girl. Even before I knew you were my sister I thought of you as one. You and I were closer than me and Ashley ever was. I trusted you. Throughout your pregnancy I was there for you. Even though I was still devastated from losing my baby, I was always there. Despite my depression and heartache I was there for you. I would be in bed crying my heart out over my breakup with Braxton or losing my baby, but you would call and I would put my hurt aside and come to you. All this time, you lie to me without a second thought. I was at the hospital crying thanking you for giving him my son's name. You smiled in my face like nothing happened."

"I'm sorry" is all Landon could say.

"Shut up!" I yelled. "Now it's all making sense. This is why Eric left. This is where all the tension came from. He found out. So now you want to get a conscience and make me miserable like you. Misery truly does love company. When did he find out?" I hissed.

Landon cries hysterically.

"Shut the hell up with all the dramatics! Now answer the damn question!" I yelled.

"A couple of months ago."

"Months, you…" I couldn't get my words together, another lie.

"I'm sorry, Yassy," Landon whimpered.

"Your son! Yours and Braxton son is named after my baby! This is some real fucked up shit! Now I find out the two people I trusted most, the people who were supposed to be there for me, comforted each other rather than me. Oooh, *I HATE* y'all asses! Both of you are so wrong! Braxton you could have…. Why did you do this to me?!" I yelled, looking at him.

Braxton steps close to me. "I'm sorry it wasn't like that."

I push him away. My mind is racing, going in different directions. Pain is in every part of my body and my head feels like it is going to explode. "Why! No! No! No! Oh my GOD! Oh my God, oh my God! No! I can't do this!" I scream.

Everything was spinning. The black dots I'd seen earlier, now were getting bigger. My chest begins to tighten and I grab it willing the pain to stop. I attempt to walk away, but my legs are wobbly.

Braxton picks me up and carries me to the couch. My helplessness gives him permission to hold me, yet his touch disgusts me. I want to scream, but I can't. Breathing is strenuous. The only thing I can do is gasp for air. My vision is blurry. I lost control, I am having an outer body experience, and everything is chaotic. I see myself struggling, but I can't do anything about it.

Landon was in my face yelling something, crying. I can't hear or focus because I feel my body shutting down. I'm mad at myself for allowing this to happen. I want to kill them, but I'm so hot. The room was spinning and I still wasn't getting any air. I'm trying to calm down but I can't. Again I try to breathe, my body still refusing to cooperate. I close my eyes and I pray, "GOD help me, GOD help me, please GOD help me, help me, help me." Slowly my body relaxes, my senses gradually return, and I'm able to allow air into my lungs. "Calm down. Yasmin" I tell myself. "1,2,3,4,5, breathe. Take control, breathe."

"Yasmin, please calm down. I'm so sorry, Yasmin!" Braxton pleads.

I finally push away from Braxton and sit up.

"Yasmin, lay down please." He attempts to hold me again, but I raise my hand to stop him.

"Please."

I ignore him and continue to take in deep breaths.

On wobbly legs, I stand and make it back to the counter. My body still trembling, I stand trying to get my head together.

"Yasmin, I know you hate me right now, but I need you to calm down. Lay down, we can talk about it later." He tries to reach out to me but I recoil.

I shake my head, no.

"Yasmin, please just lay down." He reaches out again.

113

"Do not touch me. Answer my damn questions!" I yell as tears continue to stream down my face.

"Let's go to the hospital," he pleads.

"I'm not going any fucking where with you," I wail.

"Yasmin, you're too upset and for real you're scaring me. Relax."

"How the hell can I relax? Talk, all this fucking time, all these damn lies." I was getting worked up again. Braxton grabs me.

"Landon is the real reason we broke up." I push him off of me again.

"Yeah."

"Gave me that bullshit about you wanted to see other people. Then you had the nerve to throw in, 'I would rather be honest with you than to cheat,' knowing that you already had! You don't realize how much that hurt me. Especially, since I went over there telling you I didn't want to lose you after losing our baby. Yet, you still pushed me away for her." I grab my stomach which is twisting in knots and cramps.

"I'm so sorry, Yasmin, believe me."

"Sorry? Your ass is more than sorry. I should have left you the hell alone. I'm sorry I met your ass. And I'm really sorry I let you back into my life."

"Yasmin, I know you're mad."

"Mad?!"

My momentary weakness was now replaced with venom. I was ready to beat some asses physically and emotionally.

"You don't get it. Shit, how would you like it if I fucked your friend? I could have. Do you know how many times your so called best friend, Javon tried to get me to fuck him? How many times he told me how good his dick would feel inside of me." I let my words sink in, pleased to see how his whole demeanor changes. I could see how he was overwhelmed with hurt and betrayal. I continue.

"You don't know how many times he made a point to let me know he could do a better job of fucking me than you. He made sure every chance he got that he was rubbing his hard dick against my ass. And from what I felt…"

"What the fuck? Why the hell are you just telling me this shit? What are you saying? You fucked…"

He couldn't even say it so I finished, "Javon. Did I fuck Javon?"

He rushes to me, grabbing me like he was going to hit me.

"I wish you would. It doesn't feel so good now does it? Unlike you, I was faithful. Like a dumb ass, I loved only you. Every time, he tried to get with me, even when we weren't together, I told him, no. Was it even a month after I miscarried before you fucked her?"

He releases his grip. "I'm sorry, Yasmin, I do love you. It was only that one time and I always loved you."

"Javon knows? Wow, now I understand why he was always hinting at you being with someone else. He knew it was a matter of time before I found out."

I face Landon, "What did you tell me about Javon and Braxton, Landon? Birds of a feather flock together. All of y'all asses ain't nothing but some nasty, lying ass, conniving mutherfuckers. All three of you are alike, perfect for each other. Y'all need to have a big fucking orgy, die, and get the hell out of my damn life!"

Braxton looks at me with regret and remorse, but I didn't give a damn. It just made me more determined to lash out at him.

"I told you to talk to me. When we got back together, I specifically asked you if you cheated. You're lying ass said no. I said, Braxton don't fucking lie to me. I told you tell me the truth now so I can deal with it. Still you lied to me."

"I couldn't tell you then. And I didn't even know that Eric was mine."

"Yes you could have, but you chose to lie."

"I just found out," Braxton insisted.

"Really, well you want to know what you should have done? You should have stayed the hell away from me. The story you gave me about seeing other people, you should have stuck with it. You should have went on, met somebody else, been with them."

"Yasmin?"

"Why couldn't you just stay away? Why did you have to come back, make me fall back in love with you. Why did you make me need you? I trusted your ass. I let you back in. I believed you when you told me you would never hurt me again. I fucking hate you. Just die so I don't have to see your damn face again."

He takes a deep breath. "You don't mean that. I'm sorry. I'm so sorry. I do love you. I couldn't stay away because I love you too much. I never meant to hurt you. Yasmin, I need you too."

Landon steps closer. "Yas, we all make mistakes. It should have never happened, I know."

"You know what I went through when we broke up, Bitch!" I swung at Landon. Unfortunately, I didn't get her in the face, but I got her in the neck.

Braxton restrains me again. I start yelling. "You were there encouraging me to get over him. That's why you introduced me to Chauncey. If that wasn't enough, when we were getting back together, you told me I shouldn't because you knew he cheated. Saying he used the same lines you do and the way he was acting was proof. All this time you were the other woman, the bitch!"

Braxton looks at Landon. I knew he wanted to say something but bit his tongue.

"I know I was wrong. I swear it wasn't intentional," he said, pleading with me again.

It all made sense now, stupid, stupid me. Everything started flashing in my mind: Braxton's distance after the miscarriage, his moodiness, the baby's resemblance to Braxton, Landon's comment about things left in the dark, the uneasiness.

"Yasmin, please talk to me. We have to work through this."

"Work through what? Have you lost your damn mind? I'm not doing it. Eric was my godson, then nephew, now my husband's son. A son who was conceived when I was recovering from a miscarriage, uh unprotected sex. Both of you can get the hell away from me and act like you don't know me. As far as I'm concerned, I have no husband, best friend or sister. And I mean this from the bottom of my heart, FUCK YOU BOTH!"

"Yasmin, we took vows. Remember what we said for better or worse." Braxton looks at me with tears in his eyes."

I look at both of them giving them my calmest voice. "Am I supposed to just be like, okay? I understand. I accept it and we'll just act like this never happened. You both really think it isn't serious?"

They both looked at me not saying anything.

"I can't read minds!" I yelled.

Landon approached. "Yas, I know I was wrong but we're sisters and Eric loves you. I swear to you, I'm so sorry."

I let out an aggravated sigh, when Landon approaches I grab her, hitting her in her face then I wrapped my hands around her throat. Landon tried to put up a fight, but I was too strong. I squeezed this bitch's neck, ringing it like a rag. Braxton grabs my arms and is able to get me to let her loose. I focused my attention on him while Landon was coughing in the back ground.

I turn around slapping the shit out of him. I was about to punch him, but he grabbed my arms. "That's why you had me promise you all that shit. I should have known. 'Yasmin, do you promise you will love me through the good and bad times?' You made me promise I wouldn't leave you. That was just some bullshit. Am I some joke? I told you to leave me alone. You had me thinking you loved me."

"Beautiful, I do love you. What I said that day was the truth. I meant everything I said."

"My name is Yasmin, cut that beautiful shit out." I try to move my arms but he has me restrained. "Let me go."

"Calm down, okay."

"Don't tell me what the fuck to do."

Landon started rambling too much, "Yasmin, please, it was a mistake. We felt so bad afterwards. It was just sex. We all make mistakes. It was like you and Kevin. Remember when you had sex with Kevin how bad you felt afterwards."

Braxton looks at me. "You had sex with Kevin? When was this? Brother, huh? I fucking knew it."

"Don't try to turn this on me!" I yelled at Landon.

"Yasmin, when were you with Kevin?" Braxton said as though he had a break in the case against him.

"Kevin and I are different. Braxton, you and I weren't together then. This is about you and Landon. Landon, bitch, just shut the hell up! All that wasn't necessary, it has nothing to do with how wrong you are!"

"You were reconciling and you got back together three weeks later."

"Landon, leave Kevin and me out of this. Look, I want both of you to get the fuck out."

"Yasmin, I'm not leaving you."

I started throwing any and everything. "Get out."

"Yas, I know you hate me right now but I'm sorry. I'm going to leave. I'll give you time to cool off."

"Landon, what do you think tomorrow we can all be some happy family? Just get the hell out of my house. I'm through with you and him. There's no way you can make up for this. Y'all were dead wrong. Both of you can go to hell." I continue throwing anything at these mutherfuckers.

"Yassy, I'm sorry."

"Bitch, don't say my name out your mouth again. I don't want anything to do with you. Get the hell out of my house before I kill you!" Rage full in affect, voice raw, I lurch forward. I grabbed her hair, but the bitch had it cut so short I couldn't get a good grip.

Again Braxton restrains me.

She runs out the door and Braxton thinks its okay to stay.

"Braxton get out!"

"Yasmin, you can't push me away. I told you I'm not letting you go again."

"Well you don't have to let me go. I'm letting you go. I'm getting a divorce. You can go be with Landon or whoever. I'm done with your lying ass."

"Yasmin, I love you. I want you. You and me, this is it."

"And your son with my sister, they're in this equation too now. You should have thought of that before you fucked my sister."

"Yasmin, I'm not leaving you."

I run upstairs with Braxton behind and started taking his stuff throwing it on the floor.

"Yasmin"

"Just shut up! You can't justify it. Get out! Leave me alone!"

"Yasmin."

"Braxton get the hell out of here! Leave!"

"NO!"

I took a pair of scissors and charge after him, stabbing him in the arm. Blood is pouring out but I didn't care. I pull back, was about to stab him again but Braxton is quick. He manages to pin me down and gets me to drop the scissors.

"Yasmin, calm down. I know you're hurt, I'm sorry."

"Why are you still here? Get the hell out. If you don't I will be locked up on a murder charge. Leave me the hell alone." I yelled.

"No, Yasmin"

"Leave me the hell alone! Get OUT! Leave! I don't want to see you! AHHHHHHHHHH!! Leave get the hell away from me!" I started picking up shit again and throwing it. "I need to be alone. Braxton, please, please, please just go." I plead.

Braxton hesitates.

"Braxton, I need you to go. Get the hell away from me. Now!"

"Yasmin."

"Now."

119

He looks at me, finally getting the point, and leaves.

When he did, I slid to the floor crying, yelling out my anguish calling Landon and Braxton every name I could think of. Exhausted from crying, hurting, I get on my bed to get Braxton stuff out of the nightstand. I see a picture of us in the Cayman Islands. It was just one of many wedding photos, but my favorite. I looked at the picture, picked it up and threw it, causing the crying cycle to begin all over again.

I don't know how long I stayed there or how long I cried. I do know as each second passed, the pain in my heart intensified. My heart felt as if a chainsaw was continually sawing at it. This pain was a mutha. Nothing I had ever experienced could compare to this magnitude of pain. I thought I was having a heart attack and I was about to die. I tried to reach the phone, but it was too far away. Again, I was losing the little grasp of reality I had left. I started blacking out. My breathing labored and the sawing now feeling like a sledge hammer pounding on my heart at 100 MPH. I was slowly losing my vision, alternating from bright stars to blackness. The tightness in my chest worsens. I want to breathe, call out for someone to help me, but I can't. My body won't let me. The only thing it allows is the blackness to mask me.

11

Leave Me alone

I feel Braxton's arms around me. Instantly I jump up, waking him in the process.

He gets up, attempting to comfort me. "Yasmin, let me hold you."

"Get the hell away from me. I told you I'm done, we're done."

"Yasmin, I love you, only you. I'm sorry. Let's work through this."

"Braxton, leave me the hell alone. Back off. I hate your fucking ass."

"I know you're hurt. I hurt you and I hate myself for that."

"Hurt. You lied. You had sex with my sister and have a baby. I'm beyond hurt, pissed, and mad. I hate your ass." I start hitting him.

He put me in a bear hold. "I'm sorry. Let it out, hit me, do whatever, but I'm not going anywhere."

I was tired of fighting but continued. Even hitting him in the arm, where I stabbed

him earlier, which was now bandaged. I didn't want to talk to him or for him to touch me.

"Braxton let me go," I cry.

"Yasmin, look at me. I love you."

"No, please let me go so I can breathe. Just get off of me."

"I'm not letting you go. Me and you till death," he pleads.

"It is death, death of this relationship."

"No, it's not. Stop fighting."

All I could do was cry and then I collapsed in his arms.

"I'm so sorry, believe me, Yasmin."

Braxton kisses me on the cheek. All I could do was cry more. He laid me on the bed, lying beside me, just holding me. I thought, *maybe I could deal with this*. I laid there with my heart breaking, trying to lessen my pain. I tried to justify his actions, but there was no validation for this heartache. The more I told myself to run, the more I wanted to stay. I wanted to be mad. I wanted to love him. I wanted to erase the last couple of hours, my miscarriage. I wanted to make it like it was. I don't know how long I lay there, but soon I felt Braxton place soft kisses on my neck. My head was telling me to push him away but my heart wants, shit needs him. Before I knew it, Braxton is on top of me kissing me, at first, gently on the lips, but soon the kisses become more passionate.

I don't object when he takes my clothes off, I allow it. His tongue makes its way in my mouth, I accept it, kissing him back just as hard. I never stop him when he grabs my ass and enters me slow. Instead, I open my legs wider, gasping, seizing him tightly as he pushes his hardness into my sweetness. Endlessly, I accept it as he grinds his himself in me. Each thrust he goes deeper, deeper, deeper, and deeper. Each thrust leaving me wanting more. My mind in turmoil, my body elated, betraying me, overflowing with desire. My body aches for him, needing him to give me all of him. Then he whispers how sorry he is, how much he loves me. The more he tells me he loves me, the more I cry. Tears roll down my face. My body tenses. Braxton assumes it is from pleasure, but in reality it is from pain. Images of him with Landon, then Eric, invade my thoughts. I wonder if he made love to her the way he is to me. Did he give it to her, the way he is giving it to me? I wonder if he thought of her while inside of me. If her loving gave him pleasure. The desire inside me fades, while nausea arouse. When he finally does release himself in me, part of me died. The love that always brings me so much pleasure, comfort, security is gone. It is now replaced with doubts, sorrow, and too much pain. Nothing is sacred or pure. I know I have to go.

Braxton kisses me gently. "Yasmin, I love you. I do. I'm so sorry. I promise I will make this up to you. I'll never hurt you again. You're the only one for me. I'm sorry."

He bends down kissing me on my belly. My mind screams, *NO! Why there? Why? Why did he kiss me there?* His kiss on a scar that will be with me for life, reminding me of a baby, I will never get to hold.

He lifts up, kisses me on my lips. He lies behind me, spoons me, and holds me tight, while I watch the clock.

Thirty minutes later, I hear Braxton snoring in my ear. I attempt to move but Braxton just grips on tighter, pulling me closer.

Why did I let him touch me? Why did I think he loved me? I'm a dumbass for allowing him inside. He made a mockery of our love, my love. No repercussions, no respect for self. Like a fool, I allowed him inside of me. He conceived a baby with my sister while I was mourning the loss of our son. Yet I allowed him inside of me. I had to get away from him…this. I wanted to run, go where no one could fine me. But right now, I was paralyzed in his grip, forced to watch each minute slowly fade away.

It wasn't until 12:39 I was able to break away. Braxton grip had loosened, so I slipped out of bed. Quickly, yet quietly I put on some clothes, not caring if it matched or coordinated. Grabbing only my keys and purse, I left out the door, never looking back.

12

Tears on My Pillow

Two hours later, I sat in my Armada in a daze, watching the rain fall from the sky as it did from my eyes. I still prayed the last few hours was a bad dream, but, no alarm sounded, no sun shined to wake me. This was real. Yet again, I'd been lied to, hurt, rejected. I didn't know what to do. I wanted to soak and rinse away any reminder of Braxton. I could still smell his scent on my flesh, feel his hands on my body, reminding me again of my stupidity, but I had nowhere to go. I had no best friend, no parents to comfort me. It was just me.

It was very late, 3:02 in the morning. My only option was a hotel so I stopped at an ATM to get some cash. The last thing I needed was for Braxton to check my bank statement online to find out what hotel I was in. As I pulled into the hotel, I realized I had no idea of where I was.

Once I was inside the room, I went straight to the shower. Taking at least an hour, washing, crying throwing up, I tried to get myself together, but only accomplished bruising my skin from scrubbing so hard.

Lying down only initiated more images of Landon and Braxton. My body stung from thoughts of them. My heart shattered thinking of how she pleased him to the point that he gave her a child. Did he hold her afterwards? Did he kiss her the way he kissed me? Did they spend hours and hours of lovemaking? Too many questions, too many more I knew I couldn't handle the answer to.

Why did you bring Braxton into my life? Braxton promised he would love me. He told me he would never hurt or leave me. I let go of my fears, let him in, now this. He has a baby with my damn whore ass sister. I feel so empty. My parents don't want me. My biological father gave me away without a second thought. Landon just stood by and let me suffer. Alone and so hurt, I cried myself to sleep.

Two days later, I lay in bed in the same robe, same tears. The only reason I knew it'd been two days was because of housekeeping. Apparently, they became concerned after seeing me in the same spot with the same vacant look. Dejected due to my current dilemma, I forgot to use the "Do Not Disturb" sign. The manager came down offering to call my husband. That caused a crying episode, which led to the next question, if I need psychiatric help. It was time to go. Somehow, I managed to get myself together, ignoring his question. I did thank him for his concern. I advised him that I would be leaving after I took a shower. I could see he was relieved, not wanting the "crazy" lady to do anything in his establishment. Which leads me here, the same place I was two days ago… nowhere.

Two damn days of being dazed, no recollection of anything just hurt. I don't remember, eating, drinking, crying, or even praying. The same stinging I felt in my body two days ago was present, if not stronger.

When I finally got up to take a bath, I noticed I was spotting, yet another fucking reminder of what I lost and couldn't have. Since I left the house with only the clothes on my back, I had to put the same clothes back on, that now I see are a hot damn mess. Green and white Capri's, purple shirt, complete with navy mules. Talk about humility on all levels, first the embarrassment of making a baby with my sister, now forcing me to go out in public with this outfit. Once dressed, I pulled a brush out my purse, brushed my hair into a ponytail, and attempted to look sane.

I checked my messages. Of course it wasn't accepting any messages thanks to Landon and Braxton. I deleted them. Braxton was going to try to smother me. Braxton if he could would hold me captive until I gave in. Every move I made he would be beside me, in my face. I had to get away. Several messages were from my job, they were concerned when I didn't come in or call. The last message from my job was a get well soon. Apparently, Braxton told them I was sick, needing some time off. Damn motherfucker interfering with my livelihood. They also called to confirm my business trip. I was supposed to go out of town for a couple of weeks to assist with a new contract in Minnesota. A trip I neglected to tell Braxton about because I knew he wouldn't want me to be gone for so long. Well, fuck him. I was going to go, I needed to go. Problem was, I wasn't leaving for another week.

Then there was a message from Mrs. Simms pleading with me to call. I knew she loved me, but she also loved her son. She would try to convince me to work things out with him. That message was deleted. Yes, I needed to get as far away as possible. That's when I figured out my next step. After I called the office another call came in, it was Braxton. Right now, my emotions was controlling me.

"Braxton please stop calling me. It's over. I can't be with you. Go fuck my sister. You're good at that."

He took in a deep sigh of relief, "Yasmin, thank God. Are you okay?"

"Hell no! You have a baby with my sister. You and I are over."

"No, we're not."

"Braxton, listen you fucked up, now you have to pay the consequences. It's over. You can go fuck Landon or whomever."

"You know that's not what I want."

"Really?" I said sarcastically.

"Yasmin, I need you. Come home please." He begged.

"NO!"

"I know it's a lot but we need to talk."

"I'm done with talking."

"Yasmin, come home. If you don't I'll just come to your job."

"Braxton, don't threaten me."

"I didn't mean it like that, but beautiful I need you. I can't function without you."

"Learn!" I spit, angrily.

"Yasmin, please I need you home."

"I really don't give a fuck."

"Yasmin…"

"Look, I can't deal with this. I need to get away, be away from you."

"I can't do that. I can't, I love you and I told you I'm miserable without you."

"Again, I don't give a damn. Like I SAID I'm gone. Don't bother me. That means don't call my job or me."

"Yasmin, please."

"Braxton, stop. Listen to me. Leave me the hell alone."

"No!"

I let out a frustrated sigh, "Braxton, I can't deal with this. I'm leaving town…today." I lied.

"What! You can't do that."

Well, I am. I need to get away from you…this. I took a leave of absence. You can understand that right? With all this stress, I have to get myself together. I can't come back there."

"How long will you be gone?"

"That's none of your business because like I said before you and I are done. The way I'm feeling I probably will never be back. Honestly, ain't shit here in Maryland to come back to. I need a fresh start."

"How you going to tell me some shit like this and expect me to be okay with it."

"The same way you going to tell me, you fucked my sister, had a baby with her and expect me to be okay with it. Not easy is it? Can't do it, right? Now we finally agree on something. This isn't going to work."

"Yasmin, you're my wife. I married you, no one else. I love you. Come home, please."

"Wife for the moment, but that'll be quickly fixed."

"Yasmin, don't say that."

"It's the truth. You replaced me with Landon."

"No I didn't, no one can replace you."

"Well, news flash for you, you are not irreplaceable. Maybe, I should give Chauncey a call. At least I know what I'm getting."

He was pissed just like I wanted him to be. He was breathing heavy plus I could hear him tapping on something in the background. I wanted him to hurt.

"Yasmin, I know you're hurt. But you and I both know you don't want Chauncey."

"You don't know what I want."

"Yasmin you're hurt. You should be. I know you're just bringing up Chauncey to try and get back at me."

"I don't have to use Chauncey for nothing. I was just pointing out the facts. Chauncey is a sweetheart we had some good times."

"Yasmin, I'm not worried about some damn Chauncey. This is about you and me. You know that relationship was a joke. You said it yourself. I have your heart and you have mine. Yasmin, please just come home."

He was right but I still wasn't going home. "Whatever. You don't know anything about that relationship. Now that I know the real reason we broke up, there's no reason to hold back. I never gave him a real chance."

"I told you I don't want to talk about that clown Chauncey. You know you don't want to be with him. You like your privacy. You saw how being with him caused your miscarriage to be put out there."

He went there. I went off. "Don't bring up my son. Yes, I lost him. Now I have nothing, nobody. You on the other hand, have a son. Fuck you. Go be with my sister and be one big happy family," I was crying now.

"Yasmin, I'm sorry for upsetting you. I was wrong for saying that. Our son can never be replaced."

"My son. You say that, but you wasted no time. He died. Two months later you were making another one. I hate your fucking ass. Go to hell."

"Yasmin, calm down. I'm sorry, I'm sorry, please."

"What am I supposed to do, accept your son? I get it. I couldn't have your baby, so you had one with the closest thing you could get to me"

"Yasmin, it wasn't like that. I loved Bryan."

I was silent, pissed all over again.

"I'm sorry. Please come home. We have to work this out. I love you."

This was too much. I finally speak into the phone. Calmly, I managed to say, "No. Stay the hell away from me. You don't love me. If you did, you wouldn't have had sex with Landon, and Bryan would be your only son."

"You're wrong. I do love you."

"Braxton, I can't be around you right now. It's too much. Stay far away from me. Please stop. I'm leaving Maryland and you. It's over, Braxton."

"Yasmin, please let me see you."

"Braxton you have your wallet. There's a picture of me inside. You can look at it and see me all you want."

"Yasmin, please, please come home. Let's talk face to face. Tell me what to do."

"There's nothing you can do." I said with finality.

"Yasmin come home."

"I'm not entertaining this anymore. As far as I'm concerned, this is our last conversation. I don't want to see your ass again. I don't want anything from you, other than for you to leave me the hell alone. Anything you have to say to me, say it to my lawyer. You will be contacted soon." I hung up on him.

The crying started over again. I stayed there for another hour. My body was tired numb.

I needed to talk to someone. So I swallowed my pride and went to see an old friend.

I knocked on the door and felt closed in all over again. I started having yet another anxiety attack, hyper-ventilating. I really had to get this shit under control.

"Yasmin, what's going on? Kevin asked. I felt him grab me. I vaguely remember him picking me up to carry me in his house.

"I'm going to call Braxton."

"No," I cried.

"What's going on? I just got back in town this morning. I got a dozen calls from your father, Landon, even Braxton asking if I heard from you."

"Eric," I was crying uncontrollably.

"What's wrong, did something happen to Eric?"

I shook my head no. "Landon and Braxton."

"What?"

"Eric is Braxton's son?"

"What?"

I calmed down enough to tell Kevin the story as I was told. Kevin was just as shocked as I was. He had to take several drinks on this story.

"Yas, I'm sorry. I don't know what to say." Kevin said, sincerely.

"I don't know what to do. I can't believe this. Why me? Why can't I be happy? It's like my life is supposed to be miserable. I can't trust anyone. My own parents never loved me. How can I expect my husband or best friend to? It's like I don't deserve to be loved."

Kevin came over to console me. He hugged me and kissed me on my forehead.

"Nothing changed. Be strong. You're strong. I know it hurts but you do deserve love. I know you don't believe it or want to hear it, but Landon and Braxton love you. They just fucked up big time. I feel for you. I'm here. Just take some time to clear your head before you make any decisions."

"It doesn't matter how much time I take or whatever I do the result will always be the same; my husband is the father of my sister's child. I don't know what hurts more. I can't pretend this never happened. They have a child, a constant reminder of what they did. There's nothing left to do but just end it with both of them. I am not going through the drama. I'm not sharing or putting up with this shit, fuck them. I've done that my entire life."

"Yasmin, you're angry, calm down. For now, you don't need to make any rash decisions."

"Kevin, stop trying to make it seem like it's not bad. You and I both know this is fucked up. I hate both of their asses. I don't want to see or talk to them. I'm tired of hurting."

Kevin gave me another hug allowing me to cry on his shoulder.

I took off that week and stayed with Kevin. He checked on me periodically, but respected my space and I appreciated that. I cried and cried. Landon and Braxton called my cell non-stop. Kevin said he'd gotten calls from both Landon and Braxton but he covered and said he hadn't heard from me. Just in case Braxton did a drive-by, he parked my truck in his garage. I decided to leave it there while I was on hiatus. When it was finally time for my trip, I was ready. I couldn't wait to leave Maryland.

13

Sweet Misery

Minnesota was serving its purpose, keeping me busy. I'd been here a couple of weeks, working long hours, often six days a week. By the time I did reach my temporary residence, I was exhausted so sleep was not a problem. On my off days, I would try to go somewhere, but usually end up in the bed depressed. I received so many messages from Braxton and Landon that I had my phone cut off. The only person who had the new number was Kevin but I never answered when he called. Instead, I would send a text letting him know I was alright. I didn't want any pity.

I've been feeling sick lately in addition to anxiety attacks, migraines and shortness of breath. I've noticed that I've been peeing too frequently, and often with pelvic pain. I was scared I caught something from Braxton. He proved he couldn't be trusted. So now I was sitting in the gynecologist office having all these tests done for HIV, STD's, anything. I was scared to get the results, but I had to know. One thing I know for certain, if I have caught something from him, I'm prepared to shoot Braxton and Landon, then plead temporary insanity.

"Sorry for the delay, Yasmin, but I was waiting on a couple of your tests."

I couldn't tell if she had good news or bad news so I braced myself.

"What are the results?"

"Well, all of your tests came back negative accept for one."

I'm going to jail for murder. I feel the tears coming. "Which test is that?"

"Relax, Yasmin, stress isn't good for the baby. Congratulations."

"I'm pregnant, are you sure?"

"Yes."

"Really, are you sure?"

"Yes, I'm sure," she laughs.

"I've been getting a period?" I asked, shaking my head, no.

"In the first trimester, it's not uncommon for you to have a light period or to have some spotting. Your body was just adjusting to the pregnancy. How long have you been having the migraines and anxiety attacks?"

"I don't know 3-4 months."

The doctor listened to my heartbeat, checked my pressure and did a pelvic exam.

"I want you to have an ultrasound so you can have a more accurate conception date and to check the baby's growth. Judging from the size of your uterus I would say about three to four months and the baby should be here, mid - to late May. You're pressure is up, so please take it easy, if you don't, you can lose this baby."

I left the doctor office with so many emotions and even more confused. I wanted this baby for a long time. I was happy but sad. I thanked God for my baby. All of the stress not to mention my attacks on Landon and Braxton could have easily ended up with me miscarrying. I don't know what God's plan is, but I know my baby is a blessing. He or she has a purpose and will be something beautiful that came from my relationship. It's a shame this blessing complicates things. The baby did not mean get back with Braxton, but now I'm obligated to communicate. I want to move on and forget Braxton which is easier said than done. Obviously, God has other plans.

It's been a week since I found out I was pregnant and I don't know what to do. I was really missing the family. In a couple of weeks it'll be Thanksgiving. I wanted to call Mrs. Simms, I knew she was worried. She has only treated me like a daughter, but she'll tell Braxton. I picked up the phone to dial her many times, but hung up when it rung. I just wasn't ready to talk.

I was still confused even more scared. I decided to call Kevin. He'd left me a message earlier saying to call him because it was very urgent. He said if I didn't, Braxton would be knocking on my door.

"Hello, Kevin."

"It's about time you called me back. I knew my threat would get your attention. Seriously, it time for you to come home."

"I'm not ready. Besides, I am working."

"Yas, how long do you plan on running? You've been gone almost a month. Talk to these people, please. They are getting on my nerves."

"I will talk to them."

"Soon, at least to say you're okay."

"Alright Kevin, no lectures, please."

"Yasmin, I'm warning you. It will be in your best interest to call Braxton or his mother. Lawrence and Jackie are worried too."

"I heard you the first time."

"Yasmin, did you forget how crazy your husband gets when it comes to you?"

"I don't want to talk about Braxton and stop calling him my husband."

"He is your husband."

"Yasmin, you have to see him eventually. You can't keep running."

"Kevin, I'm pregnant. If I see him he's going to cause my pressure to rise and I could lose my baby. Kevin, I can't go through that again."

"Yasmin, you have to talk to Braxton. If you tell him about the baby he should back off."

"Kevin, you know Braxton will have me hooked up to a monitor and a tracking device on my car. I can't let him know yet."

"Yas, it's unavoidable, you have to see him. He shouldn't notice anything. You're only about a month, right? You shouldn't start showing until you're like four or five months."

"I'm almost four and I'm showing a little."

"Yas, why didn't tell me you were pregnant?"

135

"Kev, I didn't know. I just found out a week ago. I noticed my stomach getting bigger, but I thought I was just gaining weight from eating junk."

"So people are noticing you're pregnant?"

"I've gotten stares, but no one has asked."

"I don't know what to tell you."

"Kevin thanks, for the warning."

"Yas, I know you have a lot going on. However, call someone. Lawrence is very worried and I know he and Braxton have talked. It's just a matter of time before they find you."

"I know. I'll be back in a few days. Can I stay with you for a couple of days until I find someplace else?"

"Yasmin, I don't like lying to your father. Eventually you have to deal with Braxton."

"Is it okay to stay there for a couple days?"

"Yeah," Kevin answered reluctantly.

"Thanks, Kevin. Thank you for everything."

"Yas, you're putting me in an awkward position. If you don't let everyone know you're okay, I will."

"Kevin..."

He stops me. "This is a bad situation. Honestly, Yasmin, did you think you could disappear without a trace and have no one look for you. I told Lawrence you left me messages on my cell saying you were okay. You know he was ready to pull my phone records to track you down. I told him to give you a little more time, but Yasmin, I don't think he listened. You need to call these people. Now!"

"I will...now."

I hung up with Kevin and didn't listen. Instead I prayed that the stress of this "bad situation" didn't cause me to lose my baby.

I was determined to be extra cautious not to let current circumstances jeopardize my baby's health. I already lost one and I couldn't handle the heartache of another. I've had enough heartache for a lifetime. I needed the little sanity I had left. This baby was my hope; the push I needed to get my life in order the best way I could.

I wasn't ready to face Braxton or Landon, but Kevin was right I couldn't hide forever. Despite what Braxton has done, he had the right to know he had a child. He would be there for this baby. I just didn't want him assuming I was cool with everything and that we were back together. This was going to be difficult, but I had to tell him…just not yet.

*

"Hello, Yasmin. You look, um, nice." Candace my co-worker walks into my office.

She must have picked up on my weight gain and her comment was her being devious. Proven no matter how many times the geography may change, the people are the same. Right now they were too damn nosy. Now Candace, this broad wanted to be the center of attention. Acting like she was more important than she really is. From all the bragging she did you would think she had an entourage of assistants. This chick claims everyone is jealous of her. Have her tell it, her boyfriend or whatever he is, is in the "entertainment business" and has connections. I know better, he was a bouncer from the club. Fortunately for her, I have real shit to deal with, but my patience is thin, especially since my phone call with Kevin.

I don't respond to her "compliment," instead I offer a hello.

"All this work and no play you're doing, you need to get out. You know, get some exercise. You should come to the club with me. Your husband is going to wonder what happened to you in Minnesota."

"He's good."

"You don't have any pictures," she looks on my desk.

"You don't seem like a happy newlywed. Did you marry for money? I give it to you. That ring is serious. Is he ugly? That's why you don't have any pictures. My boo sexy, isn't he? She shows me a picture on her phone. "Don't be jealous. I can't marry an ugly man.

My kids may come out ugly. I don't care what nobody say about personality. And who wants a man who can't lay it down in the bedroom," she rambles.

"Don't try to analyze my relationship. You're not married and you're not me."

My ring always caused stares but I keep details about my marriage at a minimum. Other than name and them knowing he is an executive was all the info I provided.

"Your problem is you need some."

"No, my problem is you in my damn business. You need to mind your own. Such as why you wearing fake Louboutins, fake Louie and fake everything. Oh, I know real such as the stitching in the Fakebouutins are double stitched. That is not authentic and the purse, let not go there. As far as your boyfriend or whatever, there's nothing attractive to me. Since you are so concerned about "image" you need to take him to the dentist and get that shit in his mouth replaced. Look, I can help you find one. I am very resourceful."

Candace sucked her teeth and left.

I just rolled my eyes.

After my irritating conversation with Candace, I went to pick up a file on another floor. Upon my return, it seemed as if all eyes were on me.

"Is everything okay?" I asked feeling uncomfortable.

"Yes." Nancy a middle-aged co-worker quickly said.

"You look a little tired." Tasha commented.

"Yes, Yasmin, you do. Go ahead home, get some rest. Girl, you've been looking worn."

"I'm fine."

"Yasmin, go ahead in your office and get your coat so you can leave. Get some rest."

These chicks must have figured out I'm pregnant. At least they didn't start asking me fifty-million questions. That damn Candace.

"Linda, I think I am going to take the rest of the day off. You don't need anything do you?"

"No, you enjoy." She said, smiling.

"We have everything under control. We understand if you don't come in tomorrow or the rest of the week for that manner."

There were snickers.

"What?" I said, offensively.

"Yasmin, relax, you've been working so hard since you got here. I know you're homesick. I would be too," Sharon said, giggling.

I look at both of them wondering what was so funny. I ignored their snickers and went into my office. I open the door and my heart skipped a beat. My hormones have been out of control and instantly the tears began to flow. For a moment, I forgot the last couple of weeks. All I wanted was for Braxton to hold me and tell me he loved me.

Braxton grabs me, pulling me into his arms, "Hey, beautiful. I missed you."

He looks so relived to be holding me.

"Damn, I missed you. Let me just hold you tight. I love you so damn much, beautiful." He says, voice cracking.

I hear the "awws" and knew my co-workers were eavesdropping. I was in shock, unable to talk...to move. Braxton just held on to me, relentlessly kissing me like the found missing person I was. Finally, I step away, and close the door. I grab my stomach, which felt queasy. The pain, the hurt, had resurfaced. I felt a panic attack coming so I closed my eyes, and took in deep breaths.

Braxton reaches out to me, but I stop him. Silently, I prayed he didn't notice my stomach. Quickly I grab my stuff, wiping away my tears.

"Come on, we need to talk." I finally said.

Of course on my way out all eyes were on me. Nosy coworkers were staring like we were walking the red carpet. I did some introductions. Purposely, I stopped at Candace's office to send the message, "Ass he is, but ugly? Most definitely not, boo." I took delight in watching her drool over him. Braxton took advantage of the opportunity grabbing on me, kissing me. He tried to grab me around my waist, but I held on to his arm. I went along with the façade until we were outside, the cold wind instantly causing me to shudder. The weather makes Braxton assume it is okay to wrap me in a bear hug.

"Get off me."

"Yasmin, I'm sorry, I know you're mad, but I need you."

"Didn't I tell you to leave me alone, don't contact me. Why the hell are you here?"

"You know why, Yasmin. I need you. I know I hurt you Beautiful, but you can't leave me."

"Braxton, I can leave you. Actually, I did. Why can't you just leave me alone? How did you find out where I was anyway?"

"Yasmin, I left you alone for a month. You know how hard that was? I didn't know where you were, if you were okay. I couldn't eat, sleep, I was losing my mind."

"Am I supposed to have sympathy for you?"

"Yasmin, let's go back to your hotel room so we can talk."

"Hold up, before I go anywhere, how did you know where to find me and how do you know where I'm staying?"

"I talked to your boss, Bob. It wasn't hard, but that's not important."

"Yes the hell it is important. Why are you involving Bob in our personal business?"

"Yasmin, come on now. I still had Bob's number from when he was handling the BET account. I told him I wanted to surprise you and forgot the hotel address."

"Why did you come to the office if you knew where I was staying?" I asked, angrily. "You know I hate scenes."

"The plan was to catch you this morning, but my flight was delayed. I waited a month to see you. I couldn't wait any longer. I told you I wasn't letting you go."

I stood there freezing trying to calm my nerves.

"You're cold, let's go to the hotel."

Since I didn't want my business broadcasted in downtown Minnesota, I allow Braxton to follow me back to my hotel. He already knew where I was staying, so there was no hiding.

Once we were inside, Braxton tries to grab me again. I was able to get away. With my back turned to him, I took off my coat. Then I walked in the kitchen and stood behind the counter. Braxton took off his coat and stood on the opposite side of the counter and just stared at me for a minute or two, then took a deep breath.

He took a deep breath.

"Stop staring at me like that."

"Yasmin, are you alright?"

"What do you think, Braxton?"

"You look different."

"Really, how so?" I asked sarcastically.

Your face is fuller, different."

"What are you trying to say, I've gained some weight? Well, I have, so drop it."

"No, not at all you're still so beautiful."

"Stop staring at me!" I yell.

"You are so beautiful, Beautiful."

"Cut the bullshit." I prayed that I would remain calm for my baby's sake.

"You are. I need you, Yasmin. Please just come home."

"Anyway, how is Eric?"

Braxton took a deep swallow, "He's good. Yasmin, I'm sorry."

"Are you seeing him regularly?"

"Yes, I am."

"How often?"

"Usually, I get him every weekend."

"Interesting. What about you and Landon? Are you going to rekindle the romance?"

"There is no Landon and Braxton, never was or will be. I'm committed to you."

"What the fuck ever."

"So does Landon stay there on the weekend too?"

"Yasmin, I don't deal with Landon. She drops him off at my mother's. I want to discuss us now. I want you back."

He was irritated and losing patience, but oh well. "Well, I'm not done with my questions. So, your mother knows? I know she must be ecstatic to have a grandson." Cool and calm I continue.

He took a deep breath and waited a minute to respond. "She's happy about her new grandson, but she isn't too pleased with me at the moment."

"Braxton, I'm not coming home. I contacted a lawyer and he's drawing up divorce papers." Which I actually did, but the baby complicated things. I didn't file any papers I just picked up a card and made a call. I could see the anger in his eyes as he shook his head.

"Yasmin, I fucked up. There's no excuse, but we're not done. You're mad and should be. But I'm not signing anything."

"Braxton, don't make this more difficult than it has to be. I'm not arguing with you. We're over. I can't do this. I'm NOT doing this."

"Yasmin, I love you. I know you still love me. Yasmin, we can get through this."

"How the hell can we get through this?" I ask, almost with a laugh. "You fucked my sister, lied to me, and had me ready to check into an asylum, blaming myself for everything. You have a son, a constant reminder for me of how you cheated. Braxton just leave. Forget you knew me and move on."

"No!"

I walked over to the desk, pulled out the card with the divorce attorney's info, handed it to him and he ripped it up.

"Braxton, I can't accept what you did. This is my lawyer. The papers are being drawn up and you will be served soon. Please, let's end this as amicably as possible. I don't want anything. I just want this marriage to be over."

"I can't do that.. Yasmin, I was fucked up, I'm sorry. It was a mistake. I love you and want you. . "

Now I was crying. Not because I was getting weak, but in fact, his words infuriated me.

"You're right Braxton. You and I…" I tried to stop the tears but they kept flowing. Braxton walked over trying to comfort me, but I stop him.

"Yasmin, let me hold you."

"Braxton, those days are over. You and I had something and I'm not going to deny the fact that I love you. As much as I wish I could forget you, us, I can't. Our love, our commitment was so strong, solid, so I thought, but you fucked it up. And because of that, you have to pay the consequences."

"Let me make it right."

"You can't make it right. I let my guard down, I let you in, loved you, thinking you loved me. Then when I lost our son and I needed you the most, you couldn't handle it. You said it was too much for you. Basically, 'Fuck Yasmin and her feelings.' So you go and fuck the person I was closest to, have a baby, and now all I get is more pain, heartache, and rejection.

"I'm sorry."

"Sorry doesn't make it better. You don't know how it feels to love someone with your all. Loving them feels so right that you thank God every day that you have them in your life and they love you. Then one day, when you need them the most, when you ready to fight and not lose what you have, he tells you he can't deal and wants to see other people."

"I was an ass. I told you then, I should have handled things differently,."

"Well, I shouldn't have taken you back. I knew how things ended, how hard that was. I should have remembered the pain and moved on. I'm not going to compromise myself anymore. It's over. If you love me like you say you do, let me go. Don't fight this divorce. Let me go," I plead.

He took several deep breaths before he spoke, "I can't let you go. I can't, I love you too much."

"Braxton, you can't make me stay."

"Yasmin, I can't let you go either."

"Braxton…"

His phone rang, interrupting us. He looked at it, cursed, and sent it to voicemail. I was tired of this scene. I wanted him gone.

"Landon checking up on you," I asked.

"No, it was my job. I don't talk to Landon."

"You have a son together. You're obligated to talk to her. Like I said, there is no room for me. I'm not dealing with the baby mama drama. I'm moving on."

"Yasmin, please come home. Let's work this out. What you want me to do?"

I took a deep breath, "Braxton, there's nothing you can do. As you said, I've been gone over a month. Nothing has changed, you and I are over. Can we please just get this divorce over quickly?"

"No!" he said shaking his head.

"Damn Braxton, you can't make me love you and be with you. I'm trying not to hate your ass, but you're making it hard. Leave me alone!" I yell in frustration.

"Yasmin, you know you still love me. We can do this."

"Oh, my God, why are you so fucking stubborn? I left because I don't want to be with you. You make me fucking sick. You and I have no ties, I said throwing my hands up in frustration."

"I'm sorry. Can't you try? Yasmin, I know this is not the end for us. You meant those vows as much as I meant mine, me and you till the end. We still got a long way to go. We can get over this obstacle. We can have more kids." He let out an uneasy chuckle.

I grabbed the counter to avoid falling. Damn. Should I tell him? No, I can't. I gave him a crazy look, hoping to throw him off.

"I hurt you in the worst way, there's no excuse, I know. I am so sorry. Let me love you, please." He stepped closer, reaching out for me, but I turned away.

"Braxton, this is going nowhere. It's time for you to leave."

"Yasmin," he came up behind me attempting to grab me around the waist. Quickly, I blocked him. Stepping away, I take refuge behind the counter again.

"Braxton, stop, you need to go. I'm tired of talking about this. My feelings are the same. You and I are done… over…finished."

"No, we're not."

"Braxton, I swear to God, if you don't get out of here in the next minute, I'm calling the police."

"And tell them what; your husband is trying to talk to you?"

I took deep breaths. I tried honesty, now time for lies. I let several minutes pass. "Alright Braxton, this is too much. Give me some space. Let me finish up my job here. Then we can talk."

He looks at me apprehensively. "When will this job be done?"

"In a week."

"Yasmin, we need to talk now. I need you to come home with me. I've already spent too many nights without you."

"I have to finish this up."

"Then, I'll stay and we can go home together."

"You smothering me is not going to help. If anything you are making me want to run away."

"You already ran away and you've been gone for a month. It's been 4 weeks, 31 days, 672 hours of hell. I didn't know where you were, if you were okay. You just left and now you want me to let you do it again."

"I will come back to talk to you. You're putting too much pressure on me right now. Give me a little more time."

"Ok, I'm staying here till Friday."

"Get out! Go get another room," I demand.

"No."

"Whatever."

No surprise, he didn't leave. He wasn't sleeping in my bed or room for that matter. I ignored him for the remainder of the evening and stayed in the bedroom. I fell asleep with pillows surrounding me.

I shivered as I felt soft lips on my neck. Familiarity. I turn, my body relaxes and reaches for comfort. I'm dreaming Braxton is here holding me. No, Braxton is here! I wake startled. Although I shake my head no, Braxton kisses me. I attempt to push him away, but he resists.

"GET OFF OF ME!"

"Relax," he soothes.

He continues to kiss me and attempts to remove my shirt.

"Stop," I plead.

He ignores me.

"Get off of me!"

He ignores me again. My mind visualizes images of him with Landon. I can't, I won't.

"What you want me to bend over so you can take it? You want to keep fucking me? Am I a joke?" I lash out.

"No, I love you. I want all of you not just sex. I'm sorry. I just needed to feel you. Hold you."

"Braxton stop. The last time we were together I kept wondering did you fuck Landon the same way you fucked me. Did you compare us? I can't do this with you."

"Yasmin not at all. It wasn't at all like you and me…our connection. It was nothing special."

"Well that's why I can't. Every time I see you I think of you and Landon. I don't feel comfortable or safe. I feel sick, disgusted. You messed it up. It's not the same."

"What can I do?"

"Nothing, just leave."

"I'm going to sleep on the couch."

I just turn my back to him.

The next morning when I walk out to the kitchen he tells me he's leaving.

He was quiet. I could tell he was contemplating his next move. Finally, after about five minutes of silence, he spoke.

"I know I put you through a lot of unnecessary shit. Bottom line, I fucked up in many ways, so I'm going to give you your time. But Yasmin, I expect to see you at home this week. I also expect you to call me every day to let me know you're okay."

This fool has lost his mind, giving me orders like I'm the one that fucked everything up. Okay, I'll let you think you're running things, anything to get you out my face.

His phone rang again and he sent it to voicemail. Not even a minute later, it was ringing again. This time he answered.

I eavesdropped on his conversation. From the sound of things, they needed him back in DC right away. Thank you, God.

"Yasmin, I have to go. My plane leaves in an hour. Promise me you won't break our agreement. When you're done, you'll come home so we can talk."

"Fine." I said, knowing I had no intention of keeping my word.

"Yasmin, come here please. Can I at least get a hug before I go?"

I didn't say anything. I stood there afraid to oblige him. Despite everything I said, I still missed his touch and knew if I let him in, I wouldn't want to let go. But if I said no, he wouldn't catch that plane and he would be in Minnesota until I came back with him.

Braxton cautiously approached me. Once he was only inches away, he pulls me into an embrace. Before I knew it, the tears were falling from my eyes again and my arms wrapped around his waist.

"I'm so sorry, Yasmin. I love you, Beautiful. I never meant to hurt you. I swear to you, I'm committed to you till death. I know it's going to be hard, but we're going to get through this. We're going to be alright. I promise I will make you happy again. You don't need to have any doubts."

Braxton's phone rang again, breaking us from our embrace. While he checked the missed call, I took the opportunity to get myself and hormones together.

"It's my job again, I have to go. I'll see you Friday."

I nod.

Braxton kisses me lightly on my cheek. I allow him to kiss me on the lips. He doesn't try anything else. Just holds me a little while longer. He tells me he loves me before he leaves out the door.

14

Cold, Cold World

I did finish up in Minnesota that week, even called Braxton. However, I checked out of that hotel room into another across town and stayed a couple more weeks. During that time, I did a little shopping for my expanding figure. For the most part, I stayed in my room sulking in misery.

For Thanksgiving, me and the baby had dinner alone. I watched movies to try and avoid thinking of Braxton, but it didn't help. I was lonely as hell, but I survived. It was hard not calling the family. I missed everyone, but calling them would be too much. I can only imagine how insistent they would be for me to come home. I would have stayed away for Christmas, but it was time to confront the present. Besides, my job was done, all of the contracts were in order.

Looking at myself in the mirror, I should have told Braxton when I had the chance. Now I have the dilemma of telling him while exhibiting an undeniably advanced pregnancy. I'm huge. I'm still in shock, seeing how much my body transformed in such a short period of time. Still I procrastinated, even with knowing the longer I waited, the harder it would be. It's more likely Braxton will go postal on my ass. Actually, there was no likely, Braxton's bi-polar ass was going to go ballistic.

Almost twenty-four hours later, I was back in Maryland. When I got to Kevin's he had company, Nicole. I knew Kevin had filled her in. I wasn't too close with her, but hey, that was his girlfriend. Thank God she was leaving. She was giving me that pathetic, sympathy look that made me want to break down. Nicole and I exchanged quick pleasantries before she left, then Kevin wasted no time grilling me.

"So, you're pregnant?"

I remove my coat. "Yes, I am."

"Damn, you huge."

"You know how to make a person feel good. You know you just don't know what to say out your mouth." I said, sarcastically.

"How could Braxton not notice your stomach?"

"I wasn't this big then. I don't know what happened. Okay, I ate everything.

"How are you and baby?"

"So far so good, but I have an appointment Friday. That's why I'm back. I figured now was a good time to confront Braxton. I'll tell Braxton about the baby Thursday."

"You should tell him now."

"Not ready."

"You need to get ready. What you waiting till you're on the way to the hospital? Call him and say, guess what, I'm having your baby?"

"Don't start."

"I'm just saying. This will be interesting."

"I have a lot to deal with. I need to figure out where I'm going to live. My condo is occupied at the moment, I can't kick my tenants out. I'm going to have to find something. Maybe I could convince Braxton to give up the house, but then again I don't want to stay there. There's too many memories."

"Yasmin, you don't need to be by yourself and knowing Braxton, he's not going to go for any of that."

"I'm not the only person to ever end up pregnant and have to make it on her own. I'll survive. As far as Braxton, his opinion doesn't matter."

"Yes, it does, he's the daddy."

"Like I said, his opinion doesn't matter. I don't want to be around him. He's just going to have to deal with the consequences. We'll work out some visitation schedule."

"You think you can handle him by yourself. I don't think so. Do you want me to come?"

"I'll be fine."

"Are you sure?"

"Yes."

"How do you feel?"

"I'm scared. I hate to admit it, but I still love Braxton. I just can't forgive him. I don't know how, but I have to get over him."

"Yasmin, you'll never get over Braxton."

"I know, but I have to keep it moving without him."

"What about Landon?"

"We're done too. I'm more hurt about her because she knew what I went through when I miscarried. She knew how depressed I was about the break-up. As usual, it was all about Landon."

"I've talked to her and she's definitely sorry."

"She should be."

Kevin put his head down like he was at a loss for words.

"You know what I don't want to talk about Braxton or Landon anymore. I have to be positive for my baby. So what's going on with your life?"

"You know me, working hard. It's been crazy in the office. I still can't believe Mr. Taylor is your father. I have a hard time looking at him. It's been uncomfortable because they know I know the truth but I'm managing. I knew I should have left you and Landon alone now I'm caught in the middle of the drama," he joked trying to get me to smile, I did.

"Sorry Kev. I see you and Nicole are on again?"

"Don't joke me about my relationship. We're taking it slow. She's still working in Virginia, but she'll be back in Maryland mid-March."

151

"Are you finally going to marry her?"

"No offense, but I'm not feeling the marriage thing. I handle divorces for a living. I will only consider it if she agrees to sign a prenuptial. Everyone needs one these days for protection."

"Well, I didn't sign one, but I will walk away with everything I came in with. I'm not going to clean Braxton out, but mother will get paid for relocating."

"See money changing my nice innocent Yasmin into a gold digger."

"Kevin, I need to slap you in the mouth for saying that. I swear you're like a Jekyll and Hyde. For the record, I am not a gold digger, but as you can see, I am pregnant. Braxton will support his child. I'm not even going to ask for child support or alimony. I know Braxton will take care of anything the baby needs. I just want my relocating expenses covered. He makes more than three times what I make, he won't miss it. He'll survive. Since, he's getting the house, I need a place for me and my child."

"That's what they all say."

"I figured you wouldn't handle my divorce, that's why I hired a lawyer in Minnesota. The paperwork is being drawn up and he should be served soon." I lied.

"You need to slow your roll. You know damn well Braxton is not signing that shit. It's going to be the war of the Roses type event. It'll take you years to end this marriage. You got a crazy one."

"Braxton is not crazy, just very over protective of me because of my past. And he loves me."

"Listen, you're still taking up for him. You don't need a divorce, you need counseling."

"Shut up, Kevin. You know if you were in this situation, you'd be gone."

He didn't say anything at first. "Yasmin look, I'm sorry about everything that went down with us."

"We're cool."

"No, I need to apologize. I shouldn't have talked to you that way, but I was mad."

"What are you talking about? Why are you bringing this up now?"

"I need to. I want to explain why I flipped on you."

"It's over, done, forget about it."

"No, I want to tell you what happened. Here I was giving you some good love. I was feeling you. I thought the feeling was mutual."

"It was," I interrupted.

"Let me finish. When we were done getting our little groove on, I was going to ask you about us, but you called me Braxton."

"I did not," I said trying to remember back to that day.

"I was there. I know what I heard. It was hard, but I finally admitted to myself you wanted the crazy man. Braxton had your heart and you know he still does. You know I'm right because three weeks later you were back with him. Four months later, you were married."

"I apologize. I didn't mean to. If it makes you feel better, you got skills." I said trying to lighten up the mood.

"I know I do. I had you for a minute. I do miss hanging with you. I just wish it wasn't under these circumstances. So we're cool now?"

"We're cool."

Kevin came over and put me in a headlock. We joked around and stayed up watching Def Comedy Jam. I was glad Kevin was back in my life, I still had one friend.

I stayed up with Kevin for another hour before crashing in his guestroom. I couldn't sleep. I wondered how Braxton was going to react to the news.

15

Battle of the Heart

A few days later, I made my dreaded call.

"Good morning, Mr. Simms office."

I took a deep breath.

"Good morning, Kim. Is Braxton available?"

"Yasmin? Is that you?'

"Yes, how are you, Kim?"

"Fine, but what's going on? Braxton has been … difficult and made it clear if you called to put you through."

I didn't want her in my business. "I had to go away on an important business trip, but I'm back. Is Braxton there?" I say brushing her off.

"He's coming now, I can hear his voice. He's talking to Ms. Stevens."

That bitch always on the prowl. I thought she was married, married my ass. "Tell him he has a very important phone call, please?"

"I know he'll want to take this call."

"Thanks, and don't tell him it's me."

I heard Braxton's voice. "Kim, I've warned you about personal calls."

"Mr. Simms, this call is for you. It's very urgent."

I could hear the annoyance in his voice. "Put them through to my office."

"Yes, sir."

I waited for a minute or two.

"Braxton Simms."

I took a deep breath. "I'm back and I need to talk with you. I'll be at the house."

He breathes sounding relieved. "Yasmin."

"Meet me at the house."

I'm on my way..."

I hung up even though he was saying something else.

I walked around my house looking to see if any changes were made. The place was the same. Nothing looked touched, well, it was messy as hell. Braxton had a few of his clothes thrown on the chair. I picked up a shirt. I could smell him. Damn, what was wrong with me? Why did I still miss him? Instantly, I recalled the feel of Braxton's arms around my body, the lips that kissed me, and the tongue that called me beautiful.

I looked at the time and realized I needed to snap out of this trance and sit somewhere to hide my belly. I didn't want him coming in looking at me crazy. This was going to be hard. I'm not even six months, but could pass for seven. I choose the dining room. Sitting there, praying everything would be okay, I still hadn't figured out how to tell him.

Ten minutes later Braxton was coming through the front door.

"Yasmin?"

"In the dining room."

He came in and stared at me. He looked a mess. Last month, he was rugged, but today he looked off. I mean he still had sex appeal, but now he possessed a worn look, bloodshot eyes, fatigue, he'd lost some weight. Part of me thought well, good, he deserves to be stressed. Looking at him pissed me off. I wanted to kill him.

"You're ready to talk?"

"Yes. I still want a divorce." I blurted out.

"I already told you, that's not going to happen." He walked closer to me.

"That's close enough. Have a seat over there." I pointed to the opposite end.

"I just want to at least sit close to you."

"Look, I can leave. Sit over there."

"Fine, the divorce isn't going to happen though. I already told you that, nothing has changed. You said through the good times and bad. We will get pass this."

"I can't trust you."

"Yes you can, they're no more secrets."

"I don't know why but I'm having a hard time believing you." Not even five minutes in the same room and he was pissing me off. Elevating my blood pressure to places it didn't need to go.

"Yasmin, I'm sorry. What do you want me to do? I miss you and I want my wife back."

"I thought about it and the time apart still has me at the same conclusion. We are over. I'm not going to go tit-for-tat with you."

Yasmin…"

"Listen, I need to talk to you about something else. That's why I called you."

"I'm sorry, really. I know I fucked you up mentally, but Yasmin, it doesn't mean I don't love you."

"You're right. Mentally I am all screwed up. You're yet another person that hurt me. You know what I went through. I told you the issues I had growing up. How I hated myself, my eyes. You were there when my mother disowned me. I went through all of that. And although it was hard, I trusted you and loved you. And this is what I got."

"Yasmin, that's why I couldn't tell you, I didn't want to see you hurt like that again and I told you I didn't know Eric was mine."

"Braxton, you lied. You had no problem looking me in my eyes telling me you never cheated. All this stuff you're saying I heard it all before and I'm tired of hearing it."

"So what are you going to do, run away again?" He asked frustrated.

"I need to."

Stop running from me, because I will find you."

"Ooh, you're trying to threaten me? Try, I will disappear without a trace."

"Yasmin, I'm not playing with you. When I left Minnesota, the agreement was for you to come back here at the end of the week so we could talk. That was three weeks ago." He barked.

"Braxton stop talking to me like I'm a child. I know what I said, but I wasn't ready."

He softened his tone. "You should have called me to tell me something. I know you're mad at me, but seriously Yasmin, you should at least have called my mother or someone to let them know you were okay. My mother is going crazy worrying about you."

I took a deep breath. "I wanted to. I tried, but I couldn't. Yeah she fusses at you all the time, but you are her baby. I didn't feel like hearing the "work-it-out" speech."

He put his head down. "Yasmin, my mother still isn't dealing with me right now. I feel bad for disappointing and hurting both of you. Now she's convinced something else is going on with you. She told me to stay away from you. She thinks me being around you will have you in the hospital."

I didn't say anything. I knew it was my opportunity to tell him I was pregnant, but I couldn't.

"Since I've been such a disappointment I kept my word and I stayed away. You know how hard that was, especially since I've known you've been back for a couple of days."

"Are you stalking me now?" I asked, feeling my pressure rise again.

"You can say that. Yes, I've hired someone to track you. So tell me, why are you staying with Kevin? Is this your way of getting back at me?"

"Are you fucking crazy? No, don't answer that, I already know the answer. Ahh…. I can't deal with this right now."

"Then answer my questions."

"Fuck you, Braxton. I'm staying there because that's where I want to be."

"I better be the only one you're fucking."

He was pissed as hell and I instigated "You lost that privilege. Who I fuck is none of your damn business."

Braxton whole demeanor changed and he looks like he's about to kirk out. He's standing, staring at me intensely not taking a blink. I took it too far and it's time for me to go. While I was sitting, I slowly zipped up my oversized coat, then I grabbed my oversized bag and placed it in front of my belly. Cautiously, I stood up being careful not to let him get a glimpse of my stomach.

"Braxton, we're both upset. I don't feel good, so I'm going to go. Call me later, we can try this again."

I turned around to leave when Braxton called out my name.

"Yasmin, come here."

I was too scared to look at him. His tone sent chills through my body, so I kept my back turned. "No Braxton, we both need to calm down."

I could feel Braxton breathing on the back of my neck and the heat exuding from his body.

"Yasmin."

I closed my eyes and slowly turned to face him, "Yeah."

He took a deep breath "You're not going anywhere. Your smartass is staying here. You had three weeks. No, you had two months of running away. It's time for you to come home."

"No, it's time for me to go. Goodbye." I turned around to leave, but he grabbed my wrist.

"I told you you're not going anywhere."

"Braxton, let me go." I said, calmly.

"No, you need to call Kevin and let him know you're staying home with your husband," he countered.

"I'm not doing shit. I'm staying with Kevin. Now let me go."

He let go of my wrist, "Yasmin, listen…"

Like a fool, I attempted to hit him with my purse, just for principle. He grabbed my wrist, and in the process I dropped my purse. With my free hand, I swung on him. As usual, he was quick and caught my other wrist.

"So you're fucking Kevin now?" I felt his grip around my wrists tighten.

"Braxton, stop, you're hurting me!" I yelled.

"Answer the question," He added more pressure to my wrist.

"Let go, you're hurting me," I said crying.

"Answer me."

"No, I'm not fucking Kevin, now let go."

He still had my wrist restrained and wasn't releasing them fast enough, so I knee him in the groin. He wasn't fast enough that time. By default, I was let go. I was halfway to the door when I realized my keys were in my purse which was now on the floor next to Braxton. Braxton was bent over on the floor trying to regain his composure. I quickly went back over to get my purse. I reached down and on my way up, Braxton grabbed my coat.

"Braxton, please, let me go." I tried to walk away and in the process my zipper broke. Quickly, I took the purse and used it as cover.

With his free hand he stood up, came behind me and pulled me close. His arms were wrapped around my shoulders. "Stay with me, I'm not going to hurt you."

"You already did, now let me go."

"I'm sorry, Yasmin, don't leave me."

I tried to grab his arms, but he wouldn't let go. "Braxton let me go. I have to go.

He held me tighter. My chest felt like it was tightening and I started having hot flashes.

"Yasmin, I'm sorry, I'm sorry. Calm down."

I was getting hotter and I could feel the sweat forming on my forehead. "Braxton let me go, I need some air."

"Yasmin, I need you, I need you, I need you. I love you and I can't lose you again."

I started to feel nauseous and my throat getting dry. "Braxton, you have to let me go, I don't feel good. Braxton let me go, let me sit down," I said as I felt my knees buckle.

He held me to prevent me from falling. "I'm sorry, are you okay?"

I shook my head, no.

 He attempts to pick me up, but I stop him. "Come, lay down on the couch." Braxton guides me into the family room. I was still hot. I dropped my purse. "Yasmin, please, relax. I'm going to take your coat off."

"No, just get me some water. I'm going to lie down."

"You're sweating, take off the coat and lay down.'

"Ok, just get me some water." I said frustrated.

While he was in the kitchen I took off my coat, and then decided to lie down on the couch. I took the coat and pillow and placed it over my belly. I closed my eyes, taking deep breaths in order to calm my nerves.

Braxton returned with my water. "Yasmin, I apologize for getting you upset..."

I stop him. "Alright, I'm tired of arguing." I close my eyes again, laying my head back.

"Why do you still have…" He pulls off my coat, which causes my pillow to fall to the floor and pauses.

I opened my eyes and saw Braxton staring at my belly. I couldn't read his emotion, so I remained quiet and let him take it in.

"Here's your water." He handed it to me and took a seat opposite of me.

He sat there alternating from shaking his head and looking at me. It looked like he went from shock to disbelief to hurt to anger. I sat up, sipped on my water and waited.

I know he had to have sat there for twenty minutes just taking deep breaths.

"How far along are you?" he finally asks.

"About five months. I have an ultrasound scheduled for tomorrow. That's what I came to talk to you about," I spoke quickly.

"Talk to me about? You didn't…" He stood up, got a drink from the bar, and came back. Taking the same seat, he picked up where he left off.

"You didn't talk to me. You were on your way out the door. You weren't going to tell me."

"I was going to tell you. I wanted to tell you today, but we started arguing."

"I saw you a month ago, you were pregnant then? Why didn't you say anything?" He chuckled. You hid the baby real well. Oversized clothes, kept your back turned avoiding me. Tonight you were going to do the same thing. I kept wondering why you had that hot ass coat on with that big ass bag."

"I wanted to tell you when you came to Minnesota, but you caught me off guard. There were a lot of emotions. I was angry, hurt, confused, and I couldn't deal. The doctor told me my pressure was high and I needed to avoid stress."

"So you decided I shouldn't know? You didn't think that if I knew that would calm me? You really think I want to hurt you or stress you out?"

"I thought my pregnancy would have calmed you down, but I knew you wouldn't get out of my face. You would have relocated to Minnesota had me under surveillance and watched my every move. Jokes on me though because you did it anyway." Braxton takes another sip from his glass.

"So you weren't going to tell me."

"I was, but being around you upsets me too much."

162

"Basically, you changed your mind and decided that I had no right to know. You were just going to walk out the door and say nothing."

I turned away and closed my eyes. I couldn't look at him. "The doctor told me to avoid stress. I couldn't risk having another miscarriage."

"You really think I purposely hurt you or would hurt…my baby?"

I turned to face him. When I opened my eyes, I saw his had tears.

"You're acting like Landon now?"

"What?"

"You're doing the same shit she did. You decided because you didn't want to deal with me, I shouldn't know. What, were you going to wait until the baby was 2, 3, 4, or never tell me? Apparently, you forgot I help get you pregnant. Meaning anything concerning my child I'm included in. Are we clear?"

"No, we're not, don't compare me to Landon. You take her reasons up with her. As for me, Yasmin, again, the doctor told me to avoid stress. Thanks to you and Landon it's inevitable. My concern is my baby and you are stressing me out. Matter of fact, it's time for me to go." I attempt to get up.

Braxton comes to sit next to me and grabbed my hand.

"Yasmin, I know I can be a little crazy and difficult. I don't want to hurt you. I did a lot of stupid stuff and I'm still doing it. Yasmin, I just love you so much and when I think about you leaving me I lose it. The last two months being without you was hell."

"Braxton, I can't pretend like you don't have a kid. I love Eric, but I'm scared to see him. I can't even look at his picture because I cry. I think about how it's not fair that I had to lose my son. How my son is gone, how my son died and is the reason he is here."

He couldn't respond to that.

I took a deep breath. "Braxton, it's late, I'm tired I'm going to go. I have a doctor's appointment tomorrow at one. You can meet me there."

Before I stood up, he stops me. "Please don't go. Sleep in our room and I'll sleep in the guestroom. I'll give you space, I need you here."

"No."

He gets down on his knees, grabbing me around the waist. He lifts up my shirt, cradles my stomach and begins kissing it. "You're having my baby. This is our baby. Me and you made this baby."

"I love you," he says.

I'm not sure if he's talking to me or our baby. His hands are still around my waist. His lips are still kissing my belly.

"Braxton, no," I remove his face from my belly. I stand up. I reach into my purse and give him my ob/gyn's card. "Meet me there at 12:30."

"Yasmin, stay."

"No." I say, firmly.

"Alright, can we drive together? We need to talk. The baby will be here in four months and we have to get everything in order."

I didn't have the strength to argue with him and I was ready to go. "Fine, I'll be here at twelve."

On my way out the door Braxton stopped me. "Yasmin, I know you think me and you are over, but we're not. Our baby was made out of love. All that time, we were trying to have a baby and nothing happened. It's not a coincidence. This baby confirms you and me, this is it. I fucked up in the worst possible way, but don't doubt my love."

"Braxton, that's bullshit. Just because I'm pregnant now doesn't mean we should be together. Was your son with Landon love too?

"You know it wasn't." He leaned down and kissed me. For a second it felt right and I wanted to stay, but reality was a mother. It was time for this to end. I pushed him away and walked out the door.

"I love you too, Beautiful."

16

Heaven Sent

The next day, I met Braxton at the house so we could drive to the doctor. During the ride we were silent. At the doctor's office it was the same thing, a lot of tension no conversation. We alternate between looking at the many pregnancy magazines to looking at the posters on the wall. Dr. Dey finally came in twenty minutes later too chipper. "Good morning, Ms. Sinclair." Braxton interrupted, "Mrs. Simms." The doctor chuckled.

"I'm sorry, Mr. Simms. Mrs. Simms how are we feeling today?"

"I'm feeling okay, but I'm just always tired. This baby is sitting right on my bladder. I feel a lot of pressure and back pain, feels like the baby is about to drop out."

The doctor looked concerned, which put me on alert. He took my pressure.

"Well your pressure is a little elevated, but not high enough to concern me."

Braxton grabbed my hand.

"Let's take a look at the baby, see how he or she is doing. Would you like to find out the sex?"

I look at Braxton, "Yes."

"Okay, let's take a look at your belly." Dr. Dey pulls up my shirt exposing my huge stomach.

"Whoa," Braxton said

I gave him a look.

"Sorry."

The doctor laughed.

"Women are sensitive about their weight when pregnant. I do have to say you are rather large to only be five months."

First, he listened to the baby's heartbeat. Listening was surreal, the beats, the sequence. The longer I listened, the more alarmed I became. It sounded a little irregular. My first instinct was to panic. Braxton saw my uneasiness, so he began to rub my shoulders. Looking at the doctor didn't help, he looked concerned as well. Next, he placed the ultrasound wand on my belly.

I saw my baby. I looked at Braxton and saw he was amazed. The screen showed our little baby. I saw what I think was an arm or leg, then a heartbeat. The doctor began moving around my belly.

"Oh my, what do we have here? Oh. I see why you have a lot of pressure. I see what the problem is?"

I automatically assume the worst and start crying.

Braxton puts his arm around me trying to console me. "What's the problem doctor?" He asks, concerned.

"No, I apologize, there's not a bad problem. You see this?" He had a picture of the baby's head on the screen.

"Yes," we both say looking at each other.

He moved the wand around my belly again. "You see this?"

"Yes, it's the baby's head." I spoke up, very irritated.

"Congratulations, it looks like you're going to have a handful. There's two heads. You're having twins."

"I'm having what?" I said as though I had been startled out of a deep sleep.

"Twins," I hear Braxton say. I look over at Braxton who is smiling ear to ear.

The doctor shows us their hearts beating.

"It looks like you're having two little girls."

Braxton leans over to kiss me.

I am unresponsive. I am still in shock. *Twins?*

"Well, everything looks good. However, I want you to take it easy. No heavy lifting. Stay off your feet when possible. I don't want your pressure to escalate. I know it can be annoying, but we want two healthy babies. I'm sure Mr. Simms will take care of you. I want to see you every two weeks."

The doctor hands Braxton pictures of the babies and left.

"Twins, I need to go lay down. Woo, I can't believe this. Just drop me off at Kevin's. I'll get my truck later."

Braxton gave me a "yeah right" look.

"I'm not taking you to Kevin's. I'm taking you and my twins' home."

"No, you're not."

"Yasmin, what's going on with us can wait. I don't want to argue with you, so just listen. My responsibility is to you and our babies. You're not going anywhere. You need to lie down and take care of my babies."

"Please don't start. I don't feel like arguing with you today."

"Yasmin, you don't need to be alone. You almost passed out yesterday.

"No. Do you realize you are the problem? The farther apart we are, the better. For now, you just meet me at my doctor's appointments."

He places his hands on my stomach, bends down kissing it before speaking, "Yasmin, I know this, but I need you to be near me."

"Braxton…"

"Yasmin, you heard the doctor. I'm sorry for the past, but unfortunately I can't change it. Right now, I'm concerned about you. I'm going to take care of you and my daughters. I can't sit around and hope that you're taking care of yourself. Let me take care of you. I owe you and my daughters that much. Yasmin, please allow me to be involved with this pregnancy."

He was right, but I didn't want to be around him.

"Yasmin, it's about our daughters. We want them to be healthy right. I promise I will give you your space."

My babies came first. "Okay," I said, defeated.

"I know the timing is bad with everything going on, but I'm glad you're pregnant. You know I didn't want any kids until you. When you were pregnant with Bryan, I started getting use to the idea of having kids. I couldn't wait until he was here." He took a deep breath. "Yasmin, when we lost Bryan, it affected me too. We were both suffering, I didn't know what to do, how to comfort you. My mind was gone. Yes, I fucked up in the worst way, then I pushed you away. Even though we weren't together, I never stopped loving you. I would get mad at myself thinking about how I lost the best thing that happened to me. We weren't supposed to be over. That day I saw you at the mall, I knew I had to get you back. That's when I confronted Landon again about Eric. She swore to me there was no possibility I was his father. I was relieved because I wanted you to be my wife and the mother of my kids. So, I made it my goal to make it a reality. Everything was going like I hoped except for you getting pregnant. Every month, you would get upset when you weren't."

"How did you know I was upset?"

"Because you are my life, Yasmin. I know you. I saw it in your face. That's why I held you tighter. I didn't say anything because I knew it would happen. I can't explain it, but I just had that feeling that we would have other kids. Of course, when all this mess with Landon came out I didn't think it was possible. Yasmin, thank you, I know you can't stand me, but I love you and my babies. Now, we have another chance and I'm happy." He smiles. "We're not having one baby, we're having twins, my daughters. I'm going to have two little girls." He pauses. "I know, Yasmin, I was wrong, there's no excuse, but you were and are the only woman I love. Please can't we be a family?"

Luckily, for me we were interrupted by the nurse. I didn't answer Braxton's question. Mentally, I was drained so much going on I couldn't think. I was still getting over the shock of twins.

Instead of going home, Braxton wanted to go shopping for the babies. We ended up at Babies R Us. He was like a big kid, telling any and every one we were having twins. I had gotten over the shock, grabbing things, enjoying the moment. It felt normal.

Braxton's cell rang. He looked at it, but didn't answer. I caught an instant attitude.

"That was my mother. A lot has happened in the last twenty-four hours. I haven't talked to her. I want to tell her the good news."

"Of course."

"I have an idea, let's surprise her."

By the time we got to his mother's, my anxiety level had increased. I wasn't sure what to say or expect. She's been leaving me messages begging me to call, but I couldn't. I was hesitant of going in at first, but knew eventually I would have to face her. Braxton and I went in through the kitchen. It was a full house, Braxton parents and two of his brothers, Vincent and Horace.

"Hey," I said feeling awkward.

Braxton's mother rushes over and grabs me. She doesn't notice my stomach because of my heavy coat and purse. "Thank you, God. I'm so happy to see you. Please don't ever run off like that again. You had us all scared, worried. I wished you would have called. I left you so many messages." She backs away then looks at me like what was that.

"Before you ask, yes I am."

The rest of the family of the family was looking like what's going on.

She starts crying, pulling my coat back to see my belly. "How far along are you?"

"Five months."

"Congratulations," they all said. Braxton's dad and brothers got up and hugged me.

"Five months? You're carrying big. This is going to be a big baby. Do you know what you're having yet?" she quizzes.

Braxton smiles and hands his mother a gift box.

"What's this?"

"You wanted to know what we're having."

She takes the box, opens it, pulling out two pink sleepers. "Yes, yes, thank you, God! I finally get a girl!" She was jumping up and down. We all laughed at her. After she finishes her dance she has more questions.

"Why did you put two sleepers in here?"

"It's more," Braxton said.

She looked in the box and pulled out two sonogram pictures along with two bibs that said, "*I love Granny.*" She looks at us confused. "I saw it was a girl. Look at my baby. Look at that face. I'm going to start a baby album. Look at her face. Isn't she precious and look at this one. Aww, they gave you two pictures of her face."

"They're not the same." Braxton informs her.

"Yes they are. There just at a different angle. This new technology is something, especially these 4-D ones. It shows so much detail. You can see everything."

"It's not at a different angle," Braxton laughed.

"Look, I know what I see. I've seen a sonogram before. This is her face and this is another picture of her face. They're at different angles," she holds up the picture.

Braxton laughed. "They are different. There are two faces for two babies. That's baby A and that's baby B. We're having twin girls."

"Oh, oh, oh, my God! Twins?! I get two girls!" she started crying.

"Congratulations," Braxton father and brothers say as they come back to give me another hug.

Regaining her composure she spoke. "Come have a sit. Have you eaten? Let me see your belly. I can't believe this. What a blessing. Twins, girls, yes. I can't believe it."

"Neither can I," I admitted

"Finally, I have girls."

I just smiled and took a seat. Braxton came over and sat next to me. I could tell he wanted to touch my belly. "It's okay" I took his hand, placing it on my swollen belly. He started rubbing my belly and talking to the babies. The baby or should I say babies kicked. I guess they knew their daddy.

He smiled. "They're kicking."

I admit I was lost in the moment, the serenity. I didn't notice or care if the family was attaching us. I forgot for a moment the hurt I felt for the last few months.

Ma made some lunch. She was so excited. I was relieved she didn't ask any questions about me and Braxton. We talked about ideas for the babies, her baby girls.

The doorbell rang and Mr. Jeff went to open it. It felt good to be back until I heard Eric.

He came running to me with the speed of lightning.

"Mimi!"

That's when it came crashing down on me like a ton of bricks. I hadn't seen him in over three months. This was my first time seeing him, as not only my nephew, but now as my husband's son. Eric reached his arms up for me to pick him up. I couldn't deny him love. So, even though it was hard as hell, I picked him up. A tear rolled down my face. I was so tired of crying. Even though he was conceived during my heartache, I still loved this little boy. He was the innocent one. I can't be mad at him because of his parent's selfish asses. I still loved him like my own. "Hey, big boy."

He grabbed me tightly and gave me a kiss. He then nestled his head on my shoulder.

Landon approached with tears in her eyes. "Yas, I'm so glad to see you, I've missed you." She looks at my stomach and smiles.

I was feeling overwhelmed and ready to just run again, but I knew I couldn't. I put Eric down, but he wasn't going anywhere. He was staring right at me like *I know you did not put me down.*

"Big boy, I'll be right back." I gave him to Braxton not sure how to address him. "Landon, we need to talk." I managed to get up and led her to the dining room for privacy.

"Yasmin, I am so sorry. I miss you, girl."

I held my hand up stopping her. "I'm still dealing with this. I would have stayed away, but my condition wouldn't allow it."

"I see. When is the baby due? Congratulations."

"It's twins, go figure, but I wanted to talk because I need you to give me space. You were a selfish conniving bitch. Truthfully, I can't stand you or Braxton right now. I love Eric to death, but now that I see him it's a reminder of this big mess. Listen, I can't risk getting stressed and endangering the health of my babies. I know you and Braxton have some type of arrangement and I respect that. I actually encourage you to allow him to bond with his son, but I told him and I will reiterate, allow me my space. Don't push. I'm tolerating you, but I don't have to."

"Okay Yasmin, I will respect that. I just want us to at least try and talk."

"Landon please, I'm not promising you anything. You know we all could have avoided a lot of this, but you chose to lie so you have to deal with it." I walked out the door leaving her with a stupid look on her face.

When I come back everyone in the kitchen is looking at me. I definitely didn't like that. I grab my coat and keys.

"Where are you going?" Braxton asked.

"For a ride."

I gave him a look that said, *if you know what's best for you, shut up and leave me alone.*

"Yasmin, I don't think that's a good idea," he responded.

"Guess what, I don't care. I'm not your child, he is, so you can keep your thoughts to yourself."

I could see him getting frustrated, but I was frustrated too.

He takes a deep breath, puts Eric down, and walks over to me. Staring me in the eyes he says, "You're right, you're not my child, but you are carrying my daughters. I can see you're upset,but I'm not letting you run off again. You don't need to be riding around like this."

Landon appears in the door. I throw my keys at him.

"Fine, I won't drive. Am I allowed to take a walk?" I ask being sarcastic.

"Actually no, it's too cold outside. You really need to calm down. Go in one of the bedrooms."

I opened my mouth to cuss him out, but I remembered his parents are there. I roll my eyes and walk out the door.

"YASMIN!" I hear him call out, but I hear his brother tell him to "let her get some air" as I continue to stroll down the driveway.

I was ten minutes into my walk when I hear my cell phone ring, it was Kevin.

"Hey Mrs. Yes. What did you do, reunite and forget about me?" he teases.

I broke down.

"Kevin, I don't think I can do it. It's too much. Braxton is already smothering me watching my every move like I'm going to run away."

"In his defense, Yasmin, you did for over two months."

"Kevin, I need a friend not a lawyer. I didn't talk to you last night. You were right, Braxton is crazy. The fool hired a PI, he knew I was staying with you. He said he stayed away because his mother made him promise."

Kevin bursts out laughing. "I told you Braxton wasn't playing with you. You're stuck with him for life."

"Kevin it's not funny, I told you I need a friend."

"You're right, I'm sorry."

"I was dealing with everything, but then Landon came with Eric and I lost it. Landon started the apologies about how she misses me and wanted to try and rebuild our friendship."

"Yas, I know it's hard. They both were dead wrong, but right now you can't let that stress you out. You have a baby that's depending on you."

"Oh, with all the commotion I forgot to tell you."

"Is everything alright?"

"Yes, the doctor said I'm having twins, two girls."

"What?"

"I know, I'm still shocked."

"Where are you?"

"I needed some air, so I'm taking a walk."

"Are you sure you want to do that in your condition."

"I'm not an imbecile."

"I know you're not, I just want you to be careful, babies first. Do you need me to come get you?"

"Thanks, but I'm okay. I'm on my way back to the house."

"Are you coming here?"

"The doctor said I need to be very careful. He doesn't want me stressed, but how can I not be? Anyway, he wants me to take it easy. Braxton wants me stay at our house. He says he will sleep in the other room, but I don't know if I can be around him that long."

"Yas, I know you don't want to hear this, but I agree. I work long hours and you need support. Go home with Braxton. You can call me at any time."

"What, are we on team Braxton now?"

"No, I'm on team, what's best for Yasmin and her two babies," he says, seriously.

"Alright Kevin, I will try. Kevin, thanks for your support."

"You know you're my girl, Mrs. Yes."

After I hung up, I walk around for about another ten minutes. I felt better after my conversation with Kevin, so I decided to go back. I look around to see I was lost. Just when I was about to call Braxton's mother, I see Braxton sitting in my truck watching me.

I just walked over, got in hoping he would just be quiet. No such luck.

"I figured you got lost. Yasmin, I'm sorry for earlier."

I stop him. "I'm so tired of you and Landon apologizing. Just give me space. I told her and I'm telling you again, leave me alone. I'm trying my best not to go off on you. Fact is, I can't stand you right now. Please take me home, so I can lay down."

He looked at me like he wanted to say something, but he didn't. Good move, I thought. We were halfway home when I asked. "Where's Eric?"

"He's staying at my parents this weekend. We need to talk and get organized. Yasmin…"

I gave him a look that said, *no more conversation.* He got the hint.

When we got home, I went straight to our room and slammed the door. Once inside, I bathed in my Carol's Daughter Coconut scrub, allowing the aroma to relax me. Since I couldn't fit anything, I grabbed one of Braxton's T- shirts. Afterwards, I got in my bed and melted. Oh how I missed my king size bed with 1000 count Egyptian threads. Soon after, I drifted off to sleep.

18

It Ain't Over Till It's Over

When I woke up the next morning, I see Braxton staring at me. He looks like he'd been watching me the whole night.

"What you do stay up all night watching me?"

"No, I've been up for a while, but I wanted to. Last time I went to sleep on you, when I woke up you were gone."

"I needed space, still do. I'm not running off. As you can see, I'm very limited."

"I just love you so much, I don't want you to leave me again. We need to work through this. We have two daughters on the way, they need us."

"Hello, I'm just getting up. You're starting already, Braxton space!" I said shooing him away.

"And many divorced parents manage to raise their kids separately."

"Yasmin, I don't want that for us." He took a deep breath. "I don't want to raise our daughters from a distance. I don't want joint custody taking turns every other weekend. I want it every weekend, every day."

"I can understand that, but you can't smother me. You made choices you have to deal with. Right now, honestly, nothing's changed."

"Yasmin you know you still love me. When we kissed the other day, you felt it. We belong together."

"I never said I didn't love you. I always will. However, I can't say I will be able to move pass this. How can I explain to my kids that your cousin is also your brother? It sounds like we belong on Jerry Springer or Maury Povich."

He didn't respond at first. "I know it's not going to be easy, but we love each other two much not to at least try. I'm not letting you go that easily. I want my wife."

"Braxton just drop it."

"Alright Yasmin, we'll discuss this later. Let's go shopping to get some things for the babies and you."

"Me?"

"Yeah, I see you have on my t-shirt not that I mind. You know I don't. I figured you needed some clothes. I want my girls to have everything they need."

I laughed. "That would be correct. You must really be excited. You want to go shopping with me."

"Yes, I am. They'll be here in a four months. We don't have much time to get their room together."

"Well if you get out, I'll get ready. I need some privacy."

"Get out, I've already seen everything. I won't get in your way."

"I don't need you staring at me while I get dressed."

"I won't."

"Yeah, right."

Braxton gave up, grabbed some clothes, and left.

I took a shower and put on a pair of black stretch pants and red baby doll top.

On the way to the mall, Braxton and I didn't say much. The radio served as conversation. At the mall, everyone was out doing there last bit of Christmas shopping, therefore it was packed. This time I didn't feel like shopping. The crowds and long lines were too much. Braxton hadn't done any shopping, so I had to help him pick out gifts for the family. I was tired of standing so I told Braxton I would be waiting on a bench outside the store. I sat there admiring the families when I hear Kevin call my name.

"Hey, Mrs. Y.E.S."

I stood up to give him a hug. "Hey Kev, I see you finishing up that last bit of shopping."

"Yup and what are you doing here by yourself?"

"I'm not, Braxton is in line. I got tired of standing." I grabbed his Victoria's Secret bag to take a peek. Inside was a pair of plain beige cotton panties and a bra. "I hope this isn't for Nicole. Kevin this is plain and ugly."

"What's wrong with it?"

"Look at this. You don't think it's plain? There's nothing sexy about this. Do you want Ms. Yasmin to pick out something for you?"

"Is it that bad?"

"Does this turn you on? Let's go."

When we walk into Victoria's Secret it's a mad house too. Even though Nicole seemed to be a little conservative, I decided she needs to spice it up. I pick out a pink lace bra set. I also handed him some Pretty in Pink body splash spray, shower gel and lotion. I also saw some things for me. Despite the fact I couldn't fit most, I couldn't resist. Chauncey gave me this fetish. New lingerie from him every week was definitely missed. I ended up with lingerie, pajamas, and ten bra and underwear sets. I forgot about poor Kevin.

"Am I boring you, Kevin? You can go to the register."

"No, how can I be bored looking at women's underwear. I'm picking up some tips. Matter of fact, you should try this blue one. "

I grabbed the gown and walked over to the mirror to compare it with my complexion. "Aww shucks, you're finally getting it. I taught you well," I say laughing

"I told you," he says, confidently.

A salesperson walks over, "Do you need any help? By the way, that's a very nice choice you have. You're lucky. I see your husband has excellent taste in lingerie as well as jewelry. Your ring is gorgeous. That's definitely a lot of love."

"Thank you very much, but he's not my husband," I laugh.

"I am," Braxton says with much attitude. He walks over to me, and puts his arm around my shoulder to claim me.

"I'm sorry," the salesperson apologizes.

"That's alright," I reply still feeling the tension.

"Hey Braxton, congratulations, I heard you're having twins, wow." Kevin says trying to alleviate some of the tension.

I could tell the salesperson felt awkward, so I let her off the hook saying, "Thank you, but I'm okay for now. I'll find you if I need help, thanks again."

The salesperson made a quick getaway. "I'm sorry again. Just let me know if you need me and congrats on the twins."

I look over to see that Braxton is completely pissed, but I don't give a damn. Now I am pissed because he didn't acknowledge Kevin.

"Yasmin, I've been out long enough. Thanks for helping me out. I'm going to let you two finish shopping," Kevin said, as he exited.

I started to hug Kevin again just to irritate the hell out of Braxton, but didn't want to make Kevin feel any more uncomfortable. He knew Landon had told him about our little fling so he expected Braxton attitude. "Alright Kev, I'll talk to you later."

Kevin walked away leaving me with Braxton.

"I thought you said you were going to be sitting on the bench?" Braxton says, getting straight to the point.

"I was, but I saw Kevin. I helped him pick out a gift for Nicole."

"So, you're a fashion consultant now?"

He's lucky we're in a store. He knows I don't do public scenes yet he still insists on aggravating me. If I didn't need any bras, I would have left. Ignoring Braxton, I gather my stuff, including the blue gown Kevin picked out and go to the register.

"Are you done shopping?" I ask once we were out of the store.

"No, but I'm ready to go."

"So am I."

*

We left and we were halfway home when I remember I needed to pick up my prenatal vitamins from the pharmacist.

"Braxton, I need to stop at market. I don't have any more prenatal vitamins."

His mood lightens up once I mention the babies. "Do you need anything else? Are you hungry?" He reaches over to rub my belly.

"I am a little hungry, but I don't want to go out. I want to go home."

"We don't have to, I'll make you something."

"Braxton, I'm not trying to end up in somebody's emergency room. You can't cook." "Yasmin, I can cook, but for your smartass, I'll buy something. Where do you want

something from?"

"It doesn't matter. While you place the order I'll do a little grocery shopping. You don't have anything in there."

"That's because my wife was gone. I had no reason to have anything. The only thing I wanted was you, Beautiful."

I ignore his comment, letting out a sigh, "Yeah, just drop me off up front and pick me up in twenty minutes."

I went in only to get a few things. But my pregnancy cravings caused me to pick up over a $100 dollars' worth of items. While I was waiting in line I saw a magazine with Chauncey on the cover. Chauncey was talking about his career and future plans. I was curious, so I purchased it. When I came out, Braxton was pulling up. Good timing.

"You were hungry," he said, startled by the amount of food I bought.

"I know. One twin wanted ice cream, the other wanted a cold cut, and I had a taste for chicken."

"My girls can have whatever they want."

"Oh no, I'm not having two spoiled little girls. I can see it now. They'll be like those girls on My Super Sweet 16."

"No, they won't. "

"Yeah, we'll see."

When we got home we ate and watched a movie. I let him pick the movie. He put in "Enemy of the State", with Will Smith and Regina King. I didn't feel like watching it, so I got my magazine with Chauncey on the cover.

Chauncey looked real good. He was doing well. He was engaged to his high school sweetheart, Toya. He had new endorsements and was on top of his game. I was proud of him. Despite his womanizing ways, he was overall a good guy. I reminisced a little about our relationship and had a few laughs to myself. I had to smile. I didn't realize Braxton was staring.

"Why do you have that shit in my house?" he barked.

"Who do you think you're talking to?"

"Don't be smart. You need to throw that shit away."

"I'm not throwing jack away."

"Either you do it or I will. First you parade Kevin in my face, now him. Hell no, the magazine is going in the trash."

"First of all, I did not parade Kevin in your face. I know your mother taught you some manners. You need to stop being rude. Kevin did nothing to you. You should have spoken. I spoke to your baby mama. That's one of your problems now, you always taking your frustration out on other people."

"You need to go somewhere with your damn orders. Why the hell is he always in your face? Picking out underwear? How the fuck that look?"

"Here we go again, I saw Kevin in the mall. I helped him pick out a gift."

"While we're on the subject, how many times?"

"How many times what?" I knew what he meant but I wanted him to say it.

"You know what I mean."

"I talk to Kevin often."

"Alright smart ass, how many times did you fuck him?"

"I don't fuck."

He got up and began pacing. "So, what are you saying, Yasmin?"

"Exactly what I said."

"How was it Yasmin? Was his dick bigger than mine? Was he better than me? How many times did you fuck him? When?"

I lay back on the couch and yawned.

"Answer me. It better be the truth. No more of your ring around the rosy games."

"The truth? Can you handle the truth? Are you sure you want to go there? Haven't you heard, don't ask questions you don't want the answer to?"

"Just answer the got damn question! I asked didn't I?"

I sat up. "Fine, unlike you I have no reason to lie. We were together right before you and I got back together. It was that one time only. It was what I needed at the time. It was special." I exaggerated.

"Alright, that's enough."

"I knew you couldn't handle the truth."

"If it was so special, then why aren't you with him?" His voice wavers

I could see the hurt on his face.

I don't say anything I just look at him. Why did I do that? His crazy ass got right in my face. Oh Shit, he's about to snap.

"Where's that smart mouth now? Answer the got damn question."

"Because of you. Kevin realized I still loved you, that you were the only one I wanted. And he was in love with Nicole."

He took a seat next to me, taking a few minutes before he spoke. "Landon was a bad mistake. I don't know why it happened."

It was my turn to be upset. "It happened because you wanted it to happen. If you didn't you would have stopped it."

"It wasn't like that.

"So what was it like then?"

183

"I felt lonely, had a drink, and basically needed a release. I wasn't thinking."

"So you pushed me away leaving me to think it was my fault?"

"I never wanted you to feel that way. It seemed like the best thing to do at the time. I was mad at myself for having sex with Landon and I realized I was hurting you. It seemed easier for you to hate me than for you to find out the truth."

"Out of all the people you could have cheated on me with, Landon? I would have been hurt yes, but Landon? It makes me wonder if you always wanted to be with Landon. So tell me, did you pick the wrong sister?"

"Yasmin, listen you're who I always wanted. I only pushed you away because I didn't want to hurt you like you are now. I hate that I hurt you like this. I tried to stay away, but I couldn't. . I couldn't tell you what happened because you were still getting over the miscarriage."

"Why didn't you use protection?"

"I got caught up in the moment. I wasn't using any with you so I didn't have a supply. We weren't using any so I had no need to buy any. It wasn't like it was planned.

"How did it happen?"

He took a moment to speak. "I went to Pearl one night for a drink. Landon was out with some guy and they had an argument. She was stranded and needed a ride home."

"How many times? Was the sex good? Never mind, obviously it was, you have Eric."

"Yasmin it was just once. It wasn't like that."

"Like I said, if it wasn't good Eric would not be your son. If I didn't have the miscarriage, I wonder how things would have turned out."

"I wondered the same thing. I hated thinking about you with someone else. I hated seeing you in magazines with Chauncey. I just kept thinking that was me, it should be me now."

184

"I hear you, but I still can't accept that Eric is your son. I was there when he was born. His name is part of our son's…" my voice drifts off.

"I know, but he is a part of my life."

"I know. I can relate. I wasn't loved as a child because of my DNA. Look at me, I was Eric. But unlike my parents, you will love him and that's the way it should be. I understand it's not his fault."

"Then why can't we move on? I want all of my kids in my life as well as you. Can we please work through this? We said for better or worse."

"Braxton, you will always be a part of my life. We have history and I pray soon to have healthy baby girls. I just can't move past this. I'm trying to be cordial and nice. Don't think because I'm here all is forgiven. We agreed I would stay here, but I can leave. I'm not going to let you stress me out. You need to understand, you and I are roommates. We are not together, married only on paper."

"Can you try?"

"No. Eric's birth did help me move pass my miscarriage. Now I think how I showed everyone pictures of my godson. It's too much, I go from godmother to aunt now stepmother. It's like the joke is on me," I said sounding defeated. "I can hear it now, my sister and I both have kids by you. You know how that would make me feel, how I do feel, stupid. I don't like this feeling. I dealt with a lot during childhood. I'm still healing. I'm not adding stupid to my pile of issues."

"Yasmin, no one thinks you're stupid."

"Well that's how I feel. This situation, no matter how you look at it isn't right. It's not fair to me. I've pushed my feelings aside and have hurt for 27 years. I'm not going through that again. I'm the one who has to deal with this. Right now, I just want to focus on having these babies. As far as the living situation, this marriage," I paused. "We need to go our separate ways. After the babies are born, we'll have to sit down to figure out some visitation arrangement."

He didn't blink or respond, he just sat there. I could see the pain in his face. Although he hurt me, I hated to hurt him like that, but at the same time I had to be honest.

185

19

Hurt Again

Lawrence called, basically, begging me to see him. He's still consistent, but I have others things going on. I told him I couldn't deal with Landon. According to him, Landon wasn't coming over until later. I rolled myself off the bed and went into my closet. My wardrobe was limited, but I put on a cream baby doll dress. I let my hair down and left Braxton a note telling him I'd see him later and headed over to Lawrence's.

I knock on Lawrence's door and was surprised to see Kevin open the door.

"New address?" I teased.

"Hey, Yassy."

I walked in and handed Kevin my coat.

"Kev, did you bring Nicole with you?"

"Nope, she's with her family. I'll probably see her later this week."

"Uh, Uh, Uh. You better stop taking Nicole for granted before she finds that man that isn't afraid to commit."

"Nicole understands how I feel. Although I piss her off, she's not going anywhere. She loves me."

"Don't get cocky, Nicole's cute. She's not going to wait for you forever."

"So how's your arrogant, jealous husband?"

"I wouldn't know, but I don't want to talk about Braxton."

"Oh, so it's alright to grill me about my relationship?"

"Sure is."

Lawrence alng with his wife, Jackie came in, greeting me with a hug. She has been consistent in showing her support with him establishing a relationship with me. I follow them along with Kevin into the living room and took a seat.

"Yasmin, how are you feeling?" Lawrence asks.

"I hear congratulations are in order," Jackie says.

"Thank you, I'm fine."

"Do you need anything? Have you started shopping yet?"

"Braxton's mother has started shopping. I know I'm in for double trouble, she's going to spoil these girls."

"I'm sure she will. She does the same thing with Eric," Jackie states.

I swallow the lump that had now formed in my throat, and try to keep from blinking, so the tears that had formed wouldn't fall.

"I'm so sorry. I didn't mean to upset you."

I put my hand up to stop her from talking. I try to talk but another lump had formed and the words were stuck. Lawrence goes into the kitchen to retrieve me a glass of water. When he returns I take a few sips to calm my nerves.

"Do you need anything else?" he asked concerned.

I shook my head no.

"Yasmin, I'm really sorry," Jackie apologized, again.

"It's a difficult situation," I manage to say.

Kevin excuses himself, giving Lawrence, Jackie and I some privacy.

"Yasmin, I know how difficult this is for you. You are a much better person than I was. Your father and I deeply regret not being involved in your life. I'm grateful, that despite everything, you're still willing to allow us to be a part of your life," Jackie said.

"Yasmin, you've suffered too much hurt for one lifetime. I blame myself. I did do the cowardly thing in abandoning you, but Yasmin, I love you," Lawrence said earnestly. "When you disappeared, I felt so much guilt and regret. I didn't know if I'd ever see you again. It made me realize how much I lost out on, even more how I want to be a part of your life. Thank you again for coming today. Please, know that I will be the father you deserve," Lawrence says, hugging me.

"Thank you, but I'm tired of the drama, this soap opera. Really, can we just have a shoulda woulda coulda free evening and talk about anything but this mess of a life I'm living."

"Of course, I just, we just, want you to know we love you and are here for you. You deserve the best and I'm going to do all I can to do for you."

"I appreciate your honesty and support. What I need from you is space because I'm overwhelmed. You can't relate to this emotional rollercoaster I've been on. Now, I'm on my way to divorce court, about to be a single mother of twins. I know, sad, depressing, which is why I don't want to talk about it," I sigh.

Lawrence sighed deeply, "Yasmin, I don't want to upset you. Listen to me, please. Right now you're upset and you have every right to be. However, I don't think you should end your marriage. I'm not by any means condoning what happened, but Braxton loves you. I know he's genuinely sorry for what happened. You two are good for each other and I know he's committed to you."

"Yes, Yasmin, when you left Braxton came to us and told us what happened. He has so much guilt and pain." Jackie cosigned.

I cut in, "He should. Everyone knows how difficult it was for me to love someone, trust them and the two people I did, hurt me in the worst way. I've dealt with being second, last, all my life. I'm done. I deserve better and should be top priority."

"With Braxton, you are. He came to me as a man, admitting his mistake. He also promised me that he would take care of Eric and you. God knows, I know what he's going through. But, unlike me, he's doing the right thing and taking care of his responsibilities. We all make mistakes."

I rolled my eyes, "I guess the same applies to Landon."

"I know how difficult this is for you." Jackie stated.

"No, you have an idea, but you don't know. Yes Lawrence, you cheated on Jackie and the result was me. However, you and my mother Michelle weren't friends or sisters. I'm tired of sacrificing my feeling to please others."

"Eric and the babies you're carrying are siblings. They will be a part of each other lives. You have to get along for their sakes. They're innocent", Jackie said, matter-of-factly.

"So was I. I was innocent. I will be cordial but that doesn't mean I have to be Braxton's wife or Landon's best friend."

The front door opens and Landon comes in with Eric running behind.

"Mimi", Eric yells, and then practically jumps into my lap.

Eric caught me off guard and starts rubbing my belly. He tries to jiggle it causing me to laugh.

"Eric, get down." Landon orders.

By now, Kevin has rejoined the group

"What's up, Diva?" Kevin says, hugging Landon.

"What are you doing here?" Landon asks.

"Your father invited me. Is that okay with you?"

"Not really," Landon teased.

"Landon, why do you always insist on giving Kevin a hard time? Leave him alone." Jackie orders.

"Mommy, Kevin likes when I give him a hard time. Hey Yas."

"Hey."

I attempt to put Eric down so I could get up, but Eric wasn't having it.

"Mimi," he whines, laying his head on my stomach.

"Big boy, what are you doing?"

"Kissey."

He kisses me on my belly and I begin to cry. I am so tired of crying.

"Yasmin, can we talk for a minute?" Landon asks.

Now Lawrence and Kevin are on both sides, rubbing each shoulder. "Leave me alone," I say to Landon.

"Please?"

"Landon, can't it wait?"

"Please, I need to say this."

"Why Mimi cry?" Eric asks.

"Mommy, daddy, can you take Eric?" Landon asks.

"Yasmin, are you sure you're going to be okay. I don't want you to get upset." Lawrence asked.

I nodded my head, yes. I grabbed Kevin's hand, signaling to him that I needed him to stay. He took a sit next to me."

"Landon, don't upset her." Lawrence warned.

Lawrence grabbed Eric and he and Jackie gave us some privacy.

"Landon, say what you have to say."

"Yasmin, I'm so sorry. I never meant to hurt you honestly."

"That's what everyone keeps saying."

"I have to tell you something."

"Say what you have to say so I can leave."

Landon took a seat opposite of me, "The night I was with Braxton, I was tipsy, but I could have stopped it."

"What, you planned this?" I began rocking, trying to prevent my blood pressure from rising. Kevin put his arm around my shoulders and squeezed them.

"I know I was wrong. No I didn't plan it. Just hear me out. I want to explain how things transpired. He brought me home, I was lonely. I know I say how I like my freedom, however at times I do get lonely. I was an only child, so I never had anyone to talk too. He was going to leave, but I asked him to stay. My intention was not to sleep with him, I just wanted someone to talk to. Anyway, we talked about life and the hardships you get sometimes. He broke down and started talking about the baby, so I went over and hugged him. He said he wanted to talk to you, but you were pushing him away." She pauses, and then takes a deep breath, "I don't know how it started, but we kissed. At first I didn't think it was possible for Braxton to be the father. We were having sex. I thought he was into it, but then he looked at me, realized what he was doing, and then stopped. I didn't think he came."

My impulse was to slap the hell out of Landon. Luckily, for her, Kevin restrained me.

"Yasmin, afterwards we both felt terrible. It meant nothing. It was a huge mistake. Braxton started rambling on about how much he loves you. How stupid he was just beating his self up. I knew then he really loved you."

"Kevin, let me go, I'm about to kill this bitch!" I yelled. I started hitting my foot on the table.

By now, Jackie and Lawrence were in the room. I was fuming but Kevin kept me down.

Landon continued to talk. "I felt so bad for what I did. I told him it never happened and I would never say anything. He said he wanted to be honest. He never lied to you and didn't want to start, but I convinced him not to. It hurt me when you used to confide in me about how distant he was. I knew I was the reason, but I was selfish. I didn't want to lose our friendship. When I found out I was pregnant, I just lied to you and Eric. Braxton was suspicious. He did confront me, but I denied it. That was the main reason I married Eric. I had feelings for him, but I didn't love him. The guilt was too much for Braxton, so he broke up with you. I really felt bad. I thought Chauncey would help you get over Braxton, but I was wrong."

I looked at Kevin. He sat there looking like this info was new to him too.

"Yasmin, I'm so, so sorry."

I took several minutes digesting this new information.

"Landon, are you capable of thinking of someone other than yourself? What you just told me does not make me feel better. In fact, it pisses me off more. I can't do this." I began rocking, "You, hurt me the most. I think of all the times I cried over Braxton and you knew the reason he left me. I doubted myself, thought I wasn't good enough. I thought he had someone else. All that time you were the other woman!" I shouted.

"Yasmin, I didn't want to upset you. I'm telling you all of this because I was wrong. Braxton loves you. I want you to forgive him. Don't let what happened destroy your relationship. Please do that for me. Braxton is good for you. You're good for him. I want you to be happy and he makes you happy. You have the girls now. You're supposed to be together."

"Excuse you? Don't tell me what to do or who I'm supposed to be with. Braxton didn't have to fuck you. You were fucking Eric. It would have saved us all grief if you limited it to one. I guess I should be glad I didn't catch anything." I stood up and began pacing. Kevin was right behind me, making sure I keep my distance from Landon.

"Yasmin, I miss my sister, my best friend. Eric misses you. He's always asking for you. We're family. For the kids' sake, we have to get along."

"I don't have to do anything." My fists were balled. Oh, I wanted to kill her. I really hate her ass.

"Yas, please."

"Landon, you were my girl. I loved you and did anything for you. Throughout my relationship with Braxton, you gave me grief. You said I could do better, he wasn't good enough. When I became pregnant, you knew how excited I was, how much I wanted my baby, my son. I was happy for once. I had Braxton to love me when I didn't even know how to love myself. It felt good to be able to give him a baby after he'd given me so much. Everything was finally working out for me, no more pain or hurt. Then, I lost our son. You don't know how empty I felt. It was like I was back in my childhood all alone. I admit I pushed Braxton away. But when I finally realized what I was doing, it was too late. Why? Because of you. You just love the dick that much. So much, you had to have it, or was it Braxton you had to have? Braxton, the man who supposedly wasn't good enough or worth the time. Joke' on me. Obviously, he was. At least you're admitting it now. After all, you gave him a son and you have the audacity to use our son's name to give Eric." I took a deep breath. "Now, my daughters have to grow up living a fucking Jerry Springer episode. No, my daughters won't see their daddy every day, just every other week. You took so much from me, my kids. I know it wasn't all you. But like you said, you could have stopped it. I refuse to let you take anything else, so stay the hell away from me and my daughters."

Landon started crying, so Jackie comforted her only child. Kevin didn't know what to do and stood there looking like he wished he was somewhere else.

"Yasmin, please forgive me."

I had some more questions for her. I'd been thinking about it for some time. "Landon, tell

the truth, do you want Braxton? I'm confused because when you were married to Eric, you decided to abort his child. I never understood that since you pretended little Eric was his."

She cries harder, "Yasmin, I swear to you, I don't want Braxton. I was being stupid and selfish. I have no feelings for him."

"Why didn't you keep Eric's baby?"

She looks down, "I wasn't sure who the father was."

We all are shocked. I grab my coat. I was ready to go. Landon was a damn selfish ass lying conniving bitch. Why? I blame Lawrence and Jackie, they created the bitch. I was on my way out the door, when Lawrence stops me.

"Yasmin, calm down, please. It isn't good for the babies. I want you to sit and calm down."

"Staying here is not going to calm me down, leaving will. This is exactly why I didn't want to come."

"I'm sorry. I didn't know Landon was coming. You're too upset to drive. Come in my office and relax."

"I'm leaving."

"Yasmin, please."

I followed Lawrence. We sat in his office in silence until he spoke.

"Yasmin, it isn't good to have hate in your heart. In life, people make mistakes. You can't change the fact that you're sisters or what happened with Braxton."

I didn't say anything. I stood up, and left out the door.

20

Mad Issues

Since our talk, it seems Braxton has purposely been avoiding me. Usually, he leaves early and comes home late with periodic two-minute calls to see how I'm feeling, or if I need anything were the norm. My hormones are out of control. One minute I can stand the sight of Braxton and was happy he was gone, but more often, I wanted him to hold me like he always did.

Even today, Christmas we did things separately. We went to his mothers, but took separate cars. Other than "hey", we didn't even talk to each other. We sat on opposite sides of the table, never looking at one another. Thankfully, everyone didn't ask about our current situation, or if we were staying together. Everyone was excited about the twins, wanting to see or touch my belly. Mrs. Simms started buying things and was showing everyone everything. Braxton was being the arrogant asshole he could be, eventually leaving.

Since I was tired and didn't feel like being alone tonight, I asked Mrs. Simms if I could stay, of course she was okay with that. Mrs. Simms always treated me like a daughter, for that, I will be forever grateful. Although, I was grateful and appreciated the love and acceptance she's shown me, I wanted my mother. I tell myself I don't care, but the reality is I do. I wanted my mother to love me, be a part of my life. It's been nine months since we last talked. I pray her resentment towards me has subsided.

My mother answered on the fifth ring.

"Hello."

"Ma…"

She cut me off, "Yasmin, what do you want?"

"I called to see how you were?"

"How I am?" I could hear the disdain in her voice.

"Yes."

"Thanks to you, miserable. Isn't that what you wanted since I made your childhood so unbearable?"

"Ma…"

"Stop right there. Last time I talked to you, you called me a dumb ass."

"I was upset, we both said things."

"None of which, I regret. On the last phone call, you said I'd gotten my wish and you were dead to me."

"I didn't call to argue with you."

"Hmph."

"Ma?"

"Also on that last call, your husband said something. Apparently, you didn't need me, you had him. He is your family." She chuckled, "Did your perfect world come crashing down? Did your family leave you, again? Are you all alone? Did he realize you're not worth the time?"

I was too hurt to speak.

"Remember, you said it, not me, you're dead to me," she said, before slamming the phone in my ear.

Ten minutes went by before I hung up the phone. Looking in the mirror adjacent to my bed, I looked at myself. and examined the tears falling that now seem to be a part of my face.

There is so much sadness, hurt in my eyes. With quivering lips, I had the talk with myself. The talk I use to have with myself, after losing Braxton and Bryan, *"I love you, Yasmin. You're beautiful, unique, and special. Your worth cannot be calculated. Anyone who has you in their life is lucky. Your love is worth holding onto. You are worth the time and love. You are here for a reason. You are special, loved and wanted."* I looked up, *"God please help me deal with the things that I cannot control. Heal my heart. Guide me to do the right things, do what is best for me. Remove any negativity or hate I have. Bless my family. Give me the strength to do the right things."*

Mrs. Simms must have heard my cries because soon after she was in the bed hugging me like the injured, hurt little girl that I am.

"It's okay, let it out. You're going to be alright. "

She let me cry and continued to soothe me until I was ready to talk.

"I, like a fool, called my mother. I'm mad at myself for allowing her to upset me. I just hoped it would be different." I cried.

"I know, sweetie. I know. You're going to be okay, I know"

"No, she wishes I was dead. She said Braxton knows I'm not worth the time. I have no family. And she's right, because of all of this going on…"

"Yasmin, calm down, listen to me. Forget about everything going on with Braxton. This is about Yasmin, how beautiful you are, how despite everything you've dealt with, you survived. How it made you so much stronger. You're a survivor, a blessing. I know right now you're hurting and feel alone but you're not. I'm here for you. I remember the first day I met you, instantly, I knew you were special and was glad God brought you into our lives. I am your family. No matter what, you will always be my daughter and a part of this family."

"Thank you," I sniffed.

"Thank you, for being part of this family. Now stop crying, be strong. You have nothing to cry about. All this love you're surrounded by. You can't forget how Uncle Charles loves his sweet thing. Braxton was an ass, I said it, but despite what he did, you know he loves you so much and will do anything for you. You are so blessed. The biggest blessings of all are my baby girls. You stay strong for them. They need their mommy. We all need their mommy."

"I love you too, Ms. Beverly."

"What I tell you about that."

"I love you too, Ma."

Mommy and I ended up staying up all night watching movies, talking, have a girls night. My overnight stay, ended up being a weekend stay, we went shopping, had spa days, lunch, a little of everything. Never did she pressure me about Braxton. She allowed me to relax, which was exactly what I needed.

During my time away from Braxton, I'd be lying if I said I didn't miss him. I missed him like harmony without the melody. Braxton has the ability to do the sweetest things that makes me love him more and more. Simple things such as those notes or gifts he would leave around. The whisper of something funny to make me laugh, followed by a soft kiss between my neck and collar bone were gone. No more strong arms wrapped around me. I can't lay my head on his chest and hear his heart beating in sync with mine. I missed our late night talks, him running his hands in my hair, my foot messages. Yeah I had the Koreans for that, but I wanted my husband. Thinking of these things we did made me want to go upside his head with a frying pan. Why did he have to fuck it up?

It wasn't fair that I was again getting cheated. This pregnancy like the last was being cheated. With Bryan, Braxton was so involved. He always rubbed my belly or kissed it. He'd be the one rubbing cocoa butter on my belly, or massaging my feet. He talked to Bryan just as much as me. I never wanted for anything. He made sure I never had any doubts about my growing figure, always making me feel beautiful. Now we can't even talk, let alone be in the same room. Our bond has been broken.

For my birthday, Braxton wanted to take me out, but I declined. He purchased a memorabilia book for me with pictures from various events and vacations we took. In the back, was a video of our wedding, his parent's party where I sang to him, along with other family events. Also attached was a note.

Yasmin,

I want you to just remember. I want you to remember the love.

Look at these pictures.

Can't you see how I adore you? My life begins and ends with you.

Seeing you in the morning is always the highlight of my day.

Holding you at night, there's nothing better.

Believe through it all, my heart is always with you.

I only want to see and make you happy.

You are my everything.

Despite my stupidity, always remember......

I LOVE YOU...

This week Braxton has been exhibiting his possession of the asshole factor. He still isn't really talking to me. For the last two weeks he's been coming home after midnight. To make matters worse, every time I throw something away there's a new alcohol bottle. Braxton's moody and difficult on a regular day. Alcohol could only make his behavior more intolerable. For his sake, I hope he acted like he had sense at work. I looked at the clock to see if it was after one. I was sitting in the kitchen, wearing a gold and pink satin chemise sleep shirt that stopped mid-thigh, stuffing my face with ice cream and chicken when Braxton and company came in.

Braxton, who was obviously drunk, comes in with the DC's wannabe pimps, Javon and Cory. Immediately, I lose my appetite, throwing my ice cream away.

"Hello, Yasmin," Javon greets.

I don't return the greeting. Instead I stare at him, waiting on an explanation on why he was at my house.

"Braxton had too much to drink. I drove him here, while Cory followed," Javon hands me the keys.

"Thank you." I take the keys, hanging them on the wall in the kitchen.

"Look at you," Braxton slurred. "Always starting something. Walking around here with no clothes."

I ignore him. I was on my way upstairs, when Braxton comes behind me and wraps his arms around my stomach.

"Braxton, get your drunk ass off me."

"You know you want some. You know you love how I give it to you. Nobody can give it to you like I can. I want to hear you call out my name," he slurs, breath hot, reeking of alcohol, instantly makes me sick.

"I'm going to count to 3, 1, 2…3."

Braxton still didn't move. His drunk ass was delayed giving me an opportunity to elbow him in his ribs. He lets go and grabs his side.

Javon and Cory chuckle. Braxton ego was bruised and he started acting more of a fool.

"Y'all mutherfuckers want to fuck my wife. All you can do is drool. Mutherfuckers wish you could have some. It's hella good too. Y'all know I've been with what, 150-200 females, if not more," he chuckles. "But that right there is the best I ever had," he says pointing at me. "Y'all remember Melania, remember we said she had the best tricks and moves? Shiiiiit she don't got shit on my wife. Melania needs to take a class. That's right drool mutherfuckers because you will never know how good it is. That's me! My pussy stays wet and tight. That's why I put not one, but two babies up there. I handle mines."

Thoroughly disgusted, I was too through and start walking upstairs. I don't believe this mutherfucker is discussing our sex life and his former sex life in front of me to these fools.

Braxton gets in front of me and kisses me. Then the fool slipped his hand up my dress, grabbing my ass, exposing my ass. That's when I knee him, he went down. Javon surprisingly, held him back. I went upstairs and slammed the door.

Five minutes later, I hear a knock on my door. I didn't respond and the knocking continued. "Braxton, get the hell away from the door before I stab you. I did it once and will not hesitate to do it again.'

"I knew you were feisty, but damn," Cory chuckled.

I opened my door. "Hey."

"Just checking to make sure you were alright."

"I'm fine other than being married to an ass."

He laughs, "He's drunk. You know fucked up in the head."

"Don't look for compassion from me. Just keep him away from me."

"Can't do that, you're married and as he says, the best he ever had. That's why you're about to have two babies."

"Not in the mood for sarcasms. Knock him out. Hell, take him with you."

"I'm sorry I didn't mean to upset you. Once he sleeps it off, he'll be fine."

"Thanks for checking on me."

"You sure you don't need anything?" he asked, staring at my breasts.

Rolling my eyes, I respond. "Me and my breasts are fine."

He laughs, "More like sexy, ass too even pregnant."

"Um, you're that horny?"

"I was just giving you a compliment. Make you feel good."

I laugh. "So you said it, but didn't mean it."

"I give it to you. You're good with the tongue. You can twist some shit around."

"Well, I don't need compliments. I know what I am."

"So do I. Braxton gave me an earful. Damn shame how you have that man whipped like that."

I shrug, "Anyway, I'm fine. You and Javon can go back to hoeing around in the city. Like I said, do whatever to Braxton, just keep him away from me."

"So mean."

"Not mean. That's what you do, hey if it makes you happy. Do you."

"You funny."

"I'm tired."

"Aw'ight shawty. Get some rest. Try not to stab your husband anymore."

I smile, "As long as you keep him away, I won't." I closed the door.

Later that day, around twelve, I decided to get out of the house. When I went downstairs I see Braxton sitting in the chair looking like crap. Looking around I see my family room is a mess. My carpet was covered with towels, reeking of vomit and alcohol. I start to cuss him out, but he was making me sick, literally. Instead, I roll my eyes and leave out the door.

*

I dreaded coming home. I pull into my driveway at eight. On my way in, Braxton was heading out, causing us to bump into one another.

"Hey," he said.

I nod, then walk past him.

"Yeah, sorry about last night."

"Sorry about feeling on me like I was a trick on the street, or the show for your friends?"

"Both."

"Just don't mutherfuckin talk to me."

"Yasmin…"

I cut him off, "Don't talk to me."

He didn't say anything, he left out the door. I heard the music blaring, the engine of his 745 Li roars as he pulled out of the driveway.

Inside my once love-filled bedroom, I cried. Never in a million years did I think I'd be here. I cried myself to sleep like I have for so many nights in the last few months.

*

It's been a week since Braxton's drunken stupor. Usually, when I see him, he's coming or going staying out like he's a bachelor. That really pissed me off. Just because I told him I was done didn't mean I wanted to know about it. No, I don't have anything concrete just speculation. But the ass works, comes home, changes, and leaves. I have no idea when he comes back because these babies usually knock me out by nine, but it's the principle. His ass hasn't attempted to talk to me. Other than, hey, you need anything or see you. The tension is ridiculous. I've had one doctor appointment since then. He came, but he didn't touch me or look at me. Even my chipper doctor knew we had issues. There were no jokes or humor, just a serious tension filled appointment.

I'd been lying in bed, trying to go to sleep so I wouldn't have to think about my many issues. My full bladder forced me to get up. Unable to go back to sleep, I looked at the clock and saw it was 4:11. I headed to the kitchen for some apple juice. On my way, I see Braxton's room is empty. I went in. From the look of things, he hadn't been home all night. Granted, I haven't spoken to him due to his drunken ass acting like a fool, but not coming home? Yeah I told him I didn't want a relationship, but he was taking it too far. Out of respect, his ass should be here. Staying out all night, he's probably between someone's legs. I don't believe him.

I don't care, I tell myself. But if I didn't care, why did I have tears rolling down my face. "Fuck you Braxton!" I yelled.

I was hurt. After about twenty minutes of being hurt over Braxton staying out, I said fuck it. He wants to be with some other chick, fine.

When I went back upstairs I noticed the phone was off the hook. I put it on, took a shower, and decided I was going to the spa. As soon as I began to lotion my body, the phone rings. It was Horace.

"Hello."

"Yasmin, where have you been? I was on my way over there. I've been trying to get a hold of you."

"The phone was off the hook."

"Listen, Yasmin. I need you to come to the hospital right now."

"What's going on?" I asked Horace.

"Yas, just come to the hospital."

"Tell me what's going on, please."

"Braxton was in an accident."

"What? What happened?"

"He was in an accident. Apparently, it looks like a case of road rage. He was beat up pretty badly."

I gasped. I just went numb. Yeah, we had plenty of issues, but I never wanted anything to happen to him. I prayed that Braxton didn't die.

"Yasmin, do you need me to come get you." Horace asks, breaking me out of my trance.

"Um no, I'm on my way. Do they know who did this?"

"No, no witnesses. An anonymous call came in and ambulance brought him here around two this morning.

"Oh my God."

"Yas, are you sure you don't need me to come get you?"

"Yes, I'm on my way."

Horace gave me the room info. I grab some pants and one of Braxton's shirts. I felt an uneasy feeling come over me. Something wasn't right. I thought of Braxton and who would hurt him. Something in my gut told me I knew who it was. I'm surprised nothing happened sooner. I pull out my cell phone and made a call. Unfortunately, I got the voice mail, but I left a message.

"Hey, it's me, Yas. Please, please, please give me a call. We need to talk. It's long overdue. I can meet you today. Call me with a time and place. It's important I talk to you. Call me anytime."

I left my cell number and headed out the door.

I prayed the whole time on my way to the hospital *"God, please make Braxton alright. I know we have problems. I don't know right now if I want to be with him, but I love him. Please don't take him. I need him, my babies need him. Give me the strength to deal with whatever I faced with. Guide me to do the right thing."*

As soon as I walked in I saw the family. Everyone looked distraught and I didn't get a good feeling. Jeff Jr. was the first to approach me and give me a hug. "Yasmin."

The way he hugged me caused me to panic, assume the worst. Hysterically, I began to cry.

Horace approaches me. "Yasmin, calm down. He's going to be fine. Relax my nieces need you to be strong."

Vincent approached me giving me a hug and kiss on the cheek. "Yasmin, listen to Horace. You can't go in there stressed. If you do, Braxton will start whining like a little girl. None of us feel like hearing Braxton whine, talking about his beautiful Yasmin."

I smile and punch Vincent.

Horace spoke, "I just need to prepare you, he's looks a lot worse than he is. He has a lot of superficial wounds, but they'll heal over time."

I took a deep breath. "What's the extent of his injuries?"

"He has a broken leg, fractured ribs, broken nose. Yasmin, I need to stress he has some swelling and doesn't look like himself."

"Okay, I'm ready."

I walk in slowly. I see mommy by Braxton's side and his father on the other side. I look at Braxton and nearly pass out. Horace grabs me.

Braxton face was swollen, both his eyes practically shut. He has a knot on his head like Hasim Rahman had after his fight with Evander Holyfield. His face hadn't been cleaned, so there was a lot of dried up blood. His nose definitely was broken. His mouth has cuts. He leg in cast.

"Yasmin, sit down." Mr. Simms coaxed.

"I'm alright."

"Yasmin, I'm glad you're here. Braxton's been asking for you." Mommy got up to hug me, but I was somewhat unresponsive from shock.

"I must have knocked the phone off the hook." I say, crying. "How long has he been asleep?"

"He's been in and out. They've given him a lot of pain medicine. He just went to sleep ten minutes ago."

I stood there looking in disbelief for I know at least twenty minutes.

"Hey, Beautiful," Braxton spoke, breaking me from my trance. I could tell from his labored breathing it was difficult to talk.

"Hey."

"I'm sorry for everything."

"Shh" I hush him.

"I love you, Beautiful. Come here, please. I can see in your eyes you're scared, but I need you. Just sit with me. Come here, please." Braxton groans.

As I was attempting to take a step, my phone went off. I grab it, seeing it was the call I was waiting on. I turn away and quickly answer the phone.

"Hello."

"I got your message. I have a lot to do today," he responds.

"It won't take long. I need to see you today... now."

"Meet me at my place in a half."

"Ok, I'm on my way."

I closed the phone, focusing back on Braxton."

"Um, I need to go."

"I'm sorry, please don't go," He coughs.

I cringe. "I need to take care of this. I promise I'll come right back."

"Yasmin, please, I need you. I want my wife."

"I'll be back."

"I lost you didn't I?"

I took a look at him, turned around quickly and exit.

I was halfway down the hall, when mommy approaches.

"Yasmin, please stay for me. I know, I know, this situation is terrible. I feel for you.

Please, Braxton messed up, but he loves you, he does. Please don't leave him now."

"Mommy, I'll be back, I need to take care of something."

"Yasmin, you need to stop running. He is still your husband. Please don't be so heartless. He's in pain, suffering."

I was taken aback at her calling me heartless, but he is her baby. "I understand that, but right now, I need to go. I will be back."

"Yasmin, don't leave."

"I'll be back." I pressed the button for the elevator.

"You're really disappointing me. If this is too much, then just walk away now."

I got on the elevator, ignoring her comments even though they cut me deep.

Vincent approaches me as I head to the hospital exit, catching me off guard.

"Calm down. Please don't go into labor on me. Although I must say sister-in -law you are big as shit, you look like you're about to bust."

I can't help but laugh.

He takes a deep breath. "Walk with me."

I follow him to less populated area in the hospital.

"Yasmin, I'm going to make this short."

"Okay."

"You need to forgive Braxton."

"Vincent, don't tell me what I need to do. I know you're use to hoeing around and this is the norm for you, but I'm not forgiving shit. Brax…"

He squeezes my hand, "Damn, you so feisty," he laughs.

I don't.

"Let me try this again. Yasmin, what Braxton did was really, really, really fucked up. I know you're hurt and everything, but he's sorry. I don't mean, none of us for that matter mean to put any extra pressure on you."

I interrupt. "Well you and everybody else are."

"Yasmin, we don't mean to. We just know how much Braxton loves you. When I say we never thought he'd settle down, I mean we never did. You love him too. Anyway you make him better. We actually like him now. Seriously, Yasmin you complement each other. My brother is crazy about you. The two months you were gone, he just about lost it, not knowing if you were alright. Some days I didn't think he would make it. Then you came back and he finds out you having twins. You belong together, stop fighting it. He wants you. You want him. Y'all about to have these babies, be happy together."

"Vincent, please. I heard this before."

"Think about it. I like having you in the family. You know you like having me as your brother. We are family, don't break it up. Forget that divorce talk. Stay together. Ask yourself this, what would you have done if something even worse happened. The way you came in here earlier says you want to be with Braxton. Would you still be sitting here debating whether or not you should forgive him or would you be spending as much time with him as you could? Think about it."

He gives me a kiss on the cheek, leaving me with my thoughts. I sit only for a minute. I have someone to meet. Once I reached my car I let the tears flow. Thirty minutes later, I was at my destination. Taking a deep breath before I rung the bell.

"Hey Yas. Come in, have a seat."

"Hey."

"So what brings you over here?"

"You know why I'm here."

"No."

"Your knuckles look a little swollen." I said noticing the bruising.

He looked down at his knuckles, "They look fine to me."

"Okay, you know I like to get straight to the point. You're the accident Braxton was in?"

"What are talking about?" He asks, never looking me directly in the eye.

"Look, I'm not going to ask you why. I know why. Truthfully, I'm surprised it didn't happen sooner. I know how you feel, but you almost killed him."

He just looked at me without blinking.

"I know how hurt you are. Please, just let it go. I'm begging you not to do anything else."

"Are you done? I told you I had things to do."

"No, are you going to leave Braxton alone?"

"I never bothered him. I still don't know what you're talking about."

"Really, I'm tired of this game. I know you're the reason Braxton is in the hospital. Now that you've made your point, can you just leave him alone?"

"Just let it go, like nothing happened. Is that what you're doing?!" he yelled.

"Truthfully, I don't know what I'm doing. I'm just tired of hurting."

"Yeah."

"Eric, we both were hurt, but you almost killed him."

"Yas, how can you sit there and take up for him?"

"I'm not. I'm just as mad as you are."

"You're not acting like it. Yas, that's your problem, you're too nice. Being nice causes people to play you for a fool."

"Eric, what happened was fucked up."

He cut me off, "That's exactly why I did what I did. No regrets, like you said I could have, but I didn't kill him."

"Looks like you tried. I just saw him. I'm going to have nightmares. You fucked him up."

Eric sat there sipping on Hennessey without blinking. I noticed he had a mellow jazz CD playing. Unfortunately, it did nothing for his mood. He had so much hate, rage, and callousness in his eyes. The sight alone caused my body to shudder. "

"I'm not denying the fact that both Landon and Braxton were wrong. I'm barely talking to either one of them. But please, stop."

He chuckled, "Landon, that bitch! Do you realize how stupid she made me look? Her crazy demands, then she punk me like I'm a joke. Her ass was always flirting with other men disrespecting me, talking to me like I wasn't shit. Yeah, that was my fault, that's the first thing they tell you when you go pro, watch the hoes, can't turn one into a housewife. Now to Braxton, his ass was in my house, smiling in my face and he knew all this time that... I can't even say it."

"Yes, they both were wrong."

"I always had my doubts, especially after Landon out of the blue decides she wanted a relationship. A month later, she's pregnant. All of a sudden she loves me. Yeah, she got me. She did any and everything. That should have told me something right there. But the hoe knew what she was doing. You know how I found out?"

"No."

"Landon couldn't keep up the façade. The bitch started doing what she did best, being a fucking whore. I don't know why she thought I wouldn't find out. I'd been in denial all that time. Finally, one day I looked at ..... Anyway I had the test done."

I felt bad for Eric. I remembered the last time I saw him. The day I offered to take Eric and he kicked me out.

"I confronted the bitch. Of course she said it was an accident, big mistake. It meant nothing. She loved me and wanted to work it out. Bitch, please! I swear if... wasn't there I would have killed her."

"I'm so sorry?"

"I'm sure you got the same story."

"Basically, yes. Landon thought he was yours. Braxton just found out the truth a couple of months ago. Not that it makes a difference, they both fucked, shit. Anyway, Landon admitted that Braxton came to her and asked if there was a possibility he was the father. Landon said no, I think Landon really thought you were."

"Landon, her lies, that bitch is going to get what's coming to her. The trick did know. I bet you didn't know Javon or some other guy was a possibility. "

My mouth drops open from shock. This was low for Landon.

"Don't look surprised, you knew your girl was a hoe. You're lucky you didn't get labeled.

Flabbergasted, appalled even I was, but I didn't want to see Landon hurt. "Eric please, don't hurt her. You've fucked up Braxton, leave Landon alone."

He looks at me with his heartless eyes given me chills, again. Eric never frightened me until today. Despite what Landon did she still is my sister. I'm not saying we will be friends, but I didn't want to visit her grave. Looking in Eric eyes, seeing what he did to Braxton, I knew it was more than possible. His eyes told me he wouldn't be satisfied, until he did.

"Yassy, you're always taking the high road. I like you, but Landon is going to pay for what she did. Yas, you're too good for any of them. Why are you still putting yourself through it? Did you forgive them?"

"No, not quite. I'd be lying if I said I didn't think about hurting them. I have my moments, but things aren't that simple. Things are complicated."

"Yas, I lost my son. You don't know how much that hurt me."

"I do, Eric. I lost my baby too. No, I wasn't able to hold him, but I carried him, we bonded. When he died, I felt so alone, empty, even now I have a void. I know how you feel. I wish it was something I could do because that pain is something I would never wish on anyone. Eric, I'm sorry."

"Yasmin, I'm sorry. I forgot. We weren't that close back then. Do you need anything?"

That's why I'm here. I'm begging you not to harm Braxton anymore. Also, I'm begging you to leave Landon alone. I'm pregnant.

My kids need their father." I opened my coat. For the first time, he noticed my belly.

"You're pregnant."

"I know, some Jerry Springer, Maury Povich shit. When I found out I ran off. I cut both of them off. One day I go to the doctor because I wasn't feeling well and she says you're pregnant. Talk about bad timing. I took it as a blessing though because you know I went through so much when I lost my son. Now I'm pregnant with twins."

For the first time Eric smiles. "Yas, congratulations."

"Thanks."

"So you and Braxton are going to work it out?"

"I wouldn't say that, I don't know. Don't get me wrong. I'm still dealing with many emotions. I still can't accept that Braxton is Eric's father. A part of me wants to just run away, forget both of them. Then there is a part that still loves Braxton. Everybody is putting pressure on me. Telling me Braxton loves me, he's sorry, and we need to be a family. I do want a family, but I don't know what I'm going to do. I'm so fucking angry that they lied. Now I have these babies to think about. I don't want them to grow up bouncing from house to house, but I can't live a lie and pretend I'm cool with all that's happened either."

"Landon lied to all of us. Believe it or not, I know Braxton wasn't in on Landon's lie. You know he just took the beating, he didn't fight back. Just kept saying he was sorry. I just lost it because Eric is supposed to be my son." I saw a tear roll down his face.

I went over to hug him, "I'm so sorry, I know it hurts. Some days I don't know if I'm coming or going."

"Yas, you know what really hurts, she killed my baby. My baby wasn't good enough to carry. She killed my baby. Why should that bitch live?"

I was at a loss for words. "Eric, I don't even have words to say." I couldn't tell him the real reason behind Landon's abortion. If I did, Landon more than likely would end up six feet under. I definitely couldn't deal with that on my conscience.

"There are no words."

"Eric, I'm begging you to just move on. Don't do anything that could jeopardize your career or freedom."

"That's just it, that bitch got my game fucked up. My mind so fucked up, I can't play. I'm a starter or I was. I'm on the bench now. She's still in my head. I'm going to get the bitch. I'm done with Braxton, Landon's ass however, I'm not making any promises. She fucked with the right person."

"Eric, please. I know Landon was wrong, but little Eric needs her, he loves her. Despite everything else, all her issues, she loves him."

He didn't say anything. I prayed I was getting through to him.

"Eric, I know you're hurt, please move on. Don't let Landon make you lose your life. I know it's hard, but let go of this hate. You're too good of a person to let them make you into the person you're becoming."

I stayed at Eric's longer than I expected to, two hours. In a strange way, it was soothing being around him. We didn't talk much, nothing physical, just sat there listening to jazz, relinquishing some of our related pain.

$$*$$

Before going to the hospital, I stopped at home. I grabbed some things for Braxton. From looking at him, it was obvious he would be there for a few days. I decided to stay with him, so I grabbed some clothes, blanket, and a real pillow. Still in need of peace after talking to Eric, not to mention my last conversation with mommy, I took a long ride. I've never seen her so mad. I made it back to the hospital at around two.

Approaching Braxton's room door was a task. Still hesitant, I pause by the door and listen. Braxton is giving the nurse hell, just being nasty, telling her to leave him alone, not eating or wanted her to clean him up. I swear he's just annoying at times. Before opening the door, I take a deep breath.

"Hello, I'm Yasmin," I extend my hand. "I apologize. My husband can be a pain in the ass. I'll wash him up and feed him. Go relax."

She looks so relieved, "Thank you. You don't have to tell me twice," she says as she quickly exits the room.

"You came back. Look, I know you're just here out of pity. I'm alright. You can go wherever."

"Oh, so you're putting me out?"

"You put yourself out when you left." He struggles to say.

"You are such a fucking baby. You act like an ass when you don't get your way."

He grunted.

"I told you I'd be back. I had to make a run."

"Where to Kevin's?"

I shook my head. "You are terrible. No, not with Kevin."

"Well, whatever. You can go. You don't want to be bothered with me anyway. Go home. You'll have the house to yourself."

"Braxton, I went to see Eric."

He was quiet.

"I figured that would get your attention. I won't ask questions. Let me just help make you better. Let's forget about what's going on with us. Focus on getting you together because in a couple of months you will be taking care of me. That includes pampers and late night feeding."

He laughs. "Don't make me laugh."

"Here eat something. I know, I'll get you some real food later. I didn't know how your mouth was.

"Fucked up like the rest of me. I deserved it though."

Ignoring his comment, I washed his mouth to feed him. Afterwards I began washing his wounds. Braxton tries to talk, but I quiet him down.

"Shhh." I took some warm water and soap and start washing him up.

"Ugh," he moans.

"I'm sorry, but I have to clean you up."

"I know, it just burns."

"Big baby," I tease.

Just as I was finishing, Braxton's parents came in.

"Hey," I said.

"Hey Yasmin" Mr. Jeff says, giving me a hug.

"Yasmin, sorry I got blood on your shirt," Braxton apologizes.

"Nice shirt isn't it? That's okay, this is your shirt."

"You're wearing my stuff now?"

"Yeah, it's comfortable. You know I can't fit mine. I decided to stretch yours out."

He laughed. I could tell it hurt.

"Yasmin, can I talk to you for a minute?" Mommy asks.

"What's going on?" Braxton asks concerned."

"Nothing, I'll be back."

Once we made it outside, mommy gave me a hug. "I'm so sorry. I apologize for talking to you like that earlier. I was out of line."

"It's ok. I know Braxton is your baby boy that's spoiled." I said, trying to lessen the tension.

"It's not ok. I was wrong. It just breaks my heart seeing him like that. What kind of person could do this?"

I didn't say anything for a while. "I'm just grateful it wasn't worse, that he's alive."

"Yes, thank God." she cried.

I gave her another hug and cried too.

"Yasmin, when I first saw him I nearly fainted. I could see the pain in his eyes, he could barely breathe. I knew he hurt. I kept telling him to calm down, but all he did was ask for you. He loves you, Yasmin, and I know you love him. When you left earlier, he became so depressed, intolerable. Sweetheart, I know you're hurt, but please don't give up on your marriage."

"I understand what you're saying, but you have to understand it's not that simple. I don't want to get into this now. I'll be here to help Braxton get better, but I can't promise that after the girls are born, that I'll stay."

"Yasmin, it breaks my heart. You have the girls to consider, you shouldn't be apart. You two been through so much. I know Bryan's death was hard on both of you, but you found your way back because you love each other. You know how miserable you were apart."

"That's why it's so hard. I lost our son then he turns his back on me. He left me when I needed him the most. All that time I blamed myself and then I find out he has a son with my sister; a son that was conceived because of my miscarriage."

Before she could respond, Mr. Jeff opened the door. "Yasmin, Braxton is asking for you."

I wiped my eyes, took a deep breath and went in. "I'm right outside, what's the problem?"

"Sit with me."

"Oh, I can tell you're going to drive me crazy. You're such a pain when you're sick."

"No, I'm not, I just want you close to me. I miss you."

I took a seat, silently praying for strength. He looked so pathetic.

"I know I look bad," he grabs my hand.

"You do."

He chuckles, "I knew you'd be honest. That mouth."

His parents came in and we watched a movie I'd brought from home. I ended up falling asleep in the chair. I was awakened by the phone. I look over at Braxton, who was knocked out from his meds.

I got up and stretched."

"Are you ok? Mr. Jeff asked.

"No, these chairs are uncomfortable and I'm cold."

"How long are you staying here tonight?" Mrs. Simms asked

"I was going to stay the night. How long do the doctors want to keep him here?"

"He had a MRI earlier. There wasn't any damage they should let him out in two days or so, Tuesday." Mr. Jeff stated

"I think I should hire a nurse to take care of him."

"You're not going to be there?" Mrs. Simms panicked.

"Yes, I'm just going to need help. I can't help him to the bathroom or lift him. My doctor has threatened to put me on bed rest if I don't take it easy."

"You're right. I can stay with you."

"No, save your energy. I'm going to need you when your baby girls come."

She smiles, getting up to rub my stomach. "How are Nana's babies?"

"Growing every second."

She lifted up my shirt. "You've gotten so big in the last month."

"I know. The only thing I want is ice cream and cake or Buffalo wings. So far, I've gained eighteen pounds. It's gone straight to my stomach, but I have fourteen more weeks to go."

"They'll be here soon. We need to get organized. Any names yet?"

"No, it's so much to do."

"We're going to get it together," Braxton said, groggily

"How are you feeling, son? How's the headache?" Mr. Jeff asked.

"It's better. Yasmin, can you come here, please?"

I walk over. "What's wrong?"

"Nothing, I just wanted my girls close." He rubs my belly. "Hey, daddy's princesses."

"I've already told him not to spoil them, but I know he's not going to listen."

"That's right. My girls can have what they want."

"Nothing's wrong with that. Nana can't wait to hold her little angels."

"Yasmin, just give it up. These two are going to drive you and me crazy. Bev didn't tell you she's bought more clothes. She has swings, cribs, and highchairs for our house. You would think she's having the babies."

We all laughed.

"How are my baby girls?" Braxton continually rubbed my stomach, talking to the babies.

My stomach began to transform as the baby moved. The babies surprisingly recognized his voice. They probably were trying to get away, all the arguing we do.

"They know daddy."

The babies continued to move around.

"That looks painful."

I laugh "It's not, it just feels funny."

We were all laughing when Landon came in. "Oh my God. Look at you. I hardly recognize you," Landon squeals, in shock with her mouth gaped open.

Braxton did look messed up, but Landon's damn dramatics didn't help. I pulled my shirt down and took a seat.

"Landon, like always, your timing is perfect," Braxton said, sarcastically.

"I'm sorry. I knew you were hurt, but I wasn't expecting this. I'm glad I didn't bring Eric."

Time for a break, I stood up, "I'm going to go get something to eat."

Braxton grabs my hand, "Yasmin, please don't go, stay."

"I'm coming back."

"I don't want you to go."

"I'm sorry, I'll leave." Landon offers.

"Bye, Landon." Braxton stated.

"I need to stretch."

"Yasmin."

"Braxton, here are my keys, wallet and coat," I said pointing to the chair. "I'll be back. I'm going to get some food."

I left out the room and saw Lawrence standing by the door.

"Hello, Yasmin."

"Lawrence."

"I wanted to see how you're holding up."

"I'm ok. I'm on my way to the cafeteria."

"Do you mind if I come?"

We walked in silence. The cafeteria didn't have anything appealing. Eventually, I grabbed a salad and some juice. Next I found a secluded corner and took a seat.

"How's Braxton?"

"He has a broken nose, leg, fractured ribs and a lot of superficial wounds. I hardly recognize him, but he'll live."

"That's what's important. Have you given anymore thought to what I said?"

"Damn. Can I breathe? What happened to the how are you. First thing out everyone's mouth, 'Have you forgiven Braxton?' "

"I apologize. However, what happened to Braxton proves time is of the essence. I don't want you to waste any of it with all this anger. It's evident to everyone there's a lot of love between you."

"And hurt, pain, lack of trust, I can go on and on."

"Yasmin, let it go."

"Forgive Landon and Braxton, act like nothing has happened?"

"It's hard, but I don't want you to hold all of the animosity inside. I'm grateful that despite what your mother and I put you through, you are a remarkable young woman."

"Well, I'm tired of letting everyone treat me like shit and then having them to expect me to get over it. I always put my feelings aside. Can't you understand? I miscarry. Landon gets pregnant and needs me. I pushed aside my feelings even though I was so depressed, I was there for Landon. All the time she's pregnant with Braxton's baby. Now Braxton's hurt, yet again, I push aside my hurt and I'm helping. What about me? Why can't I just be first for once? Why do I always have to hurt?"

Lawrence stood up, and wrapped his arms around me. "I'm sorry I didn't mean to upset you. I just know that Landon is sorry as well as Braxton and they deserve a second chance. I know they both love you. Please try."

"Lawrence, can you please, leave me alone, please."

"I'm sorry."

"All of this badgering and pressure from everyone, just give me some space."

He walked away and I fought to hold back my tears. I felt a hand on my shoulder and looked up to see Uncle Charles."

"How's my Sweet Thing?"

"I don't know Uncle Charles. I'm so tired."

"Yeah, I know you are, Braxton..."

I stopped him mid-sentence. "Please don't give me another lecture. Mommy, Mr. Jeff in so many words, Lawrence, even Vincent, already have. Braxton loves you. He is sorry, do it for the babies."

"Braxton does love you, not a question in my mind. But, I'm not telling you to forget it and move on. Braxton and Landon were dead wrong."

I hugged him and let it out. I cried and he reassured me it was okay.

"I'm so sorry. I'm just tired of everyone putting pressure on me. I have to always be the strong one, the one who does the right thing, the one who accepts everyone treating me like shit."

"Yasmin, you have to do what makes you happy. Don't compromise yourself. Do what's best for you."

"I'm so hurt and confused.. Eric, I do love him like my own, but I can't even look at him anymore without wanting to breakdown. I don't want him to feel like I don't love him. That's how I felt growing up. I never would want him to feel that. I feel so bad. I look at him, and I think that if my baby lived he wouldn't be here. My son died. I feel like they replaced him with Eric."

"Yasmin, no one tried to replace Bryan. I know you're going through hell. Like I told you, you have to do what's best for you. This

220

is your life. But know, whether you decide to leave Braxton or stay, he'll always be a part of it. Both ways Eric is a part of it. You have to decide if you can live without Braxton or with him. It must be your decision."

"Thank you, I just don't want to end up like my mother. She resents the fact I was born. She blames me for ruining her life and it's my fault John left. She told me I'm dead to her. With all of this going on it makes me think, I will always be a punching bag. Everyone keeps telling me, Yasmin, thank you, you're always there. We can count on you. Why can't I count on them? I'm so tired of being strong."

Uncle Charles hugged me. "No matter what you decide, I'm here for you. Know anytime you need to talk about anything, even a new man in your life. But don't get any ideas, Uncle Charles is here."

I laughed, "Thank you."

"Sweet Thing you get enough to eat?"

"No, can you go to a real restaurant. Like some Buffalo wings, ice cream and cake and lemonade."

He laughed. "Sure, are you going to be okay?"

Yeah, I'm going to go back to Braxton's room. I know he's wondering where I am."

"Sweet Thing, remember what I said, do what Yasmin wants."

I went back to Braxton's room and saw he was sleeping. Immediately, my heart ached. He was so messed up, he looked like his whole body ached. Part of me wanted to run over to him, tell him I love him and we'd be okay, then the other part wanted to just leave and be by myself."

221

21

Emotional Rollercoaster

Almost a month has gone by since Braxton's "accident." I'd be lying if I said I didn't have strong feelings. He still slept in the guest room, but I was lonely. I missed him being in bed with me. I'm used to waking up with Braxton's arms wrapped around me and because of this haven't had a good night's sleep.

Braxton and I were communicating, but haven't talked about us. We're trying to stay focused on the babies. He talks to them. I enjoy the time and it has brought us closer. Braxton wounds have pretty much healed up. If you look closely you can see a little bruising. Braxton grew a beard, which hid a lot of it. The beard made him look so much older. I'm not sure if I like it. I prefer the goatee, but I guess it's for the best. I'm not as quick to want to jump on his dick. Don't get me wrong, he's still handsome. My hormones were raging. I was so horny, the times I thought I would jump him, I ended up at Kevin's. With Kevin, there was no sexual attraction at all, that calmed me some. I know it bothered Braxton, but he's kept his cool.

Braxton went back to work a week ago. During his time off, he received a lot of cards with best wishes. I was surprised he was missed with his moodiness. I just told his job he was in a bad car accident. Kim was really nice. I personally couldn't tolerate Braxton as a boss. I don't know how she did it which is part of the reason I was at BET, the other was to check on Braxton. I purchased Kim a gift basket from Carol's Daughter and gave her a $1000 from me just for dealing with Braxton. It was well overdue.

Unfortunately, when I arrived Kim and Braxton were in a meeting. Because of security issues, the receptionist refused to let me pass, like I was a threat. And I know the bitch recognized me from when I came over before. Since I had Kim's basket I decided to wait.

Twenty minutes later my bladder needed relief. I walked up to the receptionist to see if she would let me use the bathroom.

"Excuse me."

"Yes," she responded, never looking up from her screen.

"Is it possible for me to use the restroom, I really need to go."

She gave me a phony smile. "As I told you before, due to security issues I can't let you past the desk."

"I understand that, however, as you can see I'm pregnant. Furthermore, my company, Legg Mason has a contract with BET, and my husband is a VP."

"Well today, it looks like it's personal. I have to verify who you say you are. Even if it was business, someone will escort you. There's a McDonald's down the street you can use.

This bitch was about to get cussed out. Before I could open my mouth I saw Braxton's boss, Mr. Johnson. I looked at the bitch. "You know what I'll just take this over your split end- raggedy-big-ass bald head."

"Mr. Johnson," I called out, as he was walking by.

He turned around. I could tell he was trying to recall where he knew me from. "Hello, Yasmin, Braxton's wife?"

"Yes, you remember."

"I never forget a pretty face. I see you're glowing, congratulations."

"Thank you, twin girls."

"Wow, congratulations, again. What brings you to BET today?"

"Two things actually, first to check on my husband and second I wanted to thank Kim. Kim by far is the best. Braxton is fortunate to have her."

"Glad to hear that, I was happy to see Braxton back as well. He's really doing a great job here."

"Braxton's glad to be back.

"Why are you waiting out here?"

"Well," I looked toward the receptionist, "She indicated due to security issues, I wasn't allowed without an escort. I understand, but as I was explaining to her. I really need to go to the bathroom." I began to rub my belly.

"Of course, follow me," he looked at the receptionist. "Anytime, Mrs. Simms comes, let her back," he ordered.

"Thank you, Mr. Johnson I apologize for calling you over."

"Nonsense, Are you ready?"

"Yes, I just need to grab my things." I looked at the receptionist and rolled my eyes.

I followed Mr. Johnson back and made small talk. When I reached Braxton's office no one was there. I went in and used his bathroom. As I was finishing up, I hear Braxton enter with Lisa Stevens. I know she's going to try me.

"Braxton, I'm so glad you back," Lisa states.

"Thanks, Lisa."

"I left you several messages. I was worried about you."

"I appreciate your concern. It was a lot going on."

"Yes, I've wanted to talk to you for quite some time. I just didn't want to pry. Maybe I should drop it. I just want you to know if you need to talk, I'm here."

Braxton says this bitch is not interested, whatever I thought.

"Thanks, but I'm okay."

"Braxton, just know I'm here. For the past couple of months, you just haven't been yourself. You've been distant, so stressed. I was the same way when my marriage ended."

No this bitch didn't, time to end this fiasco. I walk out of the bathroom.

"Hello Lisa," I coolly replied.

"Hey baby," I said, giving Braxton a hug.

"Hey Beautiful," Braxton leaned down to kiss my check I turned my head so he could kiss my lips."

"Yasmin, you're pregnant." Lisa swallows and stares at my stomach.

I turn around, placing Braxton's hands on my belly, "Yes I am."

"You're having a baby," she says, in disbelief.

"Actually no, two. Braxton and I are having twins."

Her eyes were wide, "Twins?!"

"As you can imagine, it's been crazy. We're getting everything prepared. There's no need to be concerned about Braxton. As always, I have everything under control."

"Glad to hear that."

"Thanks, Lisa," Braxton said.

"Lisa, you are done with *my* husband, right?" I turned to Braxton, "I missed you, I thought we could spend a little quality time together," I laid my head on his chest.

"Yes, I'll see you later, Braxton."

"Ok, bye. Oh and Lisa, sorry to hear about the marriage. Close the door on your way out."

She turns around and storms off.

I had to smile, I can't stand that bitch.

Braxton didn't waste any time grabbing me and kissing me. Oh shit, I took it too far, I'm not ready to commit. Oh, this feels so good. I know I shouldn't have, but I kissed him back. When he started kissing my neck I moaned, damn I miss him. He kissed me again. His hands were on my ass, I was ready to lie down and spread them.

"Braxton," Kim said, opening the door. I'm so sorry."

'Thank you, Kim' I said, to myself. "Kim, don't leave. I have something for you." I released myself from Braxton, grabbing her basket.

"Yasmin, oh my God, look at you."

"I know." I walk over and hug her.

"Why didn't you say anything? How far along are you?"

"Seven months."

"You look like you're due now. This is a big baby, it might be two," she joked.

Braxton and I laugh.

"Kim, you know everything. It's two girls. I might have to give you a raise," Braxton teased.

"She deserves it."

"Thank you, Yasmin. Oh my God, twins!"

"Kim seriously, I want to thank you for all of your support, you've really gone beyond. Most importantly, you deserve a medal for putting up with Braxton's mood swings."

"Hey," Braxton warned.

"She does, but Kim with all that being said, here's a little token of appreciation." I handed her the Carol's Daughter basket and check.

"Thank you, Yasmin. I really appreciate this, but you didn't have to," she hugged me.

"You deserve it."

"What about me, I'm sure I paid for it," Braxton teased.

"Of course, you did."

"Thank you both so much. Braxton I was just letting you know I'm going to lunch."

"Kim, take the rest of the day off."

Braxton came behind me, wrapping one around my belly. With his other hand he covered my mouth. "Hey, hey, you're taking it too far now."

Kim started laughing.

I removed his hand from my mouth, "Be nice, you know she deserves a day off."

"Alright, smart mouth. If I give Kim the day off, that means you're going to have to take her place. You'll be working for me for the rest of the day."

"Sorry, Kim, you're on your own, girl. Woo! Can't do it! Can't torture myself."

Kim busted out laughing, "I forgive you."

"I thought so," Braxton pulls me closer, kissing me on my cheek.

"Well, let me give you two some privacy. I'm going to lunch," Kim announced.

"Kim, you can have the rest of the day off," Braxton said.

I jumped from Braxton's grip, "I had to get away before the lightning struck."

"Kim, I told you, Yasmin is a smart ass. You witnessed it yourself, you believe me now. She's the reason for my mood swings."

"Don't put that on me."

Kim laughed. "Thank you both, again." She left, giving us some privacy.

After Kim left Braxton grabs me and starts where he left off.

"Yasmin, you don't know how much I've missed you."

"Braxton, I'm sorry, I'm not ready."

He abruptly stops. "What are you saying?"

"I still have issues and I still don't know if I want to be with you."

"So that was a show you just put on for Lisa?"

I didn't say anything.

"Yasmin, I'm sorry I am, but don't use me to get Lisa mad. I don't know why you talked to her like that anyway. She was concerned."

"Please, it was a desperate attempt to get you. She wants you and she's trying to use this to get you. Yes, we're having problems, but I wasn't going to let that bitch disrespect me."

"But it's ok to use me?"

"No, I apologize, however I still need time. It's a lot. I don't know. One minute I think I can deal, the next minute I can't. I'm not trying to hurt you."

"Well I'm tired of the games, I'll see you later. I have work to do."

"I'm sorry."

"I'm not getting into this here. I see you at home tonight. I'll be home at five."

Shit, he's not going to like what I say. "Actually, I'm meeting with Kevin tonight. I won't be home till late."

He stared at me for a long time. "Bye Yasmin, and shut the door on your way out."

I walked over and attempted to kiss his cheek, but he turned away. Well at least Kim doesn't have to deal with him.

22

Wishful Thinking

Denial is the unrealistic illusion in one's mind. An illusion of hope that the truth will change, a hope we hold onto, despite having all of the facts. Denial is the unwillingness to accept the reality of one's situation, particularly my situation. Each day I wake, praying that my pain will go away. Praying, that today is the day I can let go, open my heart. Yes, each day I live in denial. Knowing that one day I will have to face the truth. Yet, still I choose denial.

Another impediment has arisen. Little Eric is now spending nights over the house. As soon as the door opens, he's yelling for me. Running up to either receive or give kisses, which I give. Kids have this ability to accept anything, but with adults it's just not that easy. I don't have a problem with Eric coming here, but he expects me to stay with him and his daddy. He calls Braxton daddy now, now that hurts a lot, still adjusting to that one. For now, I do what I've been so accustomed to do, run. Usually I go out anywhere, returning when I know Eric is asleep.

To avoid the ongoing issues of my life, I keep myself busy at work. Work has been my solace. Right now a façade, everyone thinks life is perfect. Soon it will be coming to an end. At seven and a half months pregnant. I'm so swollen. I know I'll be on bed rest soon. I still haven't talked to Braxton about what he wanted to do with the rooms, or really bought anything. We need to shop now. His mother wants us to at least do a wish list but, like I said, I talk more to a stranger on the street. Time is not on my side so I need to stop procrastinating. When I walked in the door the phone rang.

"Hello."

"Hey Yasmin."

It was Landon. "Landon, Braxton isn't here. You can try him at the office."

"I want to talk to you."

Landon and I really haven't spoken. I speak when she drops Eric off, but that's it. I don't have anything to say. I do miss my crazy friend. But the bitch slept with my man. Like she said she could have stopped it. Kevin's cool but he's not Landon. Kevin stills speaks with her but has kept his opinion to himself.

"Yeah what's up?"

"Yas, I know you're still upset, which you should be, but I miss my best friend. Can we at least try to talk?"

"I have nothing to say."

"Yas, please."

"Talk about what, Braxton? How was his dick game?"

"Yas. It wasn't like that. I'm really sorry."

"You should be!"

"Yasmin, please."

"What Landon? What do you want to talk about?"

"Anything, how are you feeling?"

Pregnancy was weakening me. "Okay, you?"

"I'm maintaining. How far along are you now?"

"Seven and a half months."

"Almost there. Are you almost ready?"

"Not at all, I still haven't purchased cribs or pampers. I have a lot to do. I'm making a point to go this weekend."

"If you need help, I can help."

Now she was pushing it. "Nah, no thanks, Mommy has me covered."

She was hurt, but she tried to sound like she wasn't. "That'll be fun. Are you nervous about having the babies?"

"Hell yes. I don't know what to expect. I've seen how hard it is trying to get one baby out. Two babies, I don't know if I can do it. I'm going to make sure I have lots of anesthesia."

"I hear that. I'm not going to lie to you, it hurts like hell."

"I was there, but it was all worth it in the end." I said thinking now that it is now a bittersweet memory.

"It was."

My other line beeped.

"Landon someone is on my other line, I have to go."

"Okay, Yas thanks for talking to me. I miss that."

"I have to go," I said, clicking over.

"Hello."

"Mrs. Simms this is Dr. Dey's office calling to remind you of your 10:00 appointment for Saturday. He also has me scheduled for Lamaze class. He wants you to practice breathing for the twin's birth."

"Thanks, for the reminder, I forgot. When is the Lamaze class and how long is it?"

"Your first Lamaze class will be tomorrow at 12:00. It should be 1-2 hours and a total of 4 classes."

I hung up with the receptionist and began preparing dinner. Even though we didn't talk much, I still cooked for both of us. I decided on Chicken Alfredo with a salad.

I was already at the table eating when Braxton came in. "Hey."

"Hey, are you working tomorrow?"

"I was planning on going in for a few hours, why?"

"I forgot I have a doctor's appointment and he wants me to take a Lamaze class tomorrow."

"That'll work, I can go. I wasn't doing anything that needed urgent attention."

"We also need to decide what to do about the twins."

He came over and sat across from me. "What about them?"

Damn he's sexy as hell. He is looking too good. His beard was gone, hair wasn't cut as close. Damn, I just noticed. We really haven't seen each other. I checked to see if he was still wearing his ring. That's right he was. Whoever said pregnancy takes away sexual urges was lying. I wanted to jump on Sugar Daddy right here, right now. It has been too long. Nobody can love me like Braxton. I felt shivers along with tingling of my nipples just thinking about Sugar Daddy. I was getting so wet and felt my legs twitching. Should I just do it, but if I do he'll think we're reconciling. I can't do that. I'm so torn. I just admitted how I miss him. Oh how I miss him holding me, kissing me and...

"Yasmin, what about the twins?"

Halfway in trance, "Where they're going to stay?"

"What do you mean where they're going to stay? They're staying here."

The infamous temper, that's my Braxton.

"Calm down, I meant what room do you want to make a nursery. We have a lot to do and need to do some shopping. Your mother has been ready but I wanted to check with you."

"Yeah, I was thinking the same thing."

"When did you cut your hair?"

"About two weeks ago, I was tired of the hair on the face. Why?"

We really have been avoiding each other. "Just asking. Well, since we have to get up early. I'm going to go to sleep," I said, but was thinking I'm horny as hell and if I don't leave you'll be up in me in thirty seconds.

"See you in the morning."

I tossed and turned the whole night. Between the babies sitting on my bladder and me being horny it was terrible. After my fourth trip to the bathroom, I finally fell asleep.

"Hey Beautiful, wake up."

I opened my eyes and saw Braxton smiling at me. Um, um, um he had to wear a tank. Damn him calling me beautiful, "Hey you."

"It's time to get up we have to be at the doctor's in an hour."

234

"Ugh" I moaned.

"You didn't have a good night?"

"No, I kept going to the bathroom. It's hard to get up in the middle of the night."

"I can sleep on the couch in here tonight if you want. You know, to help you out."

I was weakening. Blame it on the pregnancy..loneliness...okay, just put it on horniness. "No, that's not necessary. This is a big bed, just stay on your side."

He looked at me like are you serious. "Are you sure, Yasmin? I can sleep on the couch."

"You know I wouldn't have asked if I wasn't sure."

"Good, because the guest bed is okay, but I miss my bed."

An hour later we were sitting in the examination room waiting for the doctor.

"How are the expectant parents feeling today?" the doctor asked.

"Everything's fine," I exclaimed.

Well let's see how the babies look today. I'm going to get more pictures to check growth. Your weight is good, so is the pressure, good. Good job, Mr. Simms."

The doctor gave me another 4D ultrasound.

"Oh my God, look Braxton!" I exclaimed.

He put his arm around me and kissed me on the forehead. Smiling, he said, "I see, she's pouting."

"That she is. Her sister must be keeping her up," Dr. Dey commented. He moved over to the other twin who was active. She had a little smile.

"Are they identical?" Braxton asked

"Yup, they sure are. It looks like baby about A is about 3lbs. 4 ozs. and baby B is 4lbs. They're looking very good. Right on target, they are an excellent size for twins."

"I believe it. I have a lot of pressure."

"That's to be expected. Don't try and do too much. Another thing, I'm not saying you can't, but be careful with sex. You may want to consider starting maternity leave."

Sex? We're not having any. I just smiled.

The doctor looked at Braxton. "Well, I want you to continue to look after her. You've been doing an excellent job. Make sure she doesn't do too much. Well I'll see you in one week." He handed us the ultrasounds and a video.

I looked at Braxton who was in awe. "How do you feel? I was in denial, but now I'm anxious nervous and scared. We're not ready. We haven't bought cribs or pampers. It's happening so fast. They're bigger, more developed."

"I know. We're going to get it together. Can't believe we're having two babies"

"I know. But believe me, it feels like it."

"Yasmin, thank you. I know I've put you through some things. I'm happy to be included."

"Braxton, I know we have issues, but no matter what I will never exclude you from our daughters' lives."

He leans over and kisses me. I didn't object, instead I welcomed it. It was sweet and gentle. Damn, I missed these lips.

"Um ummm," Dr. Dey interrupted.

"Excuse us," Braxton apologized.

"That's okay. I forgot to give you your delivery procedures. It's almost that time."

Braxton and I didn't discuss the kiss, we just went straight to Lamaze class. It felt to good having Braxton arms around me. When I felt his breath on my neck, I almost lost it. I don't remember half of what the teacher said. Luckily, they had pamphlets.

We went to lunch and kept it comfortable. We talked about work, TV, anything but us. We finally picked out baby cribs and bedding.

By the time we got home I was exhausted.

"Yasmin, go lay down. I'll bring you up something to eat. You look tired."

"You're not cooking are you?"

"Ha ha. What do you want I'll order something?"

"Just make me a sandwich."

"I got it."

I was tired so I went upstairs to take a shower. I used my Ecstasy fragrance from Carol's daughter's, lit some candles and opened the curtains just so the moonlight can creep in. I've been too lazy to curl my hair, so it was pulled up in a bun. I decided to let it down because the hairpins were killing me. My hair had grown past the middle of my back. I stood in my violet blue baby doll silk nighty that stopped mid-thigh shaking my hair out. I didn't realize Braxton was standing in the doorway staring.

"You were actually fast for once."

"Yeah, I knew you were hungry," he said, looking me up and down.

"My stomach is huge. I know I look crazy."

"No, as always, you are beautiful."

"Thank you."

"Here's your food. While you're eating, I'm going to take a shower."

"You're not hungry."

"I ate something downstairs. Go ahead, eat. I'll clean up after I get out the shower."

By the time I finished eating, Braxton was still in the shower. I lay across the bed and doze off.

"Hey beautiful, get under the covers. It's cold."

"Humph."

I felt Braxton strong arms lifting me up then putting me under the covers. I was awoke now but continued to play sleep. He got behind me cradling his body with mine. My kitty kat was thumping, ready to pounce.

He stroked my hair while whispering "I love you, Beautiful." I don't know if he was trying to wake me up or just enjoying my touch, but he started placing soft kisses on my neck.

I couldn't hold it in. I moaned, "Ummm."

"I didn't mean to wake you up."

"Yes, you did." I said groggily, rolling onto my back.

"I love you, beautiful." He kissed me at first it was gentle kisses on my face, then he started sucking on my lips.

Before I knew it my nipples were exposed and being sucked. "Ummm hmm baby that feels so good." I raked my nails up and down Braxton's back.

He took his hand and began rubbing it up and down my thigh. I opened my legs to let his finger enter me. His thumb gently massaged my clit. I wanted him. I started tugging at his pants.

Braxton got up and quickly pulled his pants down exposing his long Sugar daddy, hot damn. I got up.

"Lay down," I demanded.

He lay on his back. I lean over to kiss him. Since my stomach was huge, I was limited, but I straddle him.

"You know how I like it," he said with anticipation.

I was tired of the foreplay and needed to feel him in me, so I gently eased up so sugar daddy could enter me. My opening was a little tight, so Braxton grabbed my hips, lifted them, and then plunged in. I gasped. It was a mixture of pleasure and pain. He held his dick in me savoring my sweetness. I slowly began to rotate my hips while he glided my hips up and down, making sure I took long gentle strokes.

All I could do is pant. "Hmmm hmm hmm Ahh oh um uuh."

It felt like rockets were shooting through me as he exploded. This feeling was so good. Braxton definitely wasn't done. His dick still hard inside me, made subtle thrusts. My vaginal walls started contracting, tears were rolling down my face, I felt so complete. If only it could stay so sweet. As quick as it started, it ended. After a few more humps, Braxton was shaking, and I was screaming out of pleasure.

I rolled off of him, turning my back to him. He wrapped his arm around me. "Did I hurt you?"

"No."

"Why are you crying then?"

"Because I love you too, I've missed you. It just felt right."

"I feel the same way. I..."

"Shh, I don't want to talk. I just want you to hold me right now."

Braxton and I made love three more times before the morning light. Each time was more intense, more enjoyable than the last. He had to give me a 1000 kisses along with I love you. I took them all and reciprocated. It felt like old times. For the first time in months, I went to sleep with a smile. I felt refreshed, rejuvenated, definitely satisfied.

The ringing phone woke me from a peaceful sleep. According to the clock, it was 1:30 in the afternoon. Braxton's arms were tightly wrapped around me. He had me pinned, barely able to move. Still exhausted from last night, I decided whoever it was could wait. But, they kept calling, forcing me to maneuver out of my comfortable position. Somehow I managed to grab the phone.

"Hello."

"Yas, hey, sorry to wake you, but I need to speak to Braxton."

Back to reality, this is the shit I wasn't feeling or could deal with. Instantly, I regretted last night. Well, for an instance. My kitty was rejoicing.

"Yeah, hold on."

Placing the phone on the night stand, I started shaking Braxton. "Braxton, get up, telephone. Braxton get up."

He stretched, "Hey Beautiful."

He leaned over to kiss me, but I turned my head. "What's wrong?"

"Landon's on the phone for you." I gave him the phone and left him to go to the bathroom.

Can I deal with this? Really, can I? I mean, Chauncey had kids and I dealt with that. Listen to me trying to justify this. Here's that denial again. The truth Yasmin is Chauncey had kids prior to your relationship. You had no history with the kid's mother. This baby mama stuff is with my sister. Unh, unh. Now, Braxton and Landon, who barely said two words to each other before, now because of Eric, are obligated to communicate. I was the link, the mediator to their relationship, now I'm the trespasser, I didn't belong. I jumped in the shower, hoping to cleanse myself of my many uncertainties. Of course it didn't work.

I keep going back. I'm drawn to him. Maybe it is the dick, God knows he's always on point. Yes, it's the dick. The dick will make you look and do stupid things. My dick, my sugar daddy, always so sweet, super-sized, with plenty of stamina guaranteed to please. Why'd he have to share my dick? More importantly, why is Landon such a hoe?

I'm trying to not go off on Landon. I have cut Braxton slack because of the dick, which is wrong. With her it's more difficult. She knew how I felt about my relationship with Braxton, yet she betrays me like that?

Fast forward to the present, how do I explain to my daughters that their cousin is also their brother? I can hear it now, 'Why don't we have the same mommy?' His mommy is Aunt Landon. It's like telling them to accept that men cheat, even daddy, and it's okay. I can't accept this shit. It's not supposed to be that way. No matter how you look at it or say it, the shit is crazy. I don't want to repeat this cycle. I got out of the shower more confused.

I went in the bedroom in my robe and saw that he was fully dressed. "Yasmin, I need to talk to you."

I sat on the bed bracing myself for the drama. "What's up?"

"Landon said she needs to go away for a while. She wants me to keep Eric. I suggested her parents. I would get him every weekend, but she says she's not dealing with them right now."

"I understand. You need to take care of your son. That's fine. How long will Landon be gone?" I said ready to cry.

"She doesn't know. She says she needs to get away."

"Alright, cool where is he going to sleep?" Normally he sleeps with Braxton in the guest room. Leave it to Landon's selfish ass to create more chaos in my world.

"I haven't thought about it. I wasn't expecting this."

I started rambling, "Well I think you need to go get him a bed. For now, it looks like you're back in the guest room. You also need to figure out which bedroom to put him in. You have to decorate his room. Go get him and I'll cook something."

He walked over. "Yasmin, I know this is not easy for you. Thank you. I appreciate it." He kissed me on the cheek.

After he left, I baked chicken, made macaroni and cheese, string beans and candied yams. I left Braxton a note saying I'd be back before heading to the store. I went on and picked out a bedroom set, toys along with other accessories, it was going to be delivered the next day. It was still early, 5:30 and I wasn't ready to go home just yet, so I ended up at Kevin's.

"Hey, Mrs. Y.E.S., Braxton let you out to hang out with me?" He teased.

"No, I ran away again."

"Tell me you're lying."

I had to laugh. "I am just stressed with the situation. Eric is staying at the house indefinitely. Landon says she needs a break. Apparently, she has issues."

"Yeah, she hasn't been herself."

"Well I have issues too."

"Yas, I know you do."

"Every time I think I can deal, I get a reality check."

I told him everything that transpired between me and Braxton.

"Pretty lady, I don't envy you."

"Thanks Kevin. You words of encouragement are inspiring," I said, sarcastically.

He laughed. "I don't mean to make you feel bad it's just a complicated situation."

"I know, I'm living it."

"Seriously, Landon is sorry. She's been depressed, tense, reserved, just not Landon."

"What do you think, she should be happy she fucked my man and had a baby by him? You can really be an ass. You don't know what to say out your mouth. I was hurt too. Do you remember me crying on your shoulder?"

"Hold up. I'm not trying to ignore your feelings. I was just saying she is definitely sorry, but it seems like it's more than that. I think she has a lot of issues concerning her breakup with Eric. She's isolating herself from me and her parents. You two were so close I know she needs you."

"Here we go with what Landon needs am I just supposed to forget what happened and go to Landon's rescue. If I wasn't pregnant, I wouldn't have come back. Instead, I would have left both of them alone. I was cordial when I talked to her a few days ago. Eric is staying at my house. I have to put on a brave front and I deal with it. I've been too fucking nice. So take your opinion and put it back there." I slapped my ass.

"Calm down, I'm not trying to have you go into labor in my house. You look like you're going to pop."

"Fuck you, Kevin"

"You already did. You want more don't you?"

I had to laugh. "That's another thing, she told Braxton my business. She was really being a bitch. He definitely did not need to know that. She knows how jealous and territorial Braxton is with me."

He was laughing now. "Your hubby really can't stand me now. He be giving me that look. I'm surprised he hasn't sent a search party out for you."

„„My cell phone rang on cue, it of course is Braxton. "You jinxed me." Still laughing I answered. "Hey."

"Beautiful, I haven't heard from you. I was making sure you were okay."

Kevin was making funny gestures demonstrating how Braxton has me on lockdown.

I couldn't hold it in and laughed. "I'm fine."

"Where are you? Sounds like you're having a good time?"

"Hanging out with Kevin"

"Are you coming home soon?" I could tell Braxton was getting irritated. It just made me laugh more. It didn't help that Kevin was still joking me.

"Um, I probably will be a while. What time is it?"

"Six. How long is a while?"

"I'm not sure two, three hours."

I could hear his nostrils flaring. He was pissed.

Kevin brought me some orange juice and had cooked Pepper Steak and rice. Unlike Braxton, Kevin was a real good cook. He has skills.

"Thanks Kevin, hold on Braxton. Can you get me some food too? My babies are hungry."

"Yasmin, I am not your servant."

"Well help me up. How are you going to cook and not bring me any? You know I only like your pepper steak."

"Yasmin!" I heard Braxton call out.

Kevin starting laughing at me, making more gestures that caused me to laugh.

"Yes," I realized it sounded bad, but Kevin had me beat in the kitchen. This was a rare treat.

"If you're hungry, then you need to come home. Did you cook?"

"No, I don't want that anymore."

"Don't you think you need to come home to get some sleep?"

243

"No, but if I get sleepy I'll stay here, alright?"

"No, not alright."

"Well, I don't know what to tell you."

"Don't tell me anything, just come home."

"I will, later." I hung up on Braxton.

"Braxton didn't flip?" he teased.

"Shut up, Kevin. Did he have a bad temper in high school?"

"Actually no, he was laid back. I told you he always had the female groupies. He never was serious about any of them, always nonchalant. That's why I didn't want you dating him. I didn't want you to get hurt."

"So basically, you told me so. You knew this would happen. They say good girls like bad boys."

"That's true. However, truthfully, I see the way Braxton looks at you. Without question, he loves you. It's genuine, the real thing. You've changed him. You have that man all riled up out of character acting like a crazy man."

"What is this, get Yasmin to forget about what happened between Braxton and Landon?"

"No, I just know both of them are sorry. I know it's hard for you. You're holding up real good, especially since you're pregnant. I will admit, if I was in your predicament I wouldn't be handling it as well. Just don't make any rash decisions about Landon or Braxton."

"Ok, Dr. Kevin."

"Well, since I'm a doctor now that'll be $500 for this consultation."

I stayed at Kevin's for a couple hours. It wasn't intentional, but I didn't get home until almost eleven. I already decided I wasn't working tomorrow. I was ready for my bed. When I walked in I was greeted with the sounds of Booney James. Braxton was sitting in the chair waiting on me.

"Hey," he said calmly.

"Hey."

"What are you still doing up?"

"Couldn't sleep."

"Where's Eric?" I asked, taking a seat across from him.

"He's sleep. I put him in our bed."

This was not going to work. Eric sleeps wild and Braxton hogs the bed. *Great! Now I have to sleep in the uncomfortable bed*, I thought. Damn.

"Okay, well I'm going to go sleep in the guest room. I'm not working tomorrow so don't wake me."

"Yasmin, what's going on with you and Kevin?"

"What are you talking about?" I stood up ready to ignore him.

He was irritable now. "You know what I'm talking about. You hang out with him all day now you're coming in late. When I called you earlier, you ignored me. Now you telling me you're sleeping in the guest room. Are you still fucking him?"

"What! Are you fucking serious?" I said as a statement rather than a question.

"Well."

"Don't be making accusations about me because of your guilty conscience. Are you still fucking Landon? When you picked up Eric, did you hook up for old time's sake?"

"Hell no. I told you I don't want her. I want you."

"I said the same thing about Kevin yet you still choose not to believe me. You're the one with a child. Also, I did not hang out with Kevin all day. I have been tolerant with this situation. Very tolerant, I cooked dinner for YOUR son. I purchased a bedroom for YOUR son. I'm giving up my bed for YOUR son with my best friend slash sister. Don't question my loyalty. I've always been up front with you about Kevin. I went to his house afterwards because I needed a friend. That's what he is. I am overwhelmed with the drama you and Landon put me through."

"Well, as your husband, I don't feel comfortable with your relationship. I don't want you at his house." He was now in my face looking me in the eye.

"Braxton you better get out of my face. Remember husband for the moment. You have no authority over me. Who I choose to spend time with is my business. Remember you're the one that can't be trusted."

"I apologize again shit. I don't want Landon she doesn't want me. That was just stupidity. We just deal with each other because of Eric."

"Well if that's the case then you should understand then. I don't want Kevin he doesn't want me. We're just friends."

"I don't want to hear that shit. It's not the same. Kevin has feelings for you. He's always had feelings and has been attracted to you. I see the way he looks at you."

"Kevin is with Nicole. There is no romantic chemistry with Kevin, we figured that out a long time ago when we were both single."

"Tell you what, I'll deal with Kevin, you deal with Landon. If you had a baby with him, I would have accepted the baby. Why can't you do that?"

"Don't try to compare what went down with Landon to me and Kevin. You and I were not together. I never lied about our relationship. I used protection. You on the other hand had a son with her and I do accept Eric. I don't accept what you did."

"But you didn't tell me when we first got back together. Why, because you knew I couldn't take it and would be hurt. That's why I couldn't tell you. I didn't even know I had a son until a couple of days before you found out."

"Whatever."

"What about last night? You said it, we felt right. "

"I was horny. You heard of friends with benefits."

"That's bullshit! You know you don't even get down that way. That's not your style. You don't just have sex with anyone."

"I had sex with you the first night."

"That was different because you and I have a connection. We synch."

"Tell me anything."

"You know it's the truth. That night we met, I thought, *damn she's sexy, beautiful.* At first, I admit, I thought I'd just do the sex thing with you, but we danced and I felt something. I wanted to have sex with you, but I wanted more too," he explained. "I was caught off guard. I never had that feeling with anyone. I thought, nah, no I can't mess with you. You'll have my bachelor lifestyle all messed up. That's why I didn't get your number. I regretted it later though. Lucky for me, I saw you at work. When we went out that night, I was jealous. I never got jealous. I got tired of women, but you were different. I didn't want anyone looking or touching. When we did have sex, um, you handled it. I'm stubborn, so I didn't commit then because I thought it was infatuation, but I finally admitted it was more. You are more. I keep telling you that, you're all I want. You're my best friend, my better half, my life. I've wasted too much time without you being stubborn. I'm not letting you go. You and me, this is it. I'm in it until death. You'll really have a stalker."

"I feel you. I do love you. I never denied that. As far as me and Kevin, he's not a threat. We both were vulnerable, believe me, afterwards it was terrible. He realized I was in love with you and he would never have my heart. It's just too difficult to accept what happened with Landon. She gave you what I couldn't, I can't, a son, a first born." Tears began to roll down my face.

"Waaaa waa, I want mommy," Eric cried coming down the steps.

Braxton went to pick up his son. "Shh. don't cry man. I got you."

"I want my mommy," he started crying more.

I cried more. This is torture. Braxton was trying to calm Eric down, but it wasn't working. I wiped my tears and grabbed Eric. "Is that my baby making that noise?"

He smiled and gave me a sloppy kiss. "Mimi."

"That's my baby," I said, smiling back at him. "You want me to hold you and give you kisseys."

He started laughing.

"Let's go to bed, big boy."

When we got upstairs Eric wouldn't leave my side. He wanted me to sleep with him and his daddy. I ended up in my bed with both of them. Eric fell asleep in ten minutes clutching my hand.

"Yasmin, I appreciate everything you've done and are doing. I want us..."

I cut him off. "Braxton I'm tired of talking about us. The facts are the facts. I'm going to sleep."

"I know you're tired but we need to finish this conversation."

"I know, but I'm tired of talking. Let me think, meditate, it's a lot."

"Alright, Yasmin, but we will talk."

"I said okay. I'm pregnant with twins, big twins. I'm exhausted."

23

Love at First Sight

Little Eric stayed with us for two weeks. That was a difficult period. I'd picked up Eric a few times for Landon from daycare. Over time I became acquainted with some of the staff. They knew my husband is Braxton. Meaning since Eric now calls Braxton daddy it doesn't take a scientist to figure out the deal. I wasn't fine with that. During Eric's stay, Landon never called to speak to him. Eric however asked for her all day. I was going to say something to her, but when I saw her she looked lost. I wanted to reach out, but I didn't. Landon had the nerve to call me three days ago asking to be in the delivery room. I told her I would get back to her, but if I was her I wouldn't hold my breath.

As far as Braxton and me, I still haven't had the "us" talk. It's been some weeks and I'm still not sure what to do. I've been avoiding him in any way possible. Usually when he tried to talk, I would seduce him. Of course he couldn't turn it down. Believe me, we made up for lost time, most days, 2-3 times. With me making quite a few trips to his office, which I must say, was some of the best loving. Anyway, afterwards I would play sleep. He started to catch on, so I stayed out a little longer. I would also get him by talking about the nursery, which we just finished last week. The nursery was decorated in pink, mint green, and lavender with white Bellini canopy cribs. Definitely, no expense was spared by Nana and Daddy. They are two princesses and the room must reflect that. My daughters are going to be spoiled rotten. I was ready, finally going on maternity leave two weeks ago. Braxton had me checking in every hour, even though the doctor decided he would induce me in two weeks. For this last week, I've been taking advantage of the peace and quiet.

Braxton's birthday is tomorrow and Mommy wants to do a family dinner. I was kind of looking forward to it. I missed hanging with the family, plus, I knew Uncle Charles would keep me entertained.

I was bored…okay horny, so I decided to surprise him and take him to a pre-birthday lunch. I waddled into BET with my huge belly, but I still looked sexy from behind. From the back, you actually couldn't tell I was pregnant. I had a bigger ass, my legs still looked good. The front was all belly. I gained twenty-five pounds, but that was mostly stomach. I wore my hair out so my face wasn't as fat. My breasts were huge. I wore a baby doll dress with flat slides. Overall, I was still fly, in my opinion, to be pregnant.

It came as no surprise when I reached Braxton's office Lisa is there. I'm pissed, I see Braxton sitting in his chair facing Lisa. Lisa was leaning against his desk twirling her weave. They don't see me. I spend a few minutes eavesdropping.

"So birthday boy, what do have planned?"

"Hanging with the family, my mother is doing this big dinner."

"Is that so. Afterwards?"

"Nothing."

"You're not hanging with the fellas?"

"Nope."

"Brax, you're getting old. I guess you don't have it like you use to."

This bitch is not going to be satisfied until I slap her.

He chuckled, "No, I'm better."

"Really," She cooed.

Braxton looks up, sees me, and smiles.

"Hello, Beautiful," he says as he stands up and walks over to me.

"Hey, baby. Hi, Lisa," I said flatly.

"Yasmin," Lisa greets, looking annoyed. I laugh to myself.

Braxton wastes no time, coming up behind me and pulling me into an embrace. He kisses me on my neck and places his hands on my belly.

"Yasmin, you've gotten so big," she snickers.

"And I still look good." I say matter-of-factly.

"Yes, you do." Braxton agrees kissing my neck again.

Damn, he knows that's my spot.

"We'll see what it's like after those babies come. Some women never get their figure back after one. You're having two," she retorted.

"Well, I'm not some women. I'm Yasmin. I was sexy and beautiful before. I am sexy, beautiful now and will be after."

She laughs, "Like I said, we'll see."

"Yes, like I said, the figure will be on point. Unfortunately for you, you don't have any kids. You already have an awkward shape. I'd hate to see you pregnant."

Before any more words could be exchanged, Braxton intervened.

"Lisa didn't you say you have a meeting at one?"

She stood there giving me the, 'I can't stand your ass' look. The feeling was mutual. I gave it right back to her back and dared her to say something.

"Lisa you better get a move on it," I said to annoy her.

She hesitated, "Braxton, I'll talk to you later. Yasmin bye." She got to the door and turned to face Braxton.

"Braxton, in case I don't see you before you leave, I hope you're able to enjoy your birthday. Let me be the first to say Happy Birthday."

I had to roll my eyes, before I slipped in, "Oh, he definitely will," then I turned slightly to kiss him.

"Thanks Lisa, have a good one."

I moved from Braxton's embrace and closed the door as soon as she reaches the threshold.

Braxton shakes his head, "I don't know why you two can't get along."

"Because she's a conniving, phony ass bitch," I replied coolly.

"Lisa is not that bad."

He takes a seat at his desk.

"I can't tell."

"Yasmin."

I walk over to where he's sitting.

"Yasmin, nothing. Every time I come here she's in your face waiting on an opportunity to jump on your dick."

"For someone who doesn't want me, you're very concerned about who wants to jump on my dick."

"Braxton don't fuck with me."

"But I love fucking with you and you love fucking with me," he says pulling me into his lap.

"I'm not talking about us today. I'm tired of seeing that trick in your face."

"We work together, of course I'm going to see her."

"Braxton you and I both know that bitch wants you."

"I have no interest in Lisa."

"Really?"

"Yasmin, I don't care who wants me. I'm committed to you. There's no other woman I ever wanted but you. That's why you are my wife. My love for you never changed. I know you are still trying to figure out what you want. Yasmin, I know it hurts, but let go. Let me love you. I swear to you, I promise you, I will not hurt you."

"Braxton, I…" I didn't know what to say.

"Alright, Beautiful, no pressure, I know you love me. After my babies are born, we'll work it out. You and I till the end. Come on, Beautiful let me take you out for lunch."

Braxton and I had lunch at Dave and Buster's. Since I was limited I didn't partake in many activities. We had fun, staying for some hours and ended up eating again. Braxton was tired after that so we went home around six. I, on the other hand was restless. I felt like I could clean the whole house and I did while he slept. I was horny, so I jumped on Braxton. It didn't take much, Sugar Daddy was ready. I rode Sugar Daddy long and hard to the next day, so many orgasms.

Braxton was knocked out, but I still couldn't sleep. I finally fell asleep after one, but not for long.

My back started bothering me and I had to pee. I guess I worked it too much. After I used the bathroom and tried to lie down it was after 3a.m. and my back was getting worse. I knew it was labor. I just wasn't sure if this was false labor or the real thing. I went to the bathroom and saw I had a bloody show. When I stood up, I felt a little water trickling down my leg.

I felt icky so I jumped in the shower. So far, I had a little pain. I called Braxton's mother while I was in the bathroom and told her what was going on. She was ready. I had to calm her down. She was so excited she started to cry. After her crying spell, she said she'd meet us at the hospital.

"Braxton."

"Humph."

"Braxton."

"Braxton."

"Hunh, Beautiful, I'm tired. I'll give you some in the morning."

"Get up, Mr. Cocky. My water broke. We have to go."

It took a minute to register, but he jumped up. "Are you Okay? How do you feel?"

"I'm fine, go jump in the shower. I'll be waiting downstairs. Don't take too long."

As soon as I went downstairs, I was overwhelmed with anxiety. *"Oh my God. Am I ready? I'm scared. I can't do it. Two babies?"*

"Beautiful, you okay?" Braxton came running down the stairs.

"I'm scared."

He gave me a hug and kissed me on the cheek. "You'll be fine. I'll be there. In a couple of hours, we'll have two little girls."

By the time we got to the hospital, Braxton's mother and father were there. I was crying like a baby. "Are you in a lot of pain?" Mr. Jeff asked

"No."

Ms. Beverly walked over "It's alright. You don't have to cry. Everything is going to be alright."

Lucky for me, two family members were on staff, so my labor room was ready.

The nurse checked me and said I was 3 - 4 centimeters dilated.

By the time my doctor got there, it was six in the morning.

"How is everyone today? The babies couldn't wait I see. Are we ready for the main event?" he chuckled.

"Yes, we are," Braxton said, his mother and father agreed.

"Everyone except for me, can I get some drugs. I want to be knocked out. I've seen the video. Pushing out one is enough. I don't know if I can do two."

Everyone laughed like I was a comedian.

"I'm serious."

"Yasmin, you can do this. You don't need anesthesia yet. You can slow down the labor process." Dr. Dey said matter-of-factly.

They hooked me up to monitors to watch the babies' heartbeat. Dr. Dey did an ultrasound to see if the babies were head down. Unfortunately, only one baby was head down. The doctor completely broke my water in hopes of bringing one baby down and getting the other one to turn. A half hour later, I started feeling pain.

"I need to walk around? It's getting uncomfortable laying here."

"I think you should lie down and practice your breathing. One of the twins seems to have moved further in the birth canal. I need to monitor your pressure," the doctor advised.

"I don't need you to think, I'm getting up." I snapped, reaching for Braxton.   "Help me up, please."

"Yasmin, lay down, relax," Braxton ordered.

I ignored him, using the rails to get up. Braxton finally decides to help. We walked around for about thirty minutes. That's when I felt a sharp pain shoot from my back to my stomach. It felt like the babies were going to fall out. The pressure was terrible.

"Oowee!" I cried, grabbing Braxton to avoid falling.

"Come on, Beautiful, you're going to lie down."

It felt like the babies were going to fall out. I had so much pressure. "Call the doctor. I feel a lot of pressure." Braxton and his father helped me to the bed.

"Do you want to call Lawrence, Yasmin?" Ms. Beverly asked.

"Yeah, I think it'll be soon." I respond feeling some cramps.

Ms. Beverly called Lawrence along with the rest of the Simms family.

When the doctor came back in at 8 a.m., I knew he was going to set up for delivery. Now, I was getting anxious. The pain was annoying at this point.

"Yasmin, you're progressing a little. You're about 4-5 centimeters, almost halfway there."

I whimpered. "It's starting to hurt. I'm ready for medicine."

"OK. That's fine. I'm going to give you a little Pitocin to help speed up your delivery. Your pressure is elevating."

The anesthesiologist came in looking young and inexperienced.

"Mr. Jeff is he old enough? I hope this isn't a teaching session."

The doctor looked offended, but I was in pain.

He laughed. "Yes sweetheart, he's experienced. You're in capable hands."

After I was administered the Pitocin and anesthesia, I was comfortable again.

"Sweetheart, get some rest. We're going to get some coffee. You need as much sleep as possible," Mr. Jeff suggested.

"Ok, can I please have some juice? My throat is dry."

"Nope, you know the deal," the doctor in Mr. Jeff spoke.

"Braxton, you want anything?" his mother asked.

"Baby, go ahead and eat something. I'll be okay. I'm going to try to sleep."

"I don't want to leave you," he grabbed my hand.

"I'll be fine. I can't go anywhere." I joked.

"Alright, Beautiful," he said, kissing me on my lips.

After they left, I left a message for Kevin to let him know. I figured Kevin would spread the word to Landon. I'm still on the fence about her being here. Closing my eyes, I drifted off to sleep, but sleep didn't last because the nurses kept coming into checking my contractions, not to mention the contractions became stronger. The anesthesia was wearing off. I was feeling more pressure and started to moan.

"Hey Beautiful, how are you feeling?" Braxton said coming into the room.

"Pressure."

"That's to be expected." Mr. Jeff walked over. He looked at the monitor.

"I told you that boy didn't know what he was doing. Get a kit and give me more meds."

The doctor checked me again at 10:30 a.m., I was at six centimeters, not much change.

"Practice your breathing."

"Hey," Landon said walking in. "Thanks for calling, Braxton."

I looked at Braxton. My look let him know I didn't appreciate him calling her. Everyone got that from my stare. Braxton tried to kiss me. "Get the hell off me. Can I breathe? Damn. Move!" I yelled.

Landon walked over and sat on the opposite side of me. "You're looking good. How far along are you?"

"Only six."

"That's okay, you'll be there soon. You're still fly though, but not like the diva."

I had to laugh. I missed joking with Landon.

"You need some color to brighten up this room. Open these curtains, you need some sun."

Kevin came in. "Hello, hello, you have a full house up in here, Mrs. Y.E.S." he came over and gave me a hug, then Landon.

Everyone said hello, but Braxton of course.

"Hey Kev," Landon smiled.

"I thought you would have had the babies by now. You know I don't do the labor thing."

"I know. You left me last time with Landon."

"I wasn't that bad."

Kevin and I laughed. He told the stories of how Landon had us running around. Again everyone got a laugh but Braxton.

"Kevin you missed it though. Yas did a diva move. First of all, I had to call her, I was trying to talk. She assumed I was messing with her. She was on her date with Chauncey. She kept hanging up and had the nerve to send my calls to voicemail. I had to get Eric to track Chauncey down. So she gets there and it's obvious I interrupted her plans. Anyways, she had to cuss the receptionist out because she was star struck with Chauncey and Eric. She had my back threatening a couple of them and had the chief of staff on standby."

Landon just didn't know what to say out her mouth. She needed to shutup. She tells my dirt, but this bitch good at keeping her own secrets. Sad, but true, I really missed hanging with Landon. As I was laughing, I felt a contraction. I grabbed the side of the bed. "Aww!"

"Breathe Beautiful, remember the Lamaze."

"It hurts, oh my God. I knew that guy didn't know how to give an epidural. I need some drugs. Mr. Jeff, daddy can you hook your daughter up."

"Sorry, sweetheart, I'm not working today. I'm a grandfather today, but I'll get the doctor to come back."

"Well call someone." I snapped.

I did get more anesthesia but the contractions were still kicking my butt. It was 3 o'clock when the Doctor came in. I was only seven centimeters. The pain was worse. I couldn't handle the pressure I was shaking a little. Everyone tried to get me to calm down, but I was hurting. These babies were kicking my ass.

Lawrence was there and I had to admit it felt good to have him there, but I had other pressing issues. I was irritable. Landon was not helping with her rambling. I was tolerating her, but I was two seconds from cussing her ass out.

"Yassy, it gets better. Remember how I was with Eric? It'll be all worth it in the end. Remember how you and Eric were fighting over him? You can do it. You're going to have two little girls. Eric is going to have two little sisters. He's so excited."

That's it, I know she meant well, but I was not trying to go there.

"Landon, get out."

Everyone got quiet.

"Look, I'm not trying to go there. I'm in pain. I don't feel like thinking how my life is a Maury episode."

"Yassy, I didn't mean to upset you. I'll be quiet."

"Not now Landon, just leave."

"Yassy…"

"Landon leave," Braxton ordered.

Landon is visibly upset, but left.

Kevin came over. "Yasmin, I know she upset you, but she didn't mean it. You know Landon, she speaks before she thinks. She's really sorry."

"I know but I can't deal with that right now. I'm trying to stay positive."

"Yasmin I'm…" Kevin started.

"Damn man, didn't you hear she doesn't feel like being bothered. Why are you still in her face?" Braxton barked.

"Look Braxton, I know you have a lot of issues with me, but you're not going to disrespect me." Kevin said, sternly.

"Disrespect you. You've been disrespecting me. You can get the hell out. You're not needed. This is mine! My wife, my kids! " Braxton yelled, touching me.

"Shut the hell up!" I snapped. "I'm in labor, I don't have time to deal with this. I want everyone out. Braxton, you out now, it's yours and Landon's fault. You invited her. You both were selfish lying asses and now we're in this situation, so deal with it. Get away from me right now. I need some quiet. Kevin, you stay," I ordered.

"Hold the fuck up! I know you're not kicking me out and he's staying? Hell no! Now you want me out. You weren't saying that shit last night. It was all about me. You were loving me, couldn't get enough. That's why we're in here now."

I grabbed a cup off the dresser beside me and threw it at him. "Just get the hell out!"

"Come on, son, let her calm down. It's not good for the babies. Remember, we want two healthy babies. Don't upset her," Mr. Jeff coaxed Braxton.

As soon as he left, I broke down.

"Oh, Mrs. Y.E.S. don't start the crying thing. You know I don't do the crying thing." He came over and gave me a hug.

I punched him. I felt a contraction which caused me to grab his shirt and I ripped two buttons off.

"You know you owe me a shirt. Crying on it, now you're ripping it apart. You want me that bad," he joked.

"You shouldn't buy cheap shirts. Want you? I can't want anything I've already had."

"That's Mrs. Yes, always with a smart comeback. I have something for you."

"What?" I said feeling another contraction.

He pulled out my iPod. "You left this at my house. I know you love Jill, so I hooked you up with her songs along with some of your other favorites like Floetry and Amel Larrieux.

"Thank you, Kevin. You always know how to make me feel better," I smile.

"De nada. Listen to Jill and relax. I need to check on Landon. I'll get your crazy husband too."

"Kevin, give me a few minutes. Landon can come back, but she has to be quiet."

Kevin laughed. "You know I can't control that mouth."

Braxton along with his parents came in twenty minutes later. "Braxton don't speak, just sit down and we'll be fine."

"Braxton, listen," his mother warned. "Sweetie, how are the contractions?"

"Worse."

She paged the doctor. He checked, I was at nine centimeters. It seems like I was stuck at nine forever. They checked every half-an-hour, but still no change. Braxton's family tried to keep me calm, but labor is a bitch. Somewhere between contractions, Kevin and Landon came in. Braxton was still upset, but I didn't care. The anesthesia had worn off. I was feeling everything. The Pitocin was making things worse. One of the babies was struggling with the contractions. They stopped the Pitocin and gave me oxygen. After the oxygen, I became hysterical, screaming and shaking.

"Oww it hurts! I can't do this! Just cut me!"

Braxton held my hand through each contraction and tried to coach me. "I know, Beautiful, but breathe. It's almost over. Calm down."

I grabbed Braxton by the collar. "I can't! It hurts! I can't do it. I'm tired. I have a lot of pressure! It hurts! I need to push! AHHHHHHHH OWWWW HELP! I HAVE TO PUSH! OH MY GOD IT HURTS!" I cried.

Mr. & Mrs. Simms were rubbing my shoulder trying to calm me, but that was more irritating.

"Breathe, Beautiful, you can do this," Braxton coached.

The shaking was getting worse, the pain was excruciating. Braxton sat in bed next to me. He wrapped his arms around me. My head was on his shoulder. I just kept rocking back and forth. "OOH it hurts! UGHH!" I cried grabbing his arm. I knew I took some skin, but he didn't complain. He held me.

When the doctor came in I prayed it was time. Kevin and Landon left the room.

"Yasmin, you're 9 ½ centimeters, just a little cervix left. I want you to give me a little push. I want to see if we can get rid of the rest of your cervix. I want to take your arms and wrap them around your legs. When you feel a contraction, pull your legs back, put your chin on your chest, and push. Braxton hold her leg and push it back as she pushes." Braxton stood in position. The doctor looked at the monitor. "Here comes another contraction. On the count of three I want you to take a deep breath, hold it, and push.1, 2, 3."

I did what the doctor said. I pushed for twenty minutes and still nothing. I was exhausted. I felt dizzy. "I can't do this. I feel sick. I need to throw up!"

The nurse made it just in time before I threw up in the pan. "I can't do this."

"Yasmin, yes you can," Braxton said, kissing me on the forehead.

"Yasmin, I want you to push on the count of three."

I pushed again. On the third push I felt the baby's head pop out. "AHHH!"

"Yasmin, the head is out!" Braxton was yelling.

The pain was worse, burning. My body automatically, began to push.

"Hold it. I have to suction the baby out."

"You need to hurry up. I can't." I cried.

"Ok, on three," the doctor said.

On one I pushed again, I could feel the doctor pulling the baby out. The pain was real intense, but felt better once she was out.

"Waaaa! Waaaa!" The baby cried.

"Braxton, would you like to cut the cord?"

Braxton cut the cord smiling ear to ear with tears in his eyes.

"She's beautiful," Ms Beverly cried.

"Yes, she is." Mr. Jeff agreed.

The doctor held her up, but I was still in a daze I couldn't see one feature. The nurse took the baby to wrap her up. Everyone rushed over to the baby. They forgot about me. Everyone was excited. Mr. Jeff had the video camera taping and Ms. Beverly had the camera flashing.

Just when I thought I could relax, catch my breath I felt a sharp pain. "OOOOOOOOOOOOOOO!! AHHHHHHHHHHH!!"

Braxton rushed back over.

The doctor did a quick ultrasound. Baby B turned in the head down position. "Yasmin, we need you to push again."

I shook my head no, but when I felt that contraction, I did. "GET HER OUT! GET HER OUT!" On the eighth push, I heard my other daughter cry, then I collapsed on the bed.

Braxton was smiling as if he did the hard work. "I love you so much, thank you, thank you. They're beautiful. Thank you for my baby girls. I love you," he said kissing me all over. Seconds later, he and his parents were tending to the twins.

They took the other baby wrapped her up and cleaned her. I lie there still shaking and trying to catch my breath. I started feeling little cramps.

"Dr. Dey I need some drugs. My stomach still hurts."

"Okay, first are you ready for baby number three?"

The room was silent. I went off.

"Three! No three!. I saw two!

"Just a little joke," he chuckled.

"No one's laughing. You're a doctor not a comedian."

I hurt his feelings, but I didn't care. Childbirth was a bitch.

By now, Braxton came over to rejoin me. Two nurses followed, each holding a baby.

"They want to meet mommy and daddy," the first nurse said while handing me a baby. "This is baby A. She was born at 7:03 p.m. weighing 7lbs. 7 ozs." I look into her face the pain was worth it. She looked like Braxton's mother but with those grey eyes.

"This is baby B. She made her entrance at 7:11 p.m. weighing 7 lbs.," the second nurse said giving the baby to Braxton.

They were identical.

"They're both gorgeous," the nurse commented. "Do you have names?"

"Not yet."

The babies stayed with us briefly before going back for tests. When they returned, the battle of who gets to hold the babies began. Lawrence and Jackie stuck around giving Braxton and I congrats along with gifts for the girls. I could tell he was remorseful when he held both of the girls. Landon and Kevin gave congrats and left. Braxton was so happy he gave Kevin a hand shake and apologized for earlier. Braxton's mother couldn't stop crying. She was already showing off pictures of her granddaughters, inviting staff along with the Simms clan in. Finally, hours later, around ten, my many visitors had left with the exceptions of my in-laws.

Mommy held baby A while Mr. Jeff held baby B.

"They are so beautiful."

"They look like you." I commented.

"They do, don't they? They are my little angels. Nana is going to spoil both of you," she cried.

Mr. Jeff and I looked at each other like, "Uh oh."

"Bev, Yasmin, needs some rest. Let's go home."

She wasn't trying to hear that and stayed at least another hour. I was tired, but didn't mind. Mr. Jeff was finally able to get her to go home, but she said she'd be back early the next morning. Now it was just me and him. Braxton was holding one baby and I had the other.

"I can't believe we have two daughters."

"Who'd have thought when we met five years ago we'd end up here."

"I know so much has happened. Can you handle two girls?" I joked.

"I'm going to try. Right now, I'm cool. The dating part I'm not going to handle so well. They will be monitored."

"I think they're going to have you wrapped around their fingers. If they can't get there way with you then they'll go to Nana. She'll break you down."

He laughed, "That's the truth. You know my mother is home packing now. She's moving in temporarily. She finally has girls. I hope she doesn't drive me crazy."

"Well good, we're going to need the help." I looked at the clock and saw it was 11:45 p.m. "I almost forgot to tell you. Happy Birthday, I see you're in love with your presents."

"Thank you. You've giving me so much, daughters on my birthday. They're definitely the best gifts I'll ever get," he kissed me gently on my lips.

"Well they'll be the only presents you'll ever get from me from now on," I joked.

"I definitely have the world's greatest gifts. I have something for you though." He reaches in his pocket and retrieves a small package.

"When did you do this?" I say opening the package. Inside is a platinum and diamond heart pendant.

I told you, you had my heart. You've taken a lot of shit from me that you didn't deserve. I know no amount of gifts or I'm sorry's will take away the things I've done, but I just want you know I do love you. Every time you look at this I just want you to know my love is real and remember our love.

"I love you, Braxton."

"I love you."

"Now we need to name our daughters."

We decided to incorporate Bryan's name, Baby A, would be Khouri Bryalle Simms. Baby B, Reagan Brya Simms.

24

If I Have My Way

"Good morning, Beautiful," Braxton said to me as I walked out of the bathroom.

"Hey, you," I said getting on the bed.

Braxton laid his big head on my swollen breast causing me to flinch.

"I'm sorry, I forgot," he said, kissing my chest, then lips. He sat up grabbing me in his embrace, "How are you feeling?"

"Tired, your daughters are milking me dry."

"I know it. My mother should be bringing my babies in soon."

"I'm getting ready now. I'm so glad she's here, those midnight, and three o'clock feedings are a trip."

"Yeah, they are."

I gave him a nudge, "Like you would know, all I hear from you are snores."

Braxton starts to tickle me. He flips me over and is now on top of me gnawing on my neck.

"Watch the breasts, boy."

"I keep telling you I'm not a boy, that's why we have twins."

"You are so cocky."

"That's right." He leans down and kisses me.

I kiss him back. We lay there kissing, cuddling, as we stare at one another. It feels good being in his embrace. I can feel his love for me in his touch, see it in his eyes. I want badly to let go completely, love him and live. He kisses me again, and like I've been doing each day, I let go a little more, allowing him to love me, and it feels so good. It feels so right. We kiss until there's a knock on the door and mommy enters.

"Good Morning."

"Good morning," I said trying to get from under Braxton's body. Braxton got up, allowing me to sit up in the bed.

She walks over with one of the twins laughing. "It's been a while since I had one." She said nodding to Braxton, "But I'm pretty sure you're supposed to wait six weeks," she laughs.

"Hey, daddy's princess," Braxton said, ignoring mommy and grabbing the baby.

The baby pacifier fell out her mouth and she started to cry. She turns her head to let me know she's ready for me to nurse her. Braxton isn't handing her over fast enough and she gets frustrated.

"This is definitely Khouri."

Mommy and I laughed, the two of us could tell the babies apart almost immediately, but Braxton still had difficulty. He was right about 99% of the time, which is good because no one else could. We dressed them alike, but usually in different colors. They are now one month old, each had gained two pounds. Khouri is definitely the bossy one. She had a temper just like her daddy, quick. When she wanted to eat or play, she wanted it now and would scream. Reagan was a little calmer but could scream too. She was easier to quiet down. Having two babies was a big adjustment that I'm still trying to get use to. All I can say is, thank god for Mommy. She has been staying with us since the babies were born. Although they were a handful, I thanked God for allowing me to have them. They could never replace Bryan, but they help fill the void that remained in my heart after losing him. Just being able to hold them, kiss them, and

say, I love you was a blessing. I had no complaints; I welcomed the challenge of being their mother. They were so beautiful they looked a lot like Ms. Beverly, but it looks like their eyes were a mixture of both Braxton and mine. They had Braxton's thick wavy black hair, the nose, oval face and lips belonged to mommy and none of my features. Landon and Eric have been over twice, it was hard but I dealt with it. Right now, she's allowing us time to adjust.

The babies keep us busy. Even with mommy staying here, it's exhausting. Usually when the twins slept, we did too. Of course, we had family constantly coming over which is a chore in itself. Braxton was also on leave, so that helped out. With all the work it took to care for the twins, I haven't had time to focus on our issues. I was just so happy to finally have my babies. I pushed the issue of Landon, Braxton and Eric in the back of my head. Yes, I knew it wasn't going to disappear but I wanted to be happy, enjoy being a family, even if it is only temporarily. Having the girls really made me realize how much I want my family.

While I nursed Khouri, Braxton just gazes and smiles. He's still in awe and disbelief that this is his baby.

As soon as I finish nursing Khouri, mommy came in with Reagan. Braxton took Khouri and burped her while I nursed Reagan on my other breast.

"Alright you two, I'm about to go home and get dressed," mommy announced. Today the hospital was having a reception to honor Mr. Jeff, who recently received another prestigious award. At first I was hesitant about taking the twins, but mommy insisted. The reception will be more like a family reunion rather than a reception so I'll have plenty of help.

"Ok, ma, we'll see you later." Braxton said.

"Do you need me to get you anything before I leave?" Mommy asked.

"No, we have everything."

"Ok, see you two and my babies at four. Don't be late. Oh, I almost forgot. Put on the dresses I bought for the girls." She made sure to kiss both of the girls before leaving.

Braxton and I managed to get out of the house by 3:30. We'd taken the girls out before and knew it took a lot. We surprisingly manage to have mastered a routine. Today, I admit I was the hold up. I couldn't find anything to wear. Thanks to breastfeeding, I lost most of my baby weight except 5 – 10 pounds. The problem was my 36DD's had doubled. In every outfit I tried, my breasts looked like they were falling out. I managed to find a coral colored dress that was easy to let down for nursing. Mommy had bought the girls identical lavender sundresses, matching booties and pink barrettes. Braxton wore khakis and a green polo shirt.

Fortunately, we made it to the reception at four. We walked into the banquet hall with Braxton pushing the double stroller. When we opened the door to the hall, everyone yelled, surprise!

By instinct, I grabbed Braxton, who looked to be as shocked as I was. The babies were startled and both of them began to cry. Mommy rushed over to get her babies.

I saw my aunt Patti, the only member from my mother's side that accepted me, Lawrence, Jackie, so many others, even coworkers. It was overwhelming.

The room was beautifully decorated in the same color as the nursery, pink lavender and mint green. Mommy really outdid herself, how she found the time to arrange a baby shower, I don't know. She managed to get baby pictures of me as a baby along with Braxton. There was a huge blown up picture of our wedding in the Cayman Islands. She had pictures of us at family gatherings. She had slides of me in labor minus the actual delivery, thank God. The highlight was the twins. She had a huge banner in the center that read:

"Introducing God's most precious angels, Khouri and Reagan Simms."

Underneath she had two tables, one for Khouri, one for Reagan each displaying pictures of each girl with family. Each table had little facts, such as weight, footprints, and other differences. She spared no expense even having a photographer there to record the shower. As she says, the girls will be able to look back and see how loved they were from the very beginning.

By now Mommy held Reagan, Mr. Jeff held Khouri. Mommy was cautious making sure there was plenty of hand sanitizer, only allowing a few people to hold the girls.

"Well since we don't matter anymore, you want to get something to eat," I teased.

"Sounds like a plan, but I got a better one." Braxton says, pulling me away from the crowd.

"What's that?"

"Let's go get some sleep. We can go take an hour nap and come back."

I laughed. "You are so right."

Braxton pulls me in an embrace, "Can I get some love too? Come on lets go."

"You better get out of my face."

"Come on, Beautiful. I promise I'll pull out." He starts to kiss me on my neck.

"Stop," I say weakly.

"You don't want me to stop," he teases, kissing me more.

"Damn boy, you trying to make more babies. Yasmin, you're going to be pregnant again. I'm letting you know now don't expect any more gifts. Y'all lucky you got two," Vincent instigates, startling both of us.

"Shut up, Vince."

"Don't get mad at me."

Vince walks over and gives me a hug and kiss on the cheek."

"Alright, that's enough, get off my wife. Get your own," Braxton teases.

"Damn Yasmin, my little brother a punk."

Braxton slapped Vincent in the head. "Who the punk now," he laughed.

Vincent raises his arm to hit Braxton back, but Uncle Charles grabs it.

"You two fools better stop this horse playing. Act like you got some sense. How's my Sweet Thing today?" he asks focusing his attention on me.

"Fine," I said, giving him a kiss on the cheek.

"I'm going to see my nieces," Vince says walking away.

Braxton and I chatted with our guests. Kevin and Nicole was surprisingly lovey dovey. It was nice seeing Kim. Landon arrived right before we opened gifts, it was awkward. However, I manage to deal with her presence. Half of the people I didn't even know. They were friends of Mommy's. Although, I must say they gave us very nice gifts, ranging from certificate of deposits to jewelry to stock. I had so many clothes and gift certificates I knew we wouldn't have to buy anything until they were two.

I was sitting in Braxton's lap when my nightmare begins.

"Hello, Braxton. Yasmin."

I didn't even try to hide my annoyance, "Lisa."

"Hey Lisa, how's it going?"

"Well, thanks. I see you two are looking good. No bags under the eyes. Parenthood must be agreeing with you."

Oh, this trick is so phony. I remained quiet, Braxton conversed.

"Thanks, yes I do love my girls." He kisses me on the cheek.

"Aww isn't that sweet. We miss you at work. Are you coming back soon?" she inquired.

"Probably not for another three or four weeks. I'm doing some work at home. What's going on at the office?"

"Nothing, well I just wanted to say congratulations. Yasmin, I must admit you look good under the circumstances. Better than I would expect with everything going on."

The chick was being too nice and phony. I smile, but I don't trust the chick.

"Thanks, Lisa," Braxton said as she was walking off.

"I really can't stand that chick." I said taking a seat a chair reserved for me.

He laughs, "She was being nice."

"Whatever! You keep on trusting that trick."

The shower began to wind down around seven. Mommy opened the floor, allowing the guests to give their congratulations along with words of wisdom. Lisa stood up and it took everything in me not to take off my shoe and throw it at her. Kim and I make eye contact and both roll our eyes.

Lisa smiles before beginning. "Well, hello everyone, my name is Lisa. I am one of Braxton's close friends from work. Braxton and I go back many years," she laughs

I look at Braxton. He gives me a clueless look. The bitch better not say she fucked him. She continues.

"As many of you know it was at work he met Yasmin. I knew from the beginning, their relationship was more than platonic. Over the years, it's been a pleasure seeing how their love for one another grew and now just seeing their little babies. It's so amazing. I wish you nothing but the best. Anyway, I must say Yasmin you are really, truly wonderful. So patient, submissive and forgiving. Not many women, actually any strong women I know would accept their husband fathering a kid with their sister, a son at that, especially after you lost your son. But Yasmin, you did, had twins, wow. I just don't know how you do it with a smile. Congratulations."

If ever I wanted to run, nothing could compare to now. Somehow I held the tears back. All eyes were on me, but I refused to stare back. Instead I look ahead, watching Lisa gloat, wishing I could wrap my hands around her neck and choke the life from her.

Finally, after what seems like hours someone took the microphone. Who it was or what they said, I had no idea. I saw Lisa being escorted out of the room. I stood up, going in Lisa's direction. Braxton is on my tail. When I finally reach her, I waste no time slapping her, "You fucking pathetic bitch!"

"No, my dear you're pathetic," she tries to retaliate, but is restrained.

"You get your trifling ass out of here now!" Mommy says in a voice that lets her know, try her.

"With pleasure, I've said all I had to say."

"Well I haven't. Do you want a bow? Do you think you broke me? Your crazy, desperate ass thinks you accomplished something. The fact is, you always wanted Braxton, even before me," I spoke with venom. "The problem was he never wanted your Spongebob looking ass. When I came in the picture, like you said, you knew I wasn't a fling, so you got jealous. Even with all of your slurs, all of the flirting, you never got the time of day. I was out the picture for over a year and you still got nothing. Yet, instead of admitting it was never going to happen, you lived in lala land. Now you've lost any respect he or anyone else had for you. Yes, Braxton has a kid with my sister, but you know what, at the end of the day, you still want to be me. You wish you had half the things I do. Go ahead and take your old raggedy, miserable ass home to the person who wants to be with you, no one."

Lisa looked at me.

"What bitch, you don't have anything else to say? Has it sunk in how stupid and desperate you really look? You said all that and did all that conniving shit to prove what? What did you get? Nothing, right? Do you realize at the end of the day you're still not me, can't compete with me or be me? I am still Yasmin and I am still standing."

Lisa turned around and left without a word.

25

After All is Said and Done

It's been two weeks since the shower and Lisa's words still sting. Braxton was now irritating me. He would try to hold me, but I'd push him away. He wanted to take me out, but I'd decline. I tried to get her comments out of my head, but I couldn't. I was pissed. The reality is, the bitch really fucked my head up. What she said beared truth. I never wanted to look and feel stupid, I hated it. Staying with Braxton too many, including myself, made me look stupid. Eric has been over twice and I can't be around him. I'm not cold, I just do what I've become accustomed to…run. When I know he's coming, I make an excuse and get out of the house. I know he loves his sisters and is doing nothing wrong. I just can't accept it. And at the same time, I can't bring myself to leave.

"Yasmin, let's talk," Braxton said, startling me. He sat on the bed next to me looking me directly in the eye."

"Hello to you too."

"Yasmin no smart talk today. What are we doing?"

"What do you mean?"

"Us. One minute I think you love me, the next you act like you can't stand me."

"Post-partum."

"No, I'm not going for that."

"Braxton I just had our twins. You witnessed my labor that was love right there. What more do you want? I'm tired."

"I know you're upset about what Lisa said, but Yasmin, don't let her get to you."

I stare at him hard then roll my eyes.

"Yasmin."

"Braxton, I don't feel like talking."

"You seem to be fine when you leave out to hang with Kevin. I told you before I'm not feeling that relationship. You're my wife, the mother of my daughters, and you're with him more than me."

"That's right the mother of your daughters not all your kids. Therefore you have no right to complain about my relationship with Kevin. The wife part I'm still contemplating."

"So, it's like that? I have apologized over and over for what happened, however I love my son and I'm not going to apologize for him. The truth is fucked up but it's the truth. I have a son with Landon. I have two daughters with you. I can't change the truth no matter how much you wish things were different, they're not. I can't do anything about it. Eric is their brother. You have to accept it. They will grow up knowing that. You know for yourself how it was growing up not being accepted. I want us to be together. Fuck what people say or think. It's about us. What do you want?"

"It's easy for you to say that because you're not the one who was cheated on. You're not the one everyone looks at and says, poor Yasmin, that's messed up or why is she still there. People won't see that you were with me first. They see you had a baby with Landon and two with me later. I'm the other woman. Lisa was right."

"Fuck Lisa. You said it yourself, she's miserable. Don't let that pathetic bitch get in between us."

"Oh, now she's pathetic. When I said something before, I was crazy, it wasn't that serious. I told you she couldn't be trusted. Well the bitch pissed me off now I got to deal with everybody knowing my damn business. I have to look at them as they give me that, 'aww that's messed up' look, or 'damn, she still there?' look as they question me with their eyes."

"Yasmin, all that matters is what we think. This is about us, what we want. Everybody is going to have an opinion, but we are this relationship. We love each other, we do what we do not because of people, but how we feel. We love each other strong. You know we both belong right here together, committed. Why can't we continue to be a family?"

I heard what he was saying but I didn't have an answer. There is no doubt I love Braxton but I can't. The phone rang. I went to reach for it.

"Yasmin, we're talking."

"It might be important." I picked it up it was Kevin. "Hey, Kevin."

"Hey, Yasmin I need you to come over now it's important we need to talk."

Needing a break, I agreed. "Alright, I'm on my way. I'll be there in a few."

Braxton went from calm to crazy. "You're not going any fucking where! We're talking! I'm not done!"

"Braxton it's important. I need to think anyway. I'll be back."

"What we're talking about is not important?"

"I'm not saying that. I have to go. I promise I'll talk to you when I come back."

"So you're choosing him over me?" he asked visibly hurt.

"It's not like that."

He got up and punched a hole in the wall scaring me. "How is it Yasmin? I know I hurt you. So does that mean you have to keep throwing Kevin up in my face? He calls, you go running. I've been too damn nice about your relationship. You were with him. You won't even let me touch you. You act like you're disgusted every time I do. I ask you for a little of your time and you always have an excuse. I come in a room, you leave. How am I supposed to feel? " He punched another hole in the wall and knocked the stuff on my dresser on the floor.

His mother came rushing in our room with Khouri in a swap and Reagan in her arms. She definitely was working it.

"What's going on up here?"

"Yeah Yasmin, what's going on?" Braxton asked sarcastically.

"I need to go to Kevin's for a few a minutes, Mommy I'll be right back." I got up heading for the door.

"Hold it. You two all this chaos is uncalled for. You need to work it out for their sake. I've been quiet, but now this is getting ridiculous. Yasmin, honey I know you're hurt I can only imagine how you feel. But I know you love Braxton and he loves you. I'm not saying it's going to be easy, but you need to at least try. Despite everything that happened you were blessed with two beautiful daughters for a reason. Please try."

I looked at Braxton then at his mother with tears. "I have to go." And with that I rushed out of the house to my truck. It hurt to be like that towards Braxton, but I had to.

When I made it to Kevin's he was waiting with the door open.

"What wrong?"

"Come in."

"Something is going on with Landon."

"Kevin, I know you did not call me over here to talk about Landon. I have my own issues. I can't be concerned with Landon."

"I know. I wasn't going to say anything I know you are dealing with a lot, but I think Landon is on something."

"What?"

"Yas, have you seen her. She's lost a lot of weight and I found pills."

"What kind of pills?"

"I don't know she had them in a vitamin bottle."

"Maybe they are vitamins."

"No Yas, they wasn't. She wasn't herself, something is going on."

"Kev, seriously, I need something concrete. For real what am I supposed to do? I have enough to deal with. Landon gets herself into messes. I'm done helping her out. She a grown woman, she needs to act like it."

Unintentionally, I stayed out for a couple of hours, not arriving home until six. Although I needed more me time I went in anyway. Besides I missed my girls. Plus I knew I had to talk to Braxton.

I came in the house, surprised to see it was dark and quiet. I saw Braxton sitting on the sofa. "Where are the girls?"

Braxton didn't say anything. Instead he just looks at me. I couldn't tell if I should be scared and run, or if he was sane.

After a couple of minutes he still didn't respond. "Braxton where are my daughters?"

He jumped up and rushed over to me with tears in his eyes. "Now they're just your daughters. You want to act concerned now. You weren't concerned when you ran off to be with Kevin."

"Where are my daughters?"

"I thought you said you'd be right back. Why were you over his house all that time?"

"For air."

"You don't see anything wrong with being at his house?"

"No."

"Every damn time you get upset you run away, usually to Kevin. He's your confidante, savior, can do no wrong. You say there's no feeling, but I can't tell."

"There's not."

"You can't stand to see me in the same room with Landon all that was about was being drunk and stupid. No feelings at all. Honestly, that night it could have been anybody. No, it doesn't make it right. With you and Kevin it's different. You dated, there was an attraction. Yasmin, you fucked him. Now every time I turn around you all in his face, like y'all together."

"I was dealing with something. Now answer me, where are my daughters?"

He grabbed me scaring me. "You have got away with talking to me any kind of way too long. I'm tired of this shit. Your ass should have been home then you would know where *our* daughters are at! Fuck it. You want Kevin, fine. You're probably still fucking him anyway because you're definitely not fucking me. You can have the house. I'm gone. I'm not apologizing anymore. But I will tell you something, I don't want him around my daughters or in this house. I pay the mortgage."

"Fuck you, Braxton. I'm not you. I don't have a fight with you and run be with someone else."

"Fuck me, huh. You just can't let that shit go. I get it, I'm done. I'll be out of here soon. Remember what I said. I don't want Kevin ass in my house or around my daughters. I told you I've been too nice about his ass. Don't try me."

I was hurt. I shouldn't have gone there but I had a lot of hostility. "Don't fucking try to dictate who I can have in this house. My name is on the deed too. If I want Kevin here, then he can come, whether my daughters are here or not. Try you?! Are you forgetting that Kevin practices family law. You should be scared of me, so try me motherfucker!"

He raised his hand like he was going to hit me. I was about to scream like a bitch but remained nonchalant. He instead flipped out and started destroying the living room.

"I ADMITTED I WAS WRONG. BUT YOU'RE FUCKING WRONG SAYING THAT SHIT. I'M GONE. I NEVER THOUGHT YOU COULD BE SO SPITEFUL. BUT YOU'RE NOT MY PROBLEM ANYMORE. BRING HIS ASS IN HERE AND SEE WHAT HAPPENS."

"Whatever Braxton, What time will my daughters be home."

He walked out slamming the door.

I stood there for about ten minutes surveying the damage. All of a sudden I was overwhelmed with emptiness. My heart ached, while my head pounded. It felt like everything was in slow motion and I felt my life coming to an end. I didn't realize I fell to the ground until I felt the tears that were falling from my face soaking up the floor. Everything happened so fast and felt so final. Could I get Braxton out of my system? Could I finally let him go? Right now, my heart was screaming, hell no, but my mind reminded me of all the hurt that I ignored for the last couple of months. I couldn't deny it or run any more. The facts were the facts. I had to deal with it. I couldn't hide, fantasize or pretend anymore. I had to face reality. I would just hand him my divorce papers.

Finally, after what I knew had to be an hour, I was able to pull myself together. I cleaned up the mess Braxton made. No sooner than I finished, the back door opens. I look up to see Mommy coming in with the girls. Immediately, I began to cry. Mommy rushes over to me and hugs me.

"What's going on?"

"Braxton and I are done. I can't do it anymore. He can't do it anymore."

"Yasmin, you are upset, a lot is going on."

"No, mommy, too much has happened."

"Yasmin, you have the babies. You have to work it out."

"That's just it, I can't. It's too much to forgive. If I stay, I'm scared I'll end up treating Eric like I was treated. I won't do that to him, it's not his fault.

I saw tears in her eyes now. She didn't say anything, she didn't have to. She knew I was right.

"I'm sure. We can't keep on pretending. It's over." I answered the question her eyes asked again.

Before she could say anything, the twins interrupted. They started getting restless in their stroller. That distraction allowed me to get their daddy out of my mind temporarily.

"Yasmin, go take a bath, shower. I'll feed them. Go get yourself together."

"Thanks, but I want to feed them.

I managed to feed both babies, then took mommy's advice and took a long bath.

That night Braxton didn't come home. I heard mommy up with the babies and prayed it was him. Although in my mind I knew it was over, my heart wouldn't let the reality set in. Each second that passed my heart ached more. I wished Braxton was here beside me. Wished I could redo the last twenty four hours but I couldn't and I had to accept that.

26

What You Want

It's been two weeks since the breakup. I'd be lying if I said each day was easier. It's been hell. Every time I look at our daughters, I cry. I cry because it's not fair. I cry because I want to be a family, but I know that becoming a family will make me lose me. I couldn't deny or avoid it anymore. I don't sleep. I try not to cry myself to sleep, but all I do is think of him.

Braxton has come by a few times when I was out to grab some things and see the babies. I know because the closets that were once filled with his clothes are filled with empty hangers. Mommy has kept her opinion to herself and I am grateful. I know she's praying for a miracle. I feel bad because she's the middle man. The twins right now stay between here and her house to allow Braxton time. I haven't seen or talked to Braxton in two weeks. Mommy stays with me for four days and at her house for three days with Braxton. Although I check on them daily, usually dropping off milk, somehow we still never run into each other. We have kids and it's inevitable that eventually will come face to face. The girls left today so I was in this big house all alone. Usually I just mope around. Today, I decided to get out, even though I feel like crap, I dressed like a star. My clothes now fit and my breast just made my package look better.

As soon as I jumped into my truck my cell rang. I didn't recognize the number, but answered anyway.

"Hello."

"I just wonder…. Do you ever think of me anymore, do you?" he sang.

I smiled. "Hello Chauncey."

"Well do you?"

"Sometimes."

"Just sometimes, you miss my sexiness right?"

"You are a trip. You are a pleasant surprise what made you call me?"

"I've been thinking about you. I wanted to see how you were. I also need a huge favor."

"So you really wanted me to do you a favor and really weren't thinking about me." I laughed.

"I always think about you, I need your expertise."

"What's the problem?"

"I need you to look over my financial statements and help me manage some things."

"Chaunce, don't you have an advisor already."

"I did, but something didn't look right. I need a second opinion from someone I can trust."

"That's smart. Alright I can see what I can do. How soon do you want to see me?"

"Yassy, I know its short notice, but do you think we can meet today. I need to get this stuff straightened out."

"Chaunce…"

"I know, I tried calling your office and your cell, but I kept getting voice mail. Besides, like I said, I need to get this straightened out."

"Ok, where do you want to meet me?"

"Come to my house, you remember how to get here right?"

"I'm on my way."

It took me twenty minutes to get to Chauncey's. He obviously was waiting, as soon as I reached the door, it opens.

"Hello, Ms. Lady," he said, giving me a hug.

"Hello."

"You know you wrong."

"What are you talking about, Chauncey?"

"Coming here teasing me." He admired my short button-up orange dress.

"You called me, begging for me to see you today. I was already out."

"True, but damn you're looking good. Your breasts are popping out like they're happy to see me too. Your husband must didn't see you leaving the house."

My body tenses up and I turn my head to avoid eye contact.

"Yas, what's wrong?"

"I'm cool, what did you want me to look over?"

"Yas, me and you go way back. Are you sure?"

I smiled. "Thanks, Chauncey, but I'm cool."

"Well, back to you. You've always had much more than a mouthful, but it looks like you doubled."

"I did not come here for you to stare at my breast. I just had twins."

"Nah, you lying, when?"

"They're two months."

"What you have?"

"Two girls"

"Damn and you still look good."

I laughed, "What you expect for me to look like a hot mess."

"Yeah."

I punched him in the arm, "Well I don't. As always, I look good."

"Yes, you most certainly do," he said undressing me with his eyes making me feel uncomfortable.

"Um, excuse me, Mr. Smith what did you need help with?"

"What's the matter am I making you uncomfortable?"

I really had no interest in Chauncey, but I was feeling a little devious, "No, I know what you you're working with."

He laughed, "You're messing with me now." He walks up too close, "Don't start what you can't finish."

"Where are the papers?"

He laughed, "I thought so."

He led me into the kitchen where he had a pile laid out on the table. I took a seat never making eye contact and proceed to look over his accounts. Chauncey left me alone, allowing me to look over his financial statement, checking on me periodically to see if I needed anything. After two hours, I had a headache and was through. Basically, he was getting screwed.

"Chaunce," I called out.

"Here I come."

"Have a seat."

"That bad?"

"Bad, but I've seen worse. Basically, your accounts are being mismanaged, and you have quite a few questionable expenses, as well as missing money."

"Motherfuck! I knew something was up. Real talk, how much money is missing and I need you to fix it!" he yelled

"Calm down."

"Sorry Yas, but I work too damn hard. I got something for that motherfucker though."

"Chaunce, it's alright. You can fix it."

"Damn right, and that motherfucker is going to pay for me fixing it and then some."

"Listen, you have about $400,000 unaccounted for. Some of these investments, truthfully, were not wise. I, personally, would have invested and utilized differently, but that's just me."

"Can you help me straighten this out and manage my accounts?"

"Chaunce, this is a lot. Honestly, right now my hands are full."

"I know Yas, but like I said earlier, I can trust you. I know you're not going to try and get over. Besides, you know your stuff."

"Thanks for the compliment. I wish I could, but I have a lot, I mean a lot going on right now," I stressed. "I don't have any time. I'm still on maternity leave. Truthfully, I probably won't go back until the twins are six months."

"Yas, please, I'll pay for a nanny. You know I'll compensate you for your service. Will you help me?"

"Chauncey, you know money is not an issue with me."

"I know, but as you see I need your help."

I took a deep breath, "I'll clean this up for you, but I can't promise you that I can continue to manage your account."

"Thank you, but why can't you continue to be my advisor?"

"Hello, didn't I just tell you I had twins and have a lot going on. Speaking of my babies, I need to go home and feed them."

"You just got here, their daddy can feed them."

"No, I've been here for two hours and my breasts need to be emptied."

He smiled, "Yeah, you're right. Go ahead and get back to your family."

"I'll talk to you soon."

For the past two weeks I'd been alternating from spending time with Chauncey and the girls. His financial mishap has been what I needed to keep my mind off of Braxton. Chauncey as before was always good company. I know he noticed I wasn't wearing a ring. Thankfully, he hadn't asked me any questions about Braxton. I am grateful he respected my privacy.

I was looking in the mirror admiring my reflection. Although I was on the verge of a divorce and caring for two newborns, I looked good. I was wearing a green BCBG halter top dress that stopped just below the knees. I let my hair hang. I was stopping at mommy's for a cookout just to say hi, and then going to a party Chauncey invited me to. At first, I was hesitant. I didn't want to give him or anyone any ideas. Braxton and I hadn't been together for over a month but nothing was made official.

When I arrived at mommy's I felt awkward. Of course, I got hugs and was welcomed but there was still this uncertainty. I still hadn't seen Braxton and was nervous as hell. I went into the kitchen to see if Mommy needed anything.

"Hey Mommy."

"Hey Yasmin."

"Do you need any help?"

"No, I have everything together. You know I'm not doing much, I have to get back to my babies."

"Speaking of my daughters, where are they?"

"Braxton has them. They should be out back."

"Braxton has both of them?" I ask surprised.

She laughed, "Yes, he can handle them."

I smiled on the outside, but inside I was crying. This was just a reminder of how crazy the distance was between us. It reminded me of how us being apart wouldn't allow me to see him bond with our daughters.

I walked out to see Braxton holding one of the babies and Jeff's wife, Patrice, holding the other. My earlier content mood was quickly becoming depressing. Braxton holding the baby looking like the proud daddy he was made me want just go over and reclaim my family.

"Hey."

Braxton looked up and our eyes locked. As like the first day we met, my heart skipped beats and I lost my breath. He was just as sexy as the first day and I wanted him, but again then the reality of things surfaced and I looked away.

"Hey," Braxton solemnly responded.

Everyone looked at us awkwardly, not sure what to say.

"Hey, mommy baby," I said walking up to Patrice grabbing my baby and giving her a kiss. She must have smelled my milk, turned her trying to nurse. "Mommy baby hungry?"

I walked over to Braxton and asked him to bring Reagan so I could feed her as well.

He followed, not saying anything.

Once in the bedroom I broke the ice.

"How is it going?"

"So so. For you?"

"Same."

I fed Khouri while he held Reagan. He watched, not saying a word. It felt weird. I wasn't use to this type of tension between us. When we switched babies, he looked at me with great sadness.

"What's wrong?"

"Where's your wedding ring?"

I look away before responding. "I took it off."

"Are we dating now too?"

I sigh, "No."

"Just a matter of time though."

I didn't say anything.

"Alright, I'm going back to the party. See you."

I stayed at Mommy's for another hour feeling even more uncomfortable than before I first came. During that time, Braxton said nothing, ignoring my presence, acting as if I had no importance in his life.

The party Chauncey invited me to was at his teammate Kenyon Edwards's house. I made sure I drove my own car, not wanting to be stranded. I also made it clear to Chauncey he and I were not going to do anything; our relationship would only be platonic. While Chauncey was doing his thing, I observed. During that time I had several drinks, which wasn't a good thing.

I did not miss the party scene. Nothing had changed, all the players were there trying to fuck as many girls as possible and the groupies were endless. Amongst the wannabe pimps were Javon and Cory.

I went over to speak with Cory.

"Hello, Cory."

He turns around immediately focusing on my breasts.

"Hello, Yasmin."

"So you do remember me?"

"Yes, I do. I'll never forget your sexy ass."

"I don't know if that's a good or bad thing."

He laughed. "You get your props. I see you got rid of all that baby weight. Look likes the baby weight and the hubby is gone. I see he don't got it on lock anymore," he said running his finger over my bare finger.

"Very observant I see."

"I can't help but notice everything about you. So Yasmin can I get a dance."

"Sure."

Cory wasted no time grabbing me. We danced to Lil Wayne's, "Lollipop" and Lloyd's, "Girls Around the World".

Although I was tipsy, I knew to stop when I felt Cory's hand up my dress. I walk away, leaving him with a very hard dick.

Before I knew it, Chauncey had me intertwined in a dance. He'd gotten better since we last danced, but still couldn't keep up with me. We were facing each other. I closed my eyes, allowing the music to take me away as the Dj played Neyo's, Closer. The way I grinded up and down on Chauncey it was no surprise his dick was hard.

"You make this friend shit hard, Shorty."

His breath tickled my neck causing me to shudder.

"See what I mean. Now what am I supposed to do with this hard dick?"

"Fuck somebody."

"I want to fuck you. Let me fuck you. You going to let me fuck you?"

"No."

"Why not?"

"Because, what I need is to be fucked, I need to be fucked to the point I don't know my name. Fucked to the point I see stars and I'm crying for mercy.

"Yassy, I can do that. Let me make that happen."

I looked at him seriously, moving my lips closely to his ear. "No, Chaunce you cannot. Anyway, I can't get caught up with you or anybody right now, too many issues."

I look up to see Braxton staring me dead in the eye. If looks could kill, my ass would be six feet under right now. My ass sobered up real fast. Vincent who was with Braxton just shook his head.

I backed away from Chauncey. Chauncey not noticing Braxton pulls me back in an embrace.

"You know you wrong, Yas."

"Chauncey now is not the time," I say keeping one eye on him, the other on Braxton.

"Braxton just came in. I don't want a scene."

"Y'all not together, right?"

"Chauncey, you and I are friends the fucking is not going to happen. Get one of these groupies to suck your dick, fuck you, do whatever."

"Damn, your ass always so damn blunt, too blunt sometimes. Anyway, I still want to fuck you though."

"Nope."

"It ain't like we ain't done this before."

"Just like before those days are done and over."

He shakes his head. "Alright, go ahead to hubby."

I left Chauncey, went to the bar, ordering a shot of tequila. I gulped it down like it was water wasting no time ordering another. I made sure I kept my back turned. I didn't want to see Braxton. A few guys approached hoping for a dance, all were declined. Before I could taste my second tequila, two strong hands came from behind, pinning my arms down. His ass had definitely been to the gym taking out his frustrations. Looking at his biceps he'd definitely had a lot of frustrations, they were huge. How I didn't notice earlier is beyond me.

"What the hell is your problem?"

"Do not make a scene."

"If I make a scene it's on you."

"Braxton, please."

"I'm not trying to hear that shit. You drinking like you don't have any sense, grinding on these fools dick like a hot ass. Don't let me find out your ass fucked somebody."

"I didn't fuck anyone. I don't go to bars, get horny and fuck people just because I'm horny. I can control my urges. And if I did, I'm not your problem anymore, right?" I said with sarcasm.

"Don't start."

"You started with me. I was here minding my business."

"You are my business. Sitting here drinking, knowing damn well your ass shouldn't be drinking. Now what are my daughters going to eat? All you got is some tainted ass alcohol filled milk."

"Bye Braxton," I said removing myself from his grasp and walking away.

I ended up in the restroom. My bladder was ready to bust. One thing I hated was the way alcohol ran right through me.

Braxton came in the bathroom with me.

"Damn, are you my babysitter, now?"

"Yup, smart ass."

"Well, babysitter," after wiping myself, I stood up, bent over and said, "Kiss my ass."

Still bent over, I had to laugh until I felt his big ass hand slap my ass.

"Now that was funny," he chuckled.

"Damn, why you hit me so hard, punk," I whimpered, pulling up my panties and then washing my hands.

"Are you sobered up?"

"I'm not drunk, ass."

"I didn't hit you hard," he laughed.

"Alright, you can leave now."

"If I leave you're coming with me."

"Why are you still fucking with me? Remember you and I are over."

"I know what we are."

"Well, you need to act like it."

"Alright, you need to act like you have some damn sense."

"I do have sense. I left your cheating ass."

"Going to a party by yourself? Drinking hard liquor in a house filled with horny ass men, that makes sense?"

He walks up to me so close that when he breathes it tickles my nose. He grabs my face, lifts it, bending his down so we're eye to eye, "What else does that smart mouth of yours have to say?"

I don't speak just intently stare.

"You don't have anything to say?" he says, his lips brushing mine.

"No."

"For real, Yasmin you can't be doing dumb shit like this."

I didn't say anything.

"Right now you can't stand my ass and you should be mad. But you can't do the same dumb shit I did. You need to go home, you shouldn't even be here. Come on, Beautiful, let me take you home."

I lick my lips, licking his in the process. My lips press against his. I open my mouth to receive his tongue. Soon our lips, tongue, mouth are engaged in a seductive dance. He pushes me against the wall. I can feel him growing. I reach down to massage him. He's aching to come out. I'm so wet. I need so badly to feel him inside of me. Abruptly, he stops me. I pant.

"No."

I kiss him again.

"You know what you're doing?"

I nod.

"No regrets, later."

"The same applies to you, no regrets later."

Braxton uses both hands to grab my waist, pulling me close as he kisses me hard. Next he uses one of his hands to untie the top of my halter dress exposing my breasts. The same hand used to untie my dress is now caressing my breast. Braxton moves his lips from my mouth to my breast. With the right amount of pressure he alternates from nibbles to sucking.

I take my hands and try to unbuckle his pants. He grabs them both pinning them against the wall with just one of his. His free hand reaches up my dress to tug at my panties. He can't get them off, eventually he rips them. He rubs his hand between my thick thighs. He indicates with his hand that he wants me to spread my legs. I oblige. When he sticks his finger in my pussy, my knees buckle. Finally, he releases my arms from his grip. Securely I wrap my arms around his neck.

Braxton unbuckles his pants, allowing them to drop to the floor. I jump on him. He's prepared grabbing my ass. I wrap both legs around his waist. With both hands, he grabs my waist, slowly sliding the dick I love so much in me. Simultaneously our bodies shudder in pleasure. Damn, it's been a long time. He fills me. I can literally feel it in my back. No stomach in the way to avoid me from backing it up and receiving it all. I grind, swirl, squeeze. So wet I am, dripping in passion. With his hands still on my waist, he moves my body up and down, round and round. He backs me against the wall giving me deep and powerful thrusts. I'm crying, begging him not to stop.

"Fuck me, baby! Fuck me, baby!" I order.

He does.

I arch my back, so he can suck my nipples. I love how he reads my mind and does.

"Baby, you feel soooooo..."

He moves me from the wall to the bench in the shower. He grabs my legs, pulls me to him and picks up where he stopped. I reach out for him. I want him to kiss me, he does. My legs are wrapped around his strong arms. Each thrust he gives, his arms pull me closer. He's in so deep, he's breathing for me. My body is devoured in so much pleasure that I can't get enough, giving him the same thrusts he gives me. All my desires he's fulfilling, please don't let it stop, I pray.

He picks me up again, my legs still wrapped around his arms, his dick still in me. Pushed against the wall, our bodies rock again just as fervently as before, if not more, if that's possible. In our rendezvous, my back hits the handle in the shower. Soon warm water cascades down our backs. We're both unfazed, this isn't an interruption. We continue. I bounce up and down, holding him tight. He pounds in me, going so hard and deep I know I'm yelling, screaming, grunting, moaning, whether they're actually words I don't know. Braxton has me floating, I can't see. The loving he's giving is an illusion, too good to be real.

Minutes later my body can't take any more, it trembles pleased. Seconds later Braxton joins me letting out a loud satisfied grunt. We catch our breath. Braxton then turns off the shower. There's a noise near the door. We look up surprised at what we see, the door is wide open. Both of us unaware a crowd had formed outside the double doors. There are many stares, smiles, talk, and I don't care.

Vincent comes in loud and annoying as usual.

"Alright show's over folks. You had your peep show. Now go do your own freaky shit," he laughs closing the door.

Braxton lets my legs down. I grab him for support, my legs are jelly.

Vincent bends over in laughter. I turn my back to him, with Braxton's assistance I fix my dress. Braxton pulls his pants up.

"Damn, I wish I had my camera. I could make some more money,"

"Man, shut up," Braxton says annoyed.

"Don't get mad at me because y'all decided you wanted to be porn stars. There is a lock on the door. Y'all need to learn how to use them."

I look in the mirror, it's no surprise my hair is a mess. I take my hands to pull it off my face. Braxton and I are both drenched.

"Yeah, you look a mess. Nothing you can do to make it better."

Through the mirror I give Vincent an evil stare.

"I don't know why y'all mad at me. If I didn't come there'd still be a crowd chanting for more."

"Alright, Vince just shut up," I say.

"A thank you to your favorite brother-in-law would be nice."

I ignore his comment.

"I'm taking Yasmin home. I'll see you later."

"Handle your biz. Remember what I said though don't expect any more baby gifts."

Vision still blurry, legs wobbly I manage to walk out with Braxton's assistance. He takes me home, both of us silent on the ride home.

*

The next morning, I lay in bed nude, catching my breath. My body still tingling from the loving it just received. Yes, we did it again, all night, as a matter of fact. How could I not with love so good? I knew there were supposed to be no regrets; however I can't escape the sadness. There's sadness because this could be the last time my body feels such pleasure. I said it was over, but the fact is, our bodies just feel too right together. The way he gets into my mind, knowing what I want, how I want it, when to change positions, when I can't take anymore, and when I'm ready to cum. I lay here telling myself it's a sex thing, but I know it's definitely more.

"Yasmin, we can't keep doing this," he says interrupting my thoughts.

"I know."

He sat up, leaning his head against the headboard. "Yasmin, you know I love you."

"But…"

"I'm not going to keep going back and forth with you."

"We both knew what we were doing and said no regrets."

"Oh, I don't regret being in you. I'm just not going to be your yo-yo while you decide what you want."

I sigh, "What are you saying, Braxton?"

"I'm letting you go. I'm not going to try and persuade you to be with me. It's your choice. If you want a divorce, I won't contest it."

I now sit up, look him straight in the eye for any sign of a bluff, there is none. "So, you're not going to fight a divorce?"

"No."

"Just like that, if I want it to be over, it's over?"

"Yeah. Just promise me that before you make any decision you think it out."

"Will you really be able to handle my decision?"

"Yasmin, I will accept your decision."

"Just like that, I'm free?"

"Yup."

He kisses me on the forehead, stands and goes to the shower. When he returns, I'm wrapped in a sheet. He doesn't say anything, just dresses. When he's done he faces me.

"I'll respect your privacy. I won't be stopping by. Call me if you need anything."

I didn't say anything, nothing left to say. He left, I lay back down analyzing, accepting his words. He finally has done what I've been asking for, let me go. I should be happy.

Damn, I'm not supposed to feel like this, alone and empty, overwhelmed with regret. Feeling like I lost more than I realized. Is it really over?

27

Keep on Going

Braxton has been true to his word. He hasn't put any pressure on me. He has stopped by, only to grab some clothes, usually in and out. If he does stay, it's by my invite. He plays with the girls no longer than a half an hour.. To keep myself busy, I've been working on Chauncey's financial portfolio. I even took on Geester and Kenyon as clients. Braxton has even seen me out on different occasions with Kenyon and Chauncey. Each time he was civil.

Weeks later, I still was unsure what I wanted, not ready to commit not ready to let go.

I was walking through the mall, not paying attention when I literally bumped into John Sinclair.

He definitely was the last person I expected to see. I was apprehensive, not sure how he would react. The last time we saw each other was over a year ago, when the truth about my paternity surfaced.

"Hello Yasmin, "he says hesitantly.

"Hello."

Things are awkward. We never were affectionate towards each other so we stand.

"Are you busy? Do you have time to talk?"

I nod.

"How are you doing?" he asks once we're seated.

"Fine."

"Yasmin, I'm sorry. I owe you an apology. You were right. I never allowed myself to get close to you. I thought as long as I provided for you financially that was enough. Now that I've had time to think, I realize I wasn't fair to you. All the anger I had towards your mother I transferred to you. I was wrong. I blamed you for your mother's mistake. I never looked at it from your standpoint."

"Thank you, your apology means a lot. Thank you. I apologize for yelling at you that day," I said, sincerely.

"You don't owe me anything. I was the adult, you were the child. When I forgave your mother, I should have accepted you. I'm sorry that I never did, instead, I gave all my love to Ashley."

I was silent.

"Despite everything, you're strong, a survivor, smart. Your mother and I treated you badly, but still you did alright for yourself. You should be proud of yourself."

"Thank you, it really means a lot coming from you."

"It's ironic that I ran into you today. The other day I was looking at pictures of you and Ashley when you were younger. In all of those pictures Ashley is smiling, she so happy. When I look at your picture, you looked so sad, never happy. That's when it hit me. Your mother and I were so, so wrong. You didn't deserve that. You deserve to be happy. Your childhood was filled with so much unhappiness."

I took a deep breath listening, not bothering to wipe away the tears.

"How's Braxton? Is he still making you happy? When you started dating him, I can say that's the only time I remember seeing you happy," he smiled

I was silent. When he looked at me I spoke. "We're not together."

"I'm sorry to hear that. Is it something you can work out?"

"I'm you, 28 years ago."

He looks confused. I share my story, knowing it had to be déjà vu for him.

"I'm sorry you had to go through that. You know I know how hard it is. I know it's really hard for you since you are so close with Landon. Like I said before, you're strong. I know you're handling things better than I did."

"Not really. I'm not handling things at all. I've been in denial, hoping it'll all go away. It's too hard. I want to do the best thing for me, as well as my girls."

He looks confused.

I smile, "It has been a long time." I pull out my wallet opening to the picture of the girls. "These are my girls, Khouri and Reagan Simms. They're three months now."

"They're beautiful," he says with a tear in his eye.

"How is Ashley?"

"It's a shame you two never became close, again that's your mother and my fault. Ashley is doing well. She works at the hospital with Daniel."

"Do you talk to my mother?"

"Rarely, she has a lot of hostility."

"Towards me as well. I'm dead to her."

"Don't pay her any mind. Don't let her take your happiness. Her misery is hers and hers alone. Don't let anyone guilt you into accepting or justifying their mistakes. Do what makes you happy."

"I will."

"I know I have no right, but I want to try and right my many wrongs. If you need to talk or just to say hi, call me. We can take baby steps."

"I appreciate that."

"Well I have to get going. I'm glad I ran into you."

We both stood giving each other a quick hug.

Baby steps, not bad at all.

*

I was sitting in the restaurant having dinner, helping Kevin plan his proposal to Nicole.

"Hey Mrs. Y.E.S. It still is Mrs., right?" Kevin joked.

"Yes Kevin, as for this very moment it is Mrs."

"Damn, first Landon marriage ended, now yours. I think I'm having second thoughts about proposing."

"Kevin, don't you dare. You know the deal and my marriage isn't officially over."

"Yas, you're not wearing a ring, you're dressed like you're single, and Braxton's been gone for two months."

"Damn, all in my business. Who told you to count?" I laughed.

"So you're going to leave him?"

"Truthfully, I don't know. The custody arrangement we have has been working out well. There is no tension when I drop the girls off at his mother, no pressure. Braxton and I both are handling being apart well. I honestly can say I like the way the relationship is, we're cordial, it's good."

"And Landon?"

"Now that's a different story. I rarely see her though, which is good. I still get angry when I see her. You heard her basically admit she came on to Braxton. Yes he could have stopped, but Landon knew how I felt. Even after we broke up, she continued to lie, dragging innocent people like Eric into her mess."

"She's sorry Yassy, and she really misses you."

"I know. Unfortunately, I miss her too. However, our relationship will never be the same. Now little Eric is a different story. Even with all the drama, I can say I love him like my own. I'm glad he's here. He has a special place in my heart."

"Glad to hear that, Yassy."

"Enough about my drama, so tomorrow's the day?"

"Yeah, I'm ready."

"Well it's about time."

Kevin laughed.

"Hey Miss Lady," said a familiar voice.

I looked up to see Chauncey. I stood up to give him a hug. I was surprised to see Braxton at a nearby table as I was hugging him. It looked like he was in a business meeting, I recognized other upper management. I pretended I didn't see him, but through my peripheral vision I saw him staring."

"Chauncey, you remember Kevin."

"Hey man," Kevin shook his hand."

"You're looking real good, Ms. Lady as always," Chauncey complimented.

"Thank you. You don't look bad yourself."

"You know I stay sexy."

"Are you behaving?" I inquire.

"I should be asking you that."

Unbeknownst to Braxton and me, Kenyon had cameras throughout the house. Including the bathroom, meaning we were on camera and of course viewed not only by bystanders at the party but later by video by some folks.

I smile uncomfortably.

"You are definitely a star. You always got nothing but a rave review from me. Seeing your performance proves time has only made you better."

I laugh uncomfortably.

"Nothing funny, I'm still mad at you from the party. All that teasing you did."

"I apologize and your finances are looking real good."

"That, they are."

"Hey, do you still talk to Eric?"

A chill ran up my spine. "Not really. Is he alright?"

"Nah, I've been trying to get in contact with him. He had a real, real bad season and suffered a leg injury," he explained. "He and Landon had a crazy relationship but I wasn't expecting it to end like that. Your girl fucked him all up."

I was at a loss for words. I quickly changed the subject. "How's Toya?"

"She cool, I'm on my way to meet her now."

"Well, don't let me hold you. Have a good night."

"Later man, Ms. Lady you know I want another hug."

I obliged. Kevin couldn't wait to start.

"Damn shame, that man practically married and still trying to get some. He acted like he didn't want to let you go. And you let him. What did he mean by you being a star?"

I never told Kevin about my porn seen. I ignored his last comment. "I know, but why is Braxton over there."

Kevin glances and laughs.

"What's so funny?"

"You and Chauncey look very cozy. I felt a little jealous. Braxton has a hell of a temper. I'm curious to see what he's going to do."

"Kevin it wasn't that serious"

"I know it just look like it was," he laughed.

"I swear you have a weird sense of humor, but anyways I feel bad for Eric."

"Yeah, I do too. He's a good guy."

Kevin and I talked some more about his proposal. As we were leaving, Braxton approached us.

"Hey Kevin, how you doing?"

"Hey Braxton."

"Hello Yasmin, I just came over to speak. I had a business meeting."

"Hey Braxton, how was the meeting?" I asked.

"It was good, as you say, the normal boring executive stuff."

"It is," I smile.

He smiles back. Well, I'm going to let you two finish your dinner. I'm going to head home help my mother out with the girls."

I laughed. "She's letting you help now? She's usually carrying both of them or has them right under her."

He laughs. "She still does. She just tells me to get a bottle or a diaper. Well yesterday, she let me feed Khouri and of course I wasn't doing it right."

"Yeah that sounds about right."

"You two enjoy your evening, see you Sunday. See you later, Kevin."

Braxton walked away.

"Damn, I'm impressed. I still don't believe Braxton was that calm, friendly towards me, no jealousy."

"Shut up, I told you we're cool."

"It's really over, isn't it?"

I just laughed.

28

Love is Stronger than Pride

One week later, Kevin and Nicole are officially engaged while I'm still uncommitted. For the past week, I thought of my love for Braxton. I looked at the wedding pictures, everyday pictures of things we did. For a while, I was ready to stop fighting and go get my husband. Then I thought about all the heartache, even Bryan. I had to face and deal with what it would mean if I forgave him. I had to ask myself if I was willing to accept everything. Lisa's words still played in my head. My heart still stung. It was a hard, long process, but I have to do what is right for me. Ultimately, I knew it wasn't fair to him to make him wait around. We both were in this place too long. It was time to close this chapter and move on. I just had to first tie up another loose end before I talked to him.

Here I am standing at Landon's door waiting for her to open. When she does, she's shocked to see me. Looking at her did concern me. Like Kevin said, she didn't look like herself. I guess this really has taken a toll on her. As always, fashion wise from head to toe she was on point, but her skin, once vibrant, was now dull. Her eyes once filled with so much life look troubled.

"Yas?"

"Hello Landon, can I come in?"

"Yeah."

I went into her living room and took a seat. This was the first time I actually been to her new place. I looked around, definitely Landon's style, bright with a lot of overpriced things.

"Nice place, where's Eric?"

"Thanks. He's with daddy."

"Let me get straight to the point. I don't want to keep rehashing the past and hearing I'm sorry. You were wrong. And although this is hard for me, I forgive you."

"Yas…"

I stop her, "I forgive you, however, our relationship will never be the same. Trust is a hard thing to get, but an easy thing to lose. With that being said. I will try to build a relationship with you. Crazy but true, you are my sister. Our kids have the same father. I don't think we can be as close as we were, but we can try to make this craziness as normal as possible."

"Thank you, Yassy," she cried.

We hugged.

Landon stopped and grabbed my hand. "Yassy, I'm really grateful that you're back in my life." She stopped and started crying.

"What's wrong? I thought we were cool."

"I'm sorry I just I just feel real bad. I'm looking at your hand and see your ring is still off. I talked to Kevin and he told me it was over. I didn't want to believe it. I fucked up everything for you and the girls."

Kevin and his mouth, I thought.

"Landon, first thing my relationship with Braxton, whether there is one or not, is off limits. Braxton had a part in this mess. I've thought long and hard about my decision and I've made it. Again it's not any of your business at this time."

"You're right, I apologize. I know your life has been difficult. I am truly, deeply sorry in the part I had in making it more difficult. I thank you for allowing me to have any part big or small. I finally realize I wasted a lot of time being dumb, stupid and selfish. I hurt a lot of people in the process, especially you and Eric. For that, I will bear the pain for the rest of my life. You just don't know how much regret I have for my actions."

I was speechless.

"Listen to me. Yas, life is so precious. Time even more precious and never guaranteed. Don't let pride get in the way of your happiness. I don't want you to wake up one day to realize you have nothing but regrets. Don't take time for granted. Don't think you have time to do things right. You've always been the smart one. You've had it rough, been hurt too many times. I've seen you hurt and I've also seen when you are happy, fulfilled and alive. Remember those times? Remember what and who makes you happy."

I was taken aback. I know it's been a while since we really talked. I definitely had no idea what was going on with her or who she was seeing. But I never would expect to hear anything so deep or insightful to come from Landon's mouth. Wow, she has matured.

"Well Landon I said my peace. I need to go."

"Thank you, again."

I went to my truck, taking a minute to calm my nerves. Now, for the big decision, BET here I come.

✳

I walked into BET, waved to the receptionist who couldn't stand me and headed to Braxton's office. There are so many butterflies in my stomach. Part of me wants to turn around and do this another day. I remain strong, holding onto the papers I had drawn up. I take a deep breath. I look for Kim, but she isn't there. I walk into Braxton's office. There he is sitting at his desk. He's preoccupied looking out the window, never noticing me. I notice he's still wearing his ring. *This is going to be hard*, I thought.

"Hey."

He looks up. "Yasmin."

"Kim wasn't at her desk."

"I gave her the week off."

"What?" I said, shocked.

"Yeah, I've been told on one or more occasions how difficult I am. She deserves some time off."

"Yeah, she does."

"What brings you here, everything okay?"

"I came over to talk to you. Is it possible for us to go somewhere? I need to go over these papers with you."

He took a deep breath. "Yeah, let me just shut down my computer."

"Um, I was thinking you could follow me. Are you hungry?"

"No, not really."

"Neither am I, since we need some privacy, how about you follow me to the house."

"That's fine."

On my way home, I was so nervous that I almost pulled over to throw up several times. This was a difficult decision, but deep down I knew it was the best one for me and what I wanted.

We walked into the kitchen and both took a seat the table. I waited several moments before I spoke. I could tell Braxton was bracing himself.

"Braxton, first let me tell you, I really appreciate the time you've given me," I hesitate.

"It's okay, you can tell me how you feel." he coaxed.

"I know it was just as hard for you as it was me."

He nods.

"This has been one crazy year. Although it was difficult, we had some good, our healthy daughters."

"Yes ."

"Braxton, even when everything had spiraled out of control and I didn't want to be around you, I still loved you. When I found out I was pregnant I thought, why now. I never however, regretted being pregnant by you. We always had this crazy connection and it didn't seem right for us to be left with nothing. Having the girls made it better in a lot of ways. In a strange way it confirmed, no matter what, we would always have a bond."

He takes another deep breath.

"Let me finish please. When the truth came out, my newfound security was shattered. I never experienced happiness or love, until you. It felt so good to be wanted. I let go and I trusted you would never hurt me. Then in the blink of an eye all of that trust was gone. All the pain and hurt that I let go of was back with a vengeance. I had no one."

"I'm so sorry for that."

"I know you are. What I had to do is figure out if I could accept the past and move forward. I had to make sure it was what I wanted; something I could live with and have no doubts or regrets. I've thought long and hard about what's best for me. What would make me happy? And, I finally made my decision," I grabbed the papers and hand them to Braxton.

He took them and just looked at the envelope for several minutes. "This is it?"

I nod.

He took a deep breath, staring even longer at the envelope like it was transparent. Finally, he pulls out the papers and studies them. Confusion written all over his face, "This is for the purchase of a house?"

"I know."

"You want me to buy you a house?" he asked, even more perplexed.

"Yes," I placed my left hand on his. It took only a second for him to notice.

"Your ring?"

"It's on. I made my decision. My heart was missing its beat, I need you. I love you and I want only you. I want us to buy that villa we stayed in when we were married in the Cayman Islands. I want to take our three kids there so they can see it. But not quite yet, I think we need some alone time, it's overdue."

Braxton stood up, grabbing me in the process. He gave me a long overdue kiss. "I've missed you, Beautiful." He laughed. "I can breathe, Beautiful! You just don't know how much I need you. I can't function without you. Beautiful, you're in my blood. I promise you I will be there for you, that whatever the future holds you will always be first. Thank you for forgiving me, allowing me to love you. You won't regret it. I got my wife back, this is it. You are my life!"

"I missed you too," I laughed. "Braxton I realize now that I hurt you too in the process. I threw Kevin and Chauncey in your face."

He grabbed my face, "You don't have anything to be sorry for. My actions were the reason for you dealing with both of them. I had to pay the consequences."

"No it wasn't right. In the future I will be mindful."

"It's okay."

"Where's my bipolar husband? I can know flirt with men, get a number?" I tease.

"Ha, ha. You know you're mine for life. Nobody can love you better."

"That's my Mr. Cocky."

He kisses me again. "No cockiness. I speak the truth."

"So right you are. You know this has only made us stronger and better."

We stood there holding each other for what seemed liked hours but in reality was only ten minutes. I felt so at peace, secure, being in my baby's arms. I do love this man.

Soon, we're kissing again. Needless to say it didn't take much to arouse Sugar Daddy. He grabs my ass and lifts me. I wrap my legs around his waist allowing him to carry me to the counter. He unbuckled his pants exposing my sugar daddy. I had on a skirt so it was easy access.

"Yasmin, I just want to love you. Are you ready for some of that love?"

"Yes, I love you too, baby, but before we go any further, I need to tell you something?

He looked concerned. "What's that?"

"Don't play. Do not get me pregnant again."

He laughs.

"I'm not laughing. I'm serious. All that hard work and they come out with your temper and looks I was just the surrogate. Those girls kicked my ass, especially Khouri. She's just like her daddy, that temper, she can be so mean. Reagan, she's a little calmer, but can be just as bad."

He laughed. "You still have that smart ass mouth. Damn, I missed you. Leave my beautiful princesses alone. What you expect? We do have the same birthday?"

"I love you, Braxton."

"I love you." He kisses me passionately, before he enters me. "Beautiful, damn I missed you."

"You know this pussy was made just for this dick. It's yours, always has been."

"Always will be," he finishes. He held his dick still taking pleasure in the feeling. He made love to me nice and slow. Yes, this was right where I belonged, I was complete.

As I was riding Braxton's dick, I accidently turned on the TV. The volume was at its max:

This just in, breaking news… NBA player Eric Ayres has been arrested for attempted murder of his ex-wife, Landon Taylor. Sources say Eric Ayres came to his ex-wife's home an hour ago and shot her at point blank range. Ms. Taylor is not expected to survive.

Everything blurs. This is surreal. I'm numb, in shock. I was just with Landon.

The phone rings.

"Ok, we're on our way," Braxton says.

Final Thoughts...What is Love?

In the past few years, I've faced many obstacles. I've struggled, but I've always overcome. Through each obstacle, there is a lesson. It's our decision whether we learn from it. Five years ago, Braxton came into my life to teach me about love. Even our breakup had a purpose. During my heartache, I couldn't see the lessons. I didn't understand the pain. Now, I look back and appreciate the lesson. Understand its importance.

Although this obstacle proved to be havoc, again it had a purpose. That purpose was to teach me about forgiveness. I still have obstacles ahead of me. One is my mother.

Yes, I am disappointed that my mother isn't in my life. We both said some hurtful things and still have issues. I couldn't make her love me. I can't make her treat me like a daughter. I couldn't take back the things she did or said. Those things she did, those words she said also made me the woman I am. I do forgive her. Like Lawrence said I shouldn't have any hate in my heart. Sometimes in life people will hurt you. Often, it is those closest to you, your family. My mother has hurt me. She still hurts me, but I forgive her. I have no ill will. I pray she will one day be able to let go of her pain.

Going through this gave me insight on how John felt about me. At first, I had so much anger towards him. I didn't understand how or why he treated me like he did. I couldn't see the, ifs, ands or buts. I understand now. I see how it was possible. Unlike John, I am stronger, wiser. I am dealing with the truth.

Don't be mistaken and think I agree with what Braxton did and thinks he didn't do anything wrong because I do. What he did was wrong, very wrong. He used poor judgment. Eric is here as a result. It took a while to get through the pain, but I know Eric is not a mistake.

Many will say it is stupid of me to forgive Braxton. Many will say I should have moved on, could do better. They've formed their opinion, but are on the outside looking in. Where it seems everything is black or white, right or wrong, they don't understand the gray matter, the ifs, ands, or buts. They will say I wouldn't put up with this. I would do this, but when they are living that situation, things change. They empathize and all that talk is out of the window, because the mind thinks, but the heart knows. Their heart changes their whole perspective and like I don't know theirs, they don't know mine. Only I know my heart. I had to listen to me, not them. Do what makes me happy. Be with who made me happy. I am who matters.

It's rare to find that person who completes you. Find that person that knows you to the point that they know what you're thinking, or what your about to do before you do. That person knows something's wrong with you without you saying a word, will do anything in his power to make you happy. Braxton is that person for me. Our love is worth fighting for and holding onto. Braxton is who made me happy. He is the one I love and want. Despite his flaws and mistakes, I have no doubt if he could he would give me the world. To him I am a precious jewel and his love is real.

In the end, I can't worry about someone else's thought, or what is the logical choice. Braxton is part of me. I have no doubt of his love or commitment for me. I have no fears, nor regrets, and no doubts about choosing to stay. He *Loves Me Right*.

Stay tuned….Landon's story